WHEN THE
SHOOTING
STARTS

**Look for these exciting Western series
from bestselling authors
William W. Johnstone and J.A. Johnstone**

The Mountain Man

Preacher: The First Mountain Man

Luke Jensen: Bounty Hunter

Those Jensen Boys!

The Jensen Brand

MacCallister

The Red Ryan Westerns

Perley Gates

Have Brides, Will Travel

Will Tanner, Deputy U.S. Marshall

Shotgun Johnny

The Chuckwagon Trail

The Jackals

The Slash and Pecos Westerns

The Texas Moonshiners

Stoneface Finnegan Westerns

Ben Savage: Saloon Ranger

The Buck Trammel Westerns

The Death and Texas Westerns

The Hunter Buchanon Westerns

WHEN THE SHOOTING STARTS

WILLIAM W. JOHNSTONE
and J.A. JOHNSTONE

KENSINGTON
PUBLISHING CORP.

www.kensingtonbooks.com

KENSINGTON BOOKS are published by

Kensington Publishing Corp.
119 West 40th Street
New York, NY 10018

Copyright © 2022 by J.A. Johnstone

PUBLISHER'S NOTE

Following the death of William W. Johnstone, the Johnstone family is working with a carefully selected writer to organize and complete Mr. John-stone's outlines and many unfinished manuscripts to create additional nov-els in all of his series like The Last Gunfighter, Mountain Man, and Eagles, among others. This novel was inspired by Mr. Johnstone's superb story-telling.

All Kensington titles, imprints, and distributed lines are available at special quantity discounts for bulk purchases for sales promotion, premiums, fund-raising, educational, or institutional use. Special book excerpts or customized printings can also be created to fit specific needs. For details, write or phone the office of the Kensington Special Sales Manager: Attn. Special Sales De-partment. Kensington Publishing Corp, 119 West 40th Street, New York, NY 10018. Phone: 1-800-221-2647.

Library of Congress Card Catalogue Number: 2021948130

The K with book logo Reg. US Pat. & TM Off.

ISBN: 978-1-4967-3591-1

First Kensington Hardcover Edition: March 2022

10 9 8 7 6 5 4 3 2 1

Printed in the United States of America

WHEN THE SHOOTING STARTS

Chapter 1

"Hey, Buck! Buck West! Is that you, you old hoss thief?"

The loud, boisterous voice made Smoke Jensen come to a halt on the boardwalk. It had been a good while since he'd heard the name Buck West. When he stopped using it, he had figured he'd probably never hear it again.

But now here it was, coming from the mouth of the tall, rawboned man striding along the boardwalk toward him. The man's ugly face was wreathed in a grin. He wore a duster over canvas trousers, suspenders, and a flannel shirt. The brim of his battered old hat was turned up in front.

A holstered Colt swung on the man's right hip. Another revolver was stuck in his waistband on the left side. He had a lean, wolfish look about him that came from riding a lot of dark, lonely trails. Hoot-owl trails, some called them. Folks had started using the word "owlhoot" to describe the men who rode such trails.

Smoke had to search his memory for the name of the man who had just hailed him using that old alias. Sutcliffe, he recalled after a moment. Sort of a distinguished name for a gunman and outlaw. His nickname, Rowdy, fit him better. Smoke didn't think he had ever heard the man's real first name.

"Hello, Rowdy," he said, willing to be friendly as long as he could. "What brings you here?"

"Why, the same thing as you, I expect, Buck," replied Sutcliffe as he came to a stop and hooked his thumbs in his gun belt. "I heard that a fella name of Franklin was hirin' guns, so I come to sign on with him. This here is the town of Fontana, ain't it?"

That took Smoke by surprise. He frowned slightly and said, "You're a little behind the times. Tilden Franklin has been dead for almost a year. This is Big Rock. There's not much left of Fontana. It's fixing to dry up and blow away . . . like the memory of all the trouble that happened there."

Rowdy Sutcliffe cocked his head to the side and gave Smoke a quizzical stare.

"Franklin's dead?" he said. "Are you sure about that?"

"Pretty sure," Smoke said. He didn't add that he had been the one to hammer three slugs into the chest of the treacherous, would-be emperor of this valley.

Sutcliffe peered at him for a moment longer, then shook his head.

"Well, dadgum it. Seems like I'm always late to the party. Don't know why I didn't hear about that. O' course, I was down in old Meh-hee-co for a while, takin' my ease with the señoritas, so I weren't really payin' that much attention to what was goin' on up here in Colorado." Sutcliffe sighed. "I reckon I'm plumb outta luck." Then he brightened and went on, "Unless you got wind o' some other work for the likes o' you and me. Shoot, Buck West wouldn't be here unless hell was about to pop!"

"Sorry, Rowdy. I don't use the name Buck West anymore, and there's no gun work to be had around here. Big Rock has grown some since the railroad arrived, but it's still small enough to be pretty peaceful."

"Wait." A frown creased Sutcliffe's forehead. "Your name *ain't* Buck West?"

"That's right. That's just what I called myself for a while."

Back in the days when he had been riding the hoot-owl trails himself, searching for the men he had set out to kill. Men responsible for the deaths of several people he had loved . . .

"Then . . . what *is* your name?"

"It's Jensen. Kirby Jensen. Most folks call me Smoke."

Sutcliffe's eyes widened. "Smoke Jensen," he repeated. "Dang. I've heard that name, all right. Fella's supposed to be the fastest draw on the whole frontier. The fightin'est son of a gun anybody ever saw." He let out a low whistle. "And now, come to find out, Smoke Jensen is none other than my old pard Buck West. What do you know about that?"

Smoke shook his head and said, "We were never pards, Rowdy. We were just in the same places as the same times, every now and then."

Sutcliffe squinted now, instead of staring, as he said, "Well, that's an unfriendly sort o' thing to say. If I weren't such a for-givin' fella, I might take offense at it. Could be you're puttin' on airs, since you're really the high-an'-mighty Smoke Jensen."

"Never claimed to be high-and-mighty," Smoke replied with a shake of his head. "Just another hombre trying to make his way in life."

"Looks like you've done all right for yourself," Sutcliffe said, sneering a little.

Smoke wasn't sure what the gunman meant by that. He certainly wasn't wearing fancy duds or anything like that, just common range clothes and a dark brown, curled-brim hat that had seen better days perched on his ash-blond hair. His boots still had a little mud clinging to them. The gun belt strapped around his waist and the walnut-butted Colt that rode in the attached holster were well cared for but strictly functional.

He looked like what he was these days, a hardworking, moderately successful rancher with a small but growing spread. He and his friend Pearlie Fontaine did most of the work around the place, with Smoke's wife, Sally, pitching in when she needed to. She was learning to ride a horse and use a lariat as well as most men.

Lately, there had been enough work to do that Smoke had hired a couple of extra hands, which had prompted Pearlie to start referring to himself as the foreman. The Sugarloaf—the name Smoke had given to the ranch—was still far from being the equal of some of the massive outfits in other parts of the state. Maybe it would grow to that point someday. Smoke hoped so.

One thing he knew for sure was that he never wanted to return to the bloody, dangerous, lone wolf days of his existence as "Buck West" . . . and Rowdy Sutcliffe was a living, breathing reminder of those days, standing right in front of him.

"It was good seeing you again, Rowdy," he said as he started to turn away. That was stretching the truth considerable-like, but he wanted to end this conversation as smoothly and efficiently as he could.

"Hold on a minute," Sutcliffe said as he raised his left hand slightly.

Smoke stopped, every muscle taut.

"Least you can do is let me buy you a drink," Sutcliffe went on. "For old times' sake."

Smoke hesitated, then nodded. What harm could that do? Maybe once he'd had a drink with Sutcliffe, the gunman would decide there was no reason for him to remain in Big Rock and would move along.

"Sure," he said. "Come on down the street with me to Longmont's. It's the best saloon in town."

"Longmont's," repeated Sutcliffe as he fell in step alongside Smoke. "That wouldn't have anything to do with Louis Longmont, would it?"

"Louis owns the place," Smoke said. "Are you acquainted with him?"

"Nope, just heard tell of him. He's supposed to be mighty slick with a gun and a deck of cards, both." Sutcliffe glanced around Big Rock's main street. "What's he doin' in a little wide place in the trail like this?"

Smoke thought the town had grown enough that it was more than a wide place in the trail, but he didn't waste the time or energy to argue that point. Instead he said, "Louis has put that part of his life behind him, just like I have."

Sutcliffe clucked his tongue and shook his head. "Smoke Jensen and Louis Longmont, both settlin' down. Never thought I'd see the day."

"Living like we used to can only have one end, Rowdy, and it's not a good one."

"I hope you ain't sayin' I ought to hang up my guns!" Sutcliffe let out a bray of laughter. "That ain't gonna happen. I'll take my chances and keep on livin' like I want to."

"That's your choice," Smoke said solemnly.

"Damn right it is."

A slight air of tension remained between them as they entered Louis Longmont's establishment. Louis had told Smoke that eventually he intended to make the place as much a restaurant as it was a saloon, since he appreciated superb cooking as much as he did fine wine, a beautiful woman, a good card game, and a perfectly balanced gun. For now, however, it catered primarily to men's thirst for beer and whiskey.

Louis stood at the far end of the bar, a glass of bourbon on the hardwood in front of him and smoke curling from the thin black cigar in his mouth. He took the cheroot from his lips and used them to give Smoke a smile of welcome.

"Good afternoon, Smoke," the gambler said. "What brings you to town today?"

"Sally and I came in to pick up some supplies," Smoke replied. "She's over at the mercantile and doesn't really need my help right now, so I thought I'd stop by and say hello."

"I'm glad you did." Coolly, Louis appraised Rowdy Sutcliffe. "Who's your friend?"

Smoke didn't correct Louis's incorrect assumption that Sutcliffe was his friend. He said, "This is Rowdy Sutcliffe."

"You probably heard of me," Sutcliffe said with a confidence that bordered on arrogance.

Louis was about to inform Sutcliffe that he had no idea who he was, Smoke could tell. Before that could happen, Smoke went on, "Rowdy and I met up a few times, a while back."

"Back in the days when you was usin' the name Buck West," Sutcliffe added.

Louis cocked an eyebrow. He knew most of the story of Smoke's background, although Smoke's laconic nature meant that prying it out of him hadn't been easy.

"Well, any friend of Smoke's is a friend of mine, as the old saying goes," Louis said. "How about a drink, Mr. Sutcliffe? First one's on the house."

Sutcliffe grinned and said, "I sure won't turn that down. I favor rye, if you've got it."

"Indeed we do." Louis crooked a finger at the bartender and told the man to pour Sutcliffe a shot of rye, then said, "What about you, Smoke?"

"I'd just as soon have coffee, if you've got it."

"We always keep a pot on the stove in the back room. I'm glad most of my customers don't have your moderate habits, Smoke. I'd go broke!"

"I like to keep a clear head."

Sutcliffe picked up the glass of rye the bartender set in front of him. He threw back the drink, wiped the back of his other hand across his mouth, and said, "Whiskey don't muddle me none. I draw just as fast and shoot just as straight, drunk or sober."

"I hope for your sake you're right, Mr. Sutcliffe," said Louis. "Being mistaken about a thing like that could have serious consequences for a man."

"You mean like he might get hisself shot?" Sutcliffe gestured for the bartender to pour him another drink. The apron glanced at Louis, who gave him a tiny nod. As the bartender splashed more rye in the glass, Sutcliffe snorted disdainfully and went on, "That ain't gonna happen. I know how good I am." He picked up the glass and swallowed the second shot of fiery liquor. "I know how good the fellas I have to face down are, too. Ain't none of 'em that can match me. Not even . . ." He thumped the empty glass on the bar and sneered. "Not even the high-and-mighty Smoke Jensen."

Chapter 2

Smoke kept his face carefully expressionless in response to Sutcliffe's challenging tone as he said, "I told you about that high-and-mighty business, Rowdy. I didn't set out to get any kind of a reputation—"

"But that didn't stop you from gettin' one anyway, did it?" Sutcliffe snapped. "Ever'where I go, people talk about Smoke Jensen and how he's the fastest gun there ever was. Bull!" Sutcliffe raised his left hand and pointed a dirty-nailed index finger at Smoke. "Don't forget, mister, I knew you when you was nobody! Just a snot-nosed kid packin' an iron like you know what to do with it. Hell, you ain't much more'n a kid now."

"I reckon I'm all grown up," Smoke said, his voice flat and hard. "I've got a wife and everything, and she's probably waiting for me, so I'll mosey on. I'd say that it's been good to see you again, but—"

"You ain't moseyin' nowhere," snarled Sutcliffe. "Not until I'm finished with you. Barkeep, put some more whiskey in that glass!"

Louis Longmont held up a hand to the bartender, motioning for him to disregard Sutcliffe's order. He said, "Mr. Sutcliffe, I believe you've had enough."

"Why? Because I ain't paid for that second drink?"

"I don't care about that. It's on the house. But I think you should move on now—"

"I know all about you, too, you damn tinhorn," Sutcliffe interrupted without taking his eyes off Smoke. "You're supposed to be fast, too. But you ain't near as fast as me, and once I'm finished with Jensen, I'll prove it."

Smoke said, "You and I are already finished. You can still walk out of here, get on your horse, and ride away from Big Rock, Sutcliffe. No harm done."

"There's plenty o' harm! I been away so long, folks probably done forgot all about me." Sutcliffe's shoulders hunched a little. His right hand hovered near the Colt on his hip, ready to hook and draw. "But they'll remember, right enough, once word gets around that I'm the fella who killed Smoke Jensen. Then anybody who needs gun work done will be fallin' all over theirselves to hire me. Yes, sir, once I outdraw Smoke Jensen clean as a whistle—"

Smoke knew what the words pouring out of Sutcliffe's mouth were designed to do. They were supposed to anger him and prod him into drawing before he was ready, or else they would distract him, lull him into a split-second of unreadiness when Sutcliffe abruptly made his move.

The rant didn't accomplish either of those things. Smoke just stood there stonily, and when Sutcliffe broke off and clawed at his gun, Smoke was ready.

The walnut-butted Colt appeared in Smoke's hand as if by magic. Rowdy Sutcliffe actually was pretty fast on the draw, even with two shots of rye whiskey burning in his belly, but he had barely cleared leather when Smoke's gun roared. And to tell the truth, Smoke could have shot him a little sooner than that, but he'd waited just to make sure Sutcliffe wouldn't realize his mistake and try to stop this.

The bullet slammed into Sutcliffe's chest, twisted him half around, and made him stumble backward against the bar. He would have collapsed if it hadn't been there to hold him up. A shudder went through him. Blood welled from the corner of his mouth. Still, he stayed on his feet, held up by a combination of rage, stubbornness, and being too dumb to realize he had only seconds to live.

With his left hand, he pulled the second revolver from his waistband. With a gun in each fist, he tried to raise them. Smoke shot him again, this time drilling a neat third eye in the center of his forehead. Both of Sutcliffe's guns thundered as his fingers spasmed and jerked the triggers, but they were pointed down and hammered their slugs into the sawdust-littered floorboards right in front of his feet. A cloud of powder smoke rose from the weapons, obscuring Sutcliffe's swaying form as if he were standing behind a dirty window, doing some sort of macabre dance.

Then the guns slipped from nerveless fingers and thudded to the floor, followed a heartbeat later by Sutcliffe's lifeless husk. He sprawled face down and didn't even twitch.

Smoke shook his head and started reloading the two chambers he had just emptied.

"We both tried to talk him out of it," Louis Longmont said into the silence that gripped the room as the echoes of the shots faded away. Louis lifted the cheroot to his mouth and took a puff, then went on, "He simply wouldn't listen to reason." He looked like something had just occurred to him. "Were the two of you actually friends at one time, Smoke?"

"Not hardly," Smoke said as he slid the reloaded Colt back into leather. "He was just another two-bit gun-wolf. There are too many of them in the world."

"And they all believe it would be a wonderful thing to be the man who killed Smoke Jensen." Louis smiled humorlessly. "It must be a terrible thing to carry the hopes and dreams of so many around on your shoulders, my friend."

Around the room, the men who had dived for cover just before the shooting started were beginning to poke their heads back up. Louis waved the hand holding the cheroot to encourage them and raised his voice.

"It's all over, gentlemen. A round of drinks on the house!"

A short time later, as Smoke walked up to the Big Rock Mercantile, he saw an apron-wearing clerk loading sacks and crates of supplies into the back of the buckboard Sally had parked there earlier. Smoke's big, powerful black stallion, Drifter, was tied to a nearby hitch rail.

"Howdy, Smoke," the clerk greeted him. "Miz Jensen's inside, just finishin' up her business." The man placed the keg of nails he was carrying in the buckboard and then dusted off his hands. "Say, I thought I heard a couple of shots up the street a little while ago. You know anything about that?"

"You know me, Stan," Smoke replied with a smile. "I always try to steer clear of trouble."

"Uh-huh, sure. I just thought you might—"

"There was a little unpleasantness at Longmont's," Smoke admitted. He didn't see any point in denying what had happened. The story would be all over town in less than an hour, whether he wanted that or not. More than likely, it had spread quite a bit already.

The clerk let out a whistle. "How many of 'em did you have to shoot, Smoke?"

"Just one man. One stubborn, foolish man."

"Well, he should'a known better than to go up against Smoke Jensen."

Smoke didn't reply to that. When he and Sally had first come to this valley, not long after they were married, he had been determined to leave his gunfighting ways behind him. To that end, he had used a different name, one that people wouldn't associate with either Smoke Jensen or his previous alias Buck West.

Inevitably, though, the truth had come out, and by the time the ruckus with Tilden Franklin and his hired killers was over, everybody in these parts knew who he really was.

And as it turned out, that was a relief. Smoke never had liked secrets, and he was proud of his family name. Keeping quiet about it seemed almost like a slap in the faces of his father Emmett and his brother Luke, both of whom had died in the service of what they believed was right and honorable.

So, for better or worse, he would be Smoke Jensen from now on.

He stepped up on the store's porch and was about to go in when Sally appeared in the open doorway. She smiled when she saw him, and he was struck once again by just how beautiful this dark-haired young woman really was. She was pretty enough to take a man's breath away.

But there was a lot more to Sally Reynolds Jensen than just good looks. She was smart as could be, both in book learning and common sense, and possessed of fierce courage that wouldn't allow her to hesitate in the face of danger. In fact, Smoke wished sometimes that she was a little less courageous and more inclined to be careful.

If she'd been different, though, he might not have fallen so completely in love with her.

"Ready to go?" he asked her.

"I think so. I got everything that was on my list. Did you enjoy your visit with Louis?"

"It was all right, I reckon." He had lived through the shoot-out with Sutcliffe, so he couldn't complain too much about how the visit had gone.

The clerk was still standing on the porch. He said excitedly, ignoring the warning glance Smoke gave him, "Miz Jensen, did you hear the shootin' while you were inside?"

Sally looked at Smoke and raised her eyebrows. "Shooting?"

"I'll tell you about it once we're on the trail," he said, after scowling for a second at the clerk. The man cleared his throat, looked a little embarrassed, and retreated into the mercantile. Smoke cupped his hand under Sally's elbow and went on, "Let me give you a hand climbing up there."

She could have gotten onto the buckboard's seat just fine by herself, but she let Smoke assist her. Then she picked up the reins attached to the two horses in the team and pulled the brake lever out of its notch. Smoke untied Drifter and swung up into the saddle.

Sally waited until they were out of town and on the trail to the Sugarloaf before she said, "All right, what happened?"

"I ran into a fella I used to know a few years ago, back in the days when I was calling myself Buck West."

"An old friend?"

"No, but we weren't enemies, either . . . until he found out my real name and decided that we were."

Quickly, and without dwelling on the details, he filled her in on the deadly encounter. Sally listened in silence, but she wore a frown of concern.

He concluded by saying, "Monte Carson came down to Louis's place, took my statement, and sent for the undertaker. That's the end of it as far as I'm concerned."

Monte Carson was the sheriff of Big Rock, a former gunman himself who had been on the wrong side in the war a year earlier, until he realized that and threw in with Smoke. After that, with the founding of Big Rock, he had accepted the offer to become the new town's lawman.

"Does this man Sutcliffe have any friends or relatives who are going to come looking for you to avenge what happened to him?" asked Sally.

"Not that I know of, but honestly, I never really knew the hombre that well."

Sally sighed as she handled the team and kept the buckboard rolling along the trail while Smoke rode beside the vehicle.

"I know that by now I should be getting used to the fact

there are men roaming around who'd like to kill you," she said. "Your past is what makes you the man you are, and I knew that when I married you."

"What I used to be doesn't mean that's what I'll always be," Smoke pointed out.

"No, but it's hard to get away from all the things that have happened to us, all the things we've done. Our history lingers, no matter what we do."

"That's like saying folks can't change."

"No, not at all," Sally argued. "But changing the way you go forward doesn't change everything you've done in the past." She paused, then went on, "Smoke, don't think I'm saying I regret marrying you. I don't, not one bit! I love you and I know you don't go around looking for trouble."

"But it seems to find me anyway, doesn't it?"

She smiled and said, "I suppose that's the way it is with some people. And honestly, I wouldn't change one thing about you, even if I could! Just let me hope that someday, peace will come to this land."

"It will. I'm sure of it." Smoke gazed off into the distance. "It may be a while before it does, though."

"Well, until then, I'm glad I have Smoke Jensen by my side."

"And I'm glad to have Sally Jensen by *my* side."

They smiled at each other and traveled on, but as he rode, Smoke couldn't help but think about the things they had said.

He truly believed that peace *would* come to the frontier someday . . . but there was still a lot of blood to be spilled before that could happen.

Chapter 3

On the Kansas plains, not far from the Colorado border, the shadows of approaching evening had started to gather around the isolated ranch house belonging to Sherman and Belinda Russell. Their three sons, fourteen-year-old Kermit, eleven-year-old Harry, and eight-year-old Logan, were trying to get their chores done before it got dark. Inside the mostly sod house, Belinda and her sixteen-year-old daughter, Katie, were preparing supper.

Sherman knew those things even though he was half a mile away on horseback, chousing a couple of cows that had strayed off back toward their pen. That air of tranquility, of looking forward to supper and a good rest after a hard day's work, was how it always was in the early evening on this spread that Sherman and his wife and kids called home.

This evening, though, was going to be different.

Sherman's horse, a canny old mare he called Dixie, threw her head up and danced a little to the side. Tightening his grip on the reins, Sherman said, "Here now, what's that all about? You smell a coyote on the prowl or something?"

Something moved in the waist-high brush to Sherman's right, but it wasn't a coyote. A man stood up and regarded the rancher gravely. Sherman jerked Dixie to a stop. Instantly, he saw the feathers jutting from the pulled-back mane of black hair, the dead-white paint across the forehead of the coppery face, the horizontal streaks of black paint across the cheeks.

The man wore buckskin leggings. His muscular chest was bare. Something dark and round hung from a thong at his waist. He lifted the object with his left hand and thumped the fingers of his right hand against it several times, producing a hollow, rhythmic sound. It was a small drum painted black, Sherman realized.

His eyes took all that in right away, but for a couple of seconds, he was too stunned by the unexpected sight to react. Then the warning bells clamoring in his brain got too loud to ignore, and he let out a curse as he clawed at the revolver holstered on his hip.

What felt like a big fist punched him in the back just as he cleared leather. He gasped in pain and almost dropped the gun, but somehow he managed to hang on to it. He looked down and saw a bloody arrowhead and a few inches of the wooden shaft to which it was attached protruding from his chest. That hadn't been a fist that hit him, at all.

The Indian with the drum was still thumping on it. He started chanting along with the erratic beating on the tight-stretched hide.

More of the savages were behind him, Sherman knew. His pain-fogged brain still functioned well enough to tell him that. Acting as much on instinct as anything else, he banged his heels against Dixie's sides and gave a strangled yell. The mare lunged forward. Sherman fumbled with the gun's hammer and got it pulled back. He fired at the Indian holding the drum as he galloped past, but he didn't have any idea if he hit the man.

Home . . . he could see it ahead of him. He had to get there, had to protect his family. The boys would be outside. They would have heard the shot he had just fired and would warn their mother. Belinda knew to get everybody inside, close the thick shutters over the windows, and bar the door. The three older kids could all shoot, and Logan was good at reloading. They were prepared, as much as they could be, for trouble.

More agony ripped into Sherman's left side. Even without looking, he knew another arrow had struck him. The Indians were on both sides of him, as well as behind. He swung the revolver and blindly fired the remaining rounds. No way his family could miss that. He had warned them that trouble was on the way, if nothing else.

Dixie suddenly lurched and stumbled. Sherman moaned as he saw the arrows sticking out both sides of her neck. Blood streamed from the wounds. Sherman kicked his feet out of the stirrups just as the mare's front legs folded up under her and she went down in a rolling tumble. He flew through the air, momentum carrying him forward.

Sharp cracks sounded as he crashed to the ground and rolled. He didn't know if they came from the shafts of the arrows breaking, or if those were his bones snapping. It didn't matter anyway. He was just one huge ball of pain now, and as he came up on his knees, he sobbed.

A figure stalked out of the fading light to the east. The tall Indian had let the drum fall back to the end of its thong. He carried a tomahawk now, and as he came to a stop in front of Sherman Russell, he raised the weapon.

"I am Black Drum," the Indian said. "And I am your death."

Sherman saw the tomahawk start to fall, but that was the last thing he knew. It split his skull and cleaved deep into his brain. Black Drum pulled it loose and stepped back as Sherman toppled forward. Blood began to spread around his head and was soaked up into the Kansas dirt.

Black Drum shifted the dripping tomahawk to his left hand and idly tapped out a cadence on the drum with his right hand as he walked toward the distant homestead, dark shapes flitting forward on both sides of him in the gathering dusk.

* * *

An hour later, full night had fallen. Black Drum watched the orange flames shooting high from the ranch house roof as it burned. At his feet lay the scalped, mutilated bodies of the three boys. Off to one side, his warriors took their turns with the two white females. The woman and her daughter had stopped screaming and fighting, but Black Drum could still hear them whimpering in abject terror and misery.

The war chief's fingertips pattered on the drum. He did that almost all the time without even thinking about it, when he wasn't busy killing whites. This was the third homestead he and his men had raided during the past two weeks. Four dead here so far, and soon the two females would die, too, when his men were done with them. That made . . . how many?

Black Drum paused to add up the numbers in his head. A white teacher lady at the mission school on the reservation had taught him how to figure such things, before he raped and killed her.

Seventeen, Black Drum thought, nodding. Seventeen whites who had died since he and his men left the reservation to re-claim the glory that was rightfully theirs as Cheyenne warriors. And the teacher lady and four white men had died when they made their escape. So that came to twenty-two, in all.

It was a good start, he told himself, but no more than that. So many more would die before he was finished.

He tore his rapt gaze away from the burning building as one of his warriors called to him. When Black Drum looked around, the man said, "We are ready to ride."

"The women," said Black Drum. "Are they dead?"

The warrior shook his head.

"Cut their throats."

The warrior nodded and hurried to carry out Black Drum's orders. The chief looked at the fire again, tapped his fingers a few more times on the drum, and then turned to walk away.

Already, he was thinking about how they would strike next at the hated whites.

The locomotive barreled westward along the Kansas Pacific Railway tracks. The train had just crossed the border into Colorado. Seemingly endless plains stretched out ahead, but as engineer Chuck Barcroft leaned out the cab window and peered in that direction, he knew the mountains weren't far beyond the horizon.

Whenever he made this run, he always checked from time to time to see when he first spotted the low blue line that marked the location of the Rockies. It was a little game he played with himself to break up the monotony. The tracks actually curved a little to the northwest through here, but so slightly that they appeared to run straight through the treeless landscape covered with short grass.

There was just nothing to see out here.

Which is why Barcroft was surprised when his fireman, Ted Winslow, suddenly exclaimed, "Somethin' on the track up ahead, Chuck! Dang! It's on fire. We got to stop!"

Barcroft leaned out farther on his side of the cab and saw what Winslow had spotted. Brush had been heaped high on the tracks and set on fire, all right. Thick black smoke billowed up from the blaze a couple of hundred yards ahead.

Barcroft didn't reach for the brake, though. Instead he grasped the throttle and pressed it forward, coaxing more speed from the locomotive.

"Stoke that firebox, Ted!" he called to Winslow. "I'm givin' her all she'll take!"

"But that fire on the tracks—"

"Whoever set it wants us to stop," Barcroft said. "No tellin' if it's desperadoes or Injuns, but I don't want to mess with either one."

"But they might have damaged the tracks on the other side

of the fire," argued Winslow. "We go tearin' through there, we're liable to derail."

"Stoke that firebox, damn it! I know what I'm talkin' about. I've been on this run longer than you have, Ted."

Winslow still looked dubious, but he opened the firebox door and started shoveling coal through it. The engine's increasing rumble drowned out the roar of the flames. Sweat coated Winslow's face as the heat pounded against him.

Barcroft kept the throttle shoved ahead. He reached down and felt the hard shape of the revolver nestled in the pocket of his overalls. It was scant comfort but better than nothing.

He leaned through the window again. The gap between the locomotive and the fire on the tracks dwindled swiftly. Barcroft tried to peer through the flames to see if he could make out what was on the other side, but the smoke was too thick. He couldn't see anything. But the train was almost on top of the pile of burning brush now . . .

The locomotive's cowcatcher struck the barrier and demolished it, flinging burning branches high in the air and to both sides. Barcroft held his breath, fearful that the engine would strike some other obstacle hidden by the blaze.

Instead, the train thundered on and seconds later emerged from the cloud of smoke that stung Barcroft's eyes and nose. The track was clear. He'd been right. The fire was just a ruse to try to get the train to stop. If Winslow had been in charge, the trick would have worked.

He was too canny to have been fooled, Barcroft told himself . . . although it had been pretty nerve-racking for a few seconds.

The next instant, the engineer flinched as something flew through the cab window, zipped past his face, and bounced off the front of the cab with a clatter. He looked down and saw an arrow lying on the cab floor. With a startled yell, he turned his head to gaze out the window at several Cheyenne warriors who were racing alongside the locomotive on swiftly striding ponies.

Barcroft recovered from his shock enough to dig in his pocket for the gun he carried. He had fought off Indians before. He also knew that despite their speed over short distances, the ponies could only keep up with the train for a few moments.

He finally got the revolver out, thrust it through the window, and fired twice at the attackers, who were already starting to fall back. As far as Barcroft could tell, he didn't hit any of them.

"More of the red devils up ahead, Chuck!" cried Winslow.

Barcroft bit back a despairing groan as he gazed along the tracks and saw more mounted warriors curving toward the steel rails. Whoever was in charge of this war party was smart. He had strung out his men along the rail line so they could continue the attack even as the first raiders fell back. The Indians must have been hidden in the brush with their ponies forced to lie down next to them. Barcroft swung his gun toward this new wave of warriors, but before he could fire, more arrows flew toward the cab window.

The Cheyenne were deadly marksmen. Barcroft got off two shots before he fell back with an arrow in his chest. He gasped in pain, dropped the gun, and grabbed whatever he could find to keep from falling. That happened to be the throttle, and as he pulled it back, the train began to slow.

"Chuck!" Winslow said as he dropped his shovel and jumped to support his friend.

"Don't worry . . . about me," Barcroft struggled to say. "Keep the train . . . moving . . ."

"But Chuck—"

"Just . . . do it!"

Winslow eased Barcroft's bulky form to the cab floor and turned to the controls. He knew how to work them, of course.

He was reaching for the throttle when something thumped heavily behind him. He looked over his shoulder and saw that one of the Indians on that side of the locomotive had ridden close enough to leap from the back of his pony into the cab. The warrior had dropped a knee when he landed, but with a hate-filled screech, he surged up and threw himself at the fireman. The tomahawk in his hand rose and then flashed down at Winslow.

Winslow flung up an arm to block the blow. He screamed as the tomahawk's sharp blade bit deep into his muscles. He tried to shove the Cheyenne away with his other hand, but the warrior was too close, too strong. He chopped frenziedly at the fireman. As Winslow fell under the brutal assault, his blood splattered on the front wall of the firebox and sizzled on the hot metal.

The train continued to slow.

Even though the engineer was already dead, once the Cheyenne was finished with the fireman, he took the tomahawk to the other white man, too, striking him until the man's face barely resembled anything human. Blood was strewn all over the cab.

The warrior stepped back with a snarl twisting his face. He looked at his grisly handiwork with pride, then tapped lightly on the drum hanging at his waist. The chief of these warriors he might be, but Black Drum never asked anything of his men he was not willing to do himself. Without hesitation, he had run the risk of leaping from horseback into the locomotive's cab.

Now he reached for the brake lever and hauled back on it, slowing the train even more. He swung down to the cab's step and waited there until one of his warriors led his pony alongside again and matched the train's speed. Black Drum leaped agilely to the mount's back and whooped in blood-sated exhilaration as he veered the pony away from the roadbed.

On both sides of the slowing train, the war party peeled away. To the north, the warriors slowed and circled until they were able to cross the tracks behind the train. A few shots came from the windows of the passenger cars, but none of the bullets came close enough to worry Black Drum's men. They raced to rejoin their brother warriors.

Once everyone was back together, they sat on their mounts and watched the train dwindle in the distance to the west. When it finally coasted to a stop, some of the white men on it would venture into the cab and see what Black Drum had done.

"Did we lose any men?" asked the war chief.

"Two men fell to the shots from the iron horse," one of the warriors replied.

Black Drum nodded. "We will recover their bodies and send their spirits properly to the world beyond."

Another man said with hate dripping from his voice, "We should have stopped the train and killed all the whites."

"There are not enough of us for that," Black Drum replied. "We struck at them as best we could, and the deaths we inflicted will frighten the whites even more. The iron horses will stop coming if all are too scared to ride them."

"But how long will that take?"

"We have all the time we need," said Black Drum. "No one will stop us. And with each rising and setting of the sun, more warriors will join us. Already the size of our band has almost doubled since we left the reservation. Soon there will be enough of us for a raid that will strike real fear into the craven hearts of the whites."

He raised a hand and pointed casually to the west.

"We will move on . . . toward the mountains and our glorious destiny."

Chapter 4

The settlement of Wicker's Wells didn't amount to much, but it might someday if Claude Wicker had anything to say about it. He was the one who'd built a trading post here in eastern Colorado where two trails intersected, and he'd planned at first to call the place Wicker's Crossing because of that.

But then he'd decided to dig a well instead of relying on a nearby creek for water. The stream was small enough that it might dry up during the summer, and then nobody would be likely to stop at the trading post. They would push on until they got somewhere with more dependable water.

The well turned out to be better than Claude Wicker ever anticipated, providing a steady supply of good water. So he called the town he laid out in his mind Wicker's Wells instead, even though there was only one well. He figured it was better to be optimistic, and he could always dig more wells later, as the town grew.

That was what happened. In the five years since Wicker had built his trading post and sunk that well, the population of the settlement had grown to almost a hundred people. In addition to the trading post, it boasted a blacksmith, a saddle and harness shop, a livery stable and an adjoining freight line depot, a stagecoach stop, two saloons, and a whorehouse. In addition, more than a dozen sod houses were scattered around the cluster of businesses. Pretty soon, Claude Wicker mused as he stood on the trading post porch and surveyed the settlement, he was going to have to dig that second well.

He spied a cloud of dust rising from the trail leading to the east. That caused a small frown to appear on Wicker's face. It wasn't the right day for a train of freight wagons to come through, and the westbound stage wasn't due until late that afternoon. A group of cowboys riding in from one of the ranches in the area might cause some dust, but it wasn't Saturday, when the cowboys usually came to town. Also, to raise that much dust would require close to fifty riders, and none of the spreads around here had crews that big.

So Wicker was puzzled but not alarmed by the approaching horsemen. Nobody else moving around the settlement's single street even appeared to notice the dust. He was just borrowing trouble, Wicker told himself.

Then, when the riders were about two hundred yards away and suddenly goosed their mounts into a flat-out run toward the settlement, Wicker began to be able to make out some details about them. His eyes widened, and he bellowed, "Indians! Indians!"

He turned and plunged back into the store to get his Henry rifle.

By the time he reached the porch again, the savages were at the edge of town. The street was deserted now. Everyone had raced for cover. Arrows fired from the backs of the racing ponies arched toward the buildings. Wicker saw to his horror that the heads of some of those shafts were ablaze. Those fire arrows thudded into roofs and walls and lodged there.

Wicker knelt behind a barrel and rested the Henry across the top of it. As the raiders swept past him, he fired the rifle as fast as he could work its lever, cranking out half a dozen shots. Unfortunately, the dust had followed the renegades into town, so he couldn't tell if he hit any of them.

Shrill whoops rose above the swift rataplan of hoofbeats.

Women screamed and men shouted curses. Flames crackled as roofs caught fire and the sun-dried wood burned fiercely.

The Indians raced on through the settlement without slowing down. Wicker hoped they would just keep going. It was almost inconceivable to him that they would attack the town in broad daylight like this. He might not believe it if he hadn't seen it with his own eyes.

The evidence was right in front of him, though. As the dust cleared, he saw smoke rising from buildings all over town. Frontier settlements feared fire more than anything else. Once a blaze got going good, it was almost impossible to put it out until it had destroyed all or at least most of a town.

The trading post wasn't burning, and Wicker was thankful for that. He stood up and ran toward the livery stable, thinking he could help the owner put out that fire. But before he got there, he saw the riders wheeling around just west of town and realized the savages weren't done with Wicker's Wells just yet.

He turned and ran back the way he had come as the Indians charged again.

Wicker had just leaped onto the trading post's porch when an arrow skewered his left thigh. He screamed in pain, dropped the Henry, and tumbled to the planks. Another arrow thudded into the porch a few feet from him and stuck there. Groaning, he reached for his fallen rifle, grasped the barrel, and pulled it toward him. He used the Henry to brace himself as he pushed up and turned, rolling into a position where he leaned on his right side, so he wouldn't put any pressure on the shaft still sticking out from his left leg.

There they were, the unholy savages! He jerked the Henry to his shoulder and opened fire. One of the Indians flew backward off his pony as Wicker's shot punched into his chest. Wicker felt a second of triumph at the sight.

The next instant, two arrows drove into his chest and a third caught him in the guts. He toppled over, his face frozen in an agonized grimace, and died on the porch of his trading post.

At least that way he didn't have to watch as everything he had dreamed of went up in flames, or hear the screams of the settlement's inhabitants as they either burned in the inferno that consumed Wicker's Wells or tried to escape and were caught in the open by the Cheyenne war party. Some of those were killed outright when they tried to put up a fight. A number of others were captured, dragged out of town to get away from the heat and smoke, and killed at leisure, with a great deal more screaming.

The driver of the stage that approached from the east late that afternoon saw tendrils of smoke still rising from the ruins of the settlement and stopped while the vehicle was still half a mile away. He carried a spyglass with him, so he took it out, extended it, and studied the devastation through the lenses.

"What's wrong, driver?" one of the passengers called from inside the coach. "Why have we stopped? We haven't reached town yet, have we?"

"Ain't no town to reach," the driver muttered as he closed the spyglass. "We're gonna go around what's left of it." As he ignored the startled questions from the passengers and slapped the reins against the back of the team to get the horses moving again, he added under his breath, "And we'd better hope these nags still got some runnin' in 'em if the devils who did that are still anywheres around here."

Lieutenant Samuel Brant tapped on the door of Colonel Reeve Walker, the commanding officer of Fort Lyon, Colorado. Walker's aide wasn't at his desk in the colonel's anteroom, or else he would have announced Brant. The orderly who had brought word to Brant that Colonel Walker wanted to see him, though, had said that the summons was urgent, so Brant wasn't going to wait for the aide to return.

"Come in," Walker called from the other side of the door. Brant opened it and entered the office, saw the burly, mostly bald colonel sitting behind his desk with an angry, frustrated expression on his beefy face.

"Lieutenant Brant reporting as ordered, sir," Brant said as he saluted.

Walker sketched a salute in return, then jerked his hand toward the empty chair in front of the desk. "At ease, and sit down, Lieutenant." He lifted a piece of paper and looked like he wanted to crumple it. "I know you've seen this."

"The report from Wicker's Wells, sir? Yes, I'm the one who sent it over, because I knew you'd want to give it your personal attention."

"What I want is not to have to deal with headaches like this," Walker snapped. "An entire town almost wiped out. From a population of ninety-seven, six people remain alive, and two of them are wounded badly enough that they may not survive. It was a massacre, Lieutenant."

Wicker's Wells was a settlement approximately a hundred miles north-northeast of Fort Lyon. Or rather, it had been a settlement, Brant amended to himself.

Now, according to reports not only from a stagecoach driver but also a sheriff's posse that had ridden out to confirm the jehu's grim testimony, Wicker's Wells was just a collection of burned-out buildings. The deputies had been busy for a couple of days burying the victims of the atrocity.

"Yes, sir, it was, indeed," Brant said in reply to the colonel's angry comment. "I've been talking to some of our scouts and checking other reports from the past few weeks. This isn't the first such outrage, although it's the worst one so far."

Walker leaned back in his chair and clasped his hands on his rounded belly. "I knew I could count on you to look into this, Lieutenant. What have you found out?"

The studious junior officer stood up and stepped over to the wall where a large map of Colorado hung. On the right-hand, or eastern, side of the map, a fairly large area of Kansas was delineated, as well.

Brant rested a fingertip on the map and said, "A number of homesteads here in western Kansas were raided and the families who lived on them wiped out. Since those farms and ranches were rather isolated, the attacks weren't discovered until well after they occurred. While we can't be absolutely certain of the order in which they took place, it appears that the sites lead in a line from southeast to northwest"—Brant moved his finger along the map—"which, if we follow it back to its probable source, indicates that the renegades came from somewhere in Indian Territory."

Walker frowned and asked, "Don't I remember seeing something about a group of renegades jumping the Cheyenne reservation down there?"

"Yes, sir. A group of a dozen or more Southern Cheyenne led by an Indian called Black Drum attacked the local agency, killed several people, including a woman, and fled."

"A dozen savages couldn't wipe out an entire town, though, even a small one like Wicker's Wells," Walker said.

"No, sir, but as we've seen in the past, whenever a group of Indians does something like this, it emboldens others to slip off from the reservations and join them. Not only that, but Black Drum's group might have attracted some of the hold-outs who never went to the reservation to start with. We've had reports of Arapaho renegades in that area, and the Arapaho and Cheyenne are close allies."

Walker grunted. "You're saying this blasted Black Drum could have gathered himself an army by now."

"Maybe not a force large enough to be called an army," Brant said with a shrug. "But a significant war party, certainly." The lieutenant tapped the map again. "Which brings me to the Kansas Pacific Railway."

"What about it?"

"One of their trains was attacked recently by Indians. The only casualties were the engineer and fireman, but the train was stopped for a while before it was able to proceed on to its destination. Wicker's Wells was about thirty miles west of where the train was attacked."

"Black Drum again?"

"Some of the eyewitness reports from the train's crew and passengers mentioned seeing an Indian who carried some sort of drum on a sling. And if I can back up for a moment, there *was* one survivor from that string of raids on the homesteads in Kansas . . . a young boy who was out hunting with his dog when the savages struck. He was able to hide in a little cave in the side of a bluff, and he saw an Indian playing a drum while the family was slaughtered and their home burned."

"You said there were a few survivors at Wicker's Wells. Did *they* see that damn drumming savage?"

Brant nodded. "They did, sir." He hesitated. "They also estimated the number of renegades as at least fifty, quite possibly more. And by now, the way word spreads on the plains among the hostiles . . . Black Drum could easily have seventy-five or eighty warriors at his command. Perhaps as many as a hundred, although that seems unlikely. That's the direction in which things are headed, though."

"And speaking of directions . . . trace that route for me again, Lieutenant."

Brant placed his finger on the map in Indian Territory, not far across the line from Kansas, moved it north, curved to the northwest, and then made a slashing motion to the west.

"It appears that Black Drum is driving toward the center of the state, which is more heavily settled and populated," said Walker. "He has a force large enough now to do considerable damage, and from what you've said, it's likely to grow even more."

"That seems like an accurate assessment to me, Colonel."

"Then our course is simple, Lieutenant." Walker's clenched fist came down hard on the desk. "We have to find this Black Drum and stop him, whatever it takes."

Chapter 5

Smoke was back in Big Rock for the first time since he'd been forced to gun down Rowdy Sutcliffe. A month had gone by, and while it was unusual for Smoke not to visit the settlement for that long, it certainly wasn't unheard of. There was always a lot of work to do around the Sugarloaf, especially considering that Smoke was keeping the ranch going with just himself and one full-time hand—Pearlie—and a couple of cowboys who worked for him when he needed extra help.

When he and Sally had first come to this valley four years earlier, not long after their marriage, there hadn't been a town, and the Sugarloaf was one of the few spreads in the area. In those days, they might go months without leaving the ranch. Smoke had known that Sally was lonely at times, but for the most part, they had been happy. They had in each other the only thing they really needed to keep going.

Smoke might have been satisfied with such solitude from now on, but for Sally's sake, he was glad when other ranchers started moving into the valley, as well as prospectors looking for gold and silver. Then somebody had started up a town—Fontana—and Smoke had been even happier for Sally. Now she would have a place to shop, to see other women, to carry on a somewhat normal existence.

Unfortunately, Fontana hadn't worked out too well in the long run, since it was founded by a ruthless, greedy criminal, but since the death of Tilden Franklin, the abandonment of the town he started, and the establishment of Big Rock, things were looking up. It appeared that Big Rock would grow into the settlement Smoke had hoped Fontana would be. He and Sally had a lot of good friends there already, and more people were moving in all the time.

Smoke nodded and said hello to many of the townsfolk he passed on his way to Longmont's. As before, Sally was at the mercantile, seeing to the supplies they needed, while Smoke intended to pay a visit to Louis and catch up on any news the gambler might have.

He just hoped there wouldn't be any gunplay involved this time.

Smoke slowed his pace when he spotted Sheriff Monte Carson crossing the street toward him. Monte was somewhat older than Smoke, and the precarious life as a hired gun that he had led for a number of years had aged him even more. Despite that, he was still a vital man in the prime of his life.

"Howdy, Smoke," he said as he lifted a hand in greeting. "I'm glad I ran into you. I just got word that some army fella is waiting at my office, wanting to talk to me. How about coming along?"

"I'd be happy to, but why?" Smoke asked. "I don't have anything to do with the army."

"I know, but if something affects Big Rock, I figure you ought to find out about it, too. The town wouldn't even be here if it wasn't for you."

Smoke shook his head and said, "I don't know if I'd go so far as to say that."

"Well, I would," Monte insisted. "If not for you, we'd all still be under Tilden Franklin's thumb, over there in Fontana."

Smoke didn't want to rehash all that old, violent history, so he said, "Let's go see what the army wants."

They crossed to the other side of Center Street and headed back along it toward the sheriff's office. A horse with a Mc-Clellan saddle was tied at the hitch rail in front of the squat building that housed both Monte Carson's office and the jail. A man in blue trousers with a yellow stripe up the sides, blue blouse, and tan slouch hat paced impatiently back and forth on the porch.

He must have spotted Smoke and Monte approaching, because he stopped his pacing instead of swinging around. With a frown, he watched them come closer, then said, "Sheriff Carson?" as they stepped up onto the porch.

"That's right," Monte replied with a nod. "What can I do for you, Captain?"

Smoke had recognized the bars on the man's shoulder straps that designated the visitor a captain, and Monte had, too.

"My name's Skinner," the officer replied. "Captain Adam Skinner, second-in-command of the First Colorado Rifle Brigade."

Smoke didn't recall ever hearing anything about that unit, but he'd never had much to do with the army.

Skinner was a tall, powerfully built man with a thatch of dark blond hair under his hat and rather coarse, sun-reddened features. He went on, "My commanding officer, Colonel Talbot, sent me to fetch you out to our camp. He needs to have some words with you."

Smoke saw Monte bristle a little at the captain's high-handed tone. Monte Carson was no junior officer who could be ordered around.

"What camp is that?" Monte asked coolly. "I didn't know the army had sent any men to these parts."

"We're just getting settled in now, a short distance east of town," Skinner said. "Colonel Talbot sent me to inform you of our presence, according to standard protocol where civilian authorities are concerned, and, uh . . ." It seemed to pain the captain a little to do so, but he made his tone more deferential as he went on, "And to request that you accompany me back to the camp so that he can discuss our mission with you personally."

Monte thought it over, then nodded. "I reckon I can do that. Does this Colonel Talbot of yours want to see me right away?"

"As soon as possible, Sheriff."

Monte glanced over at Smoke and asked, "What do you think? Want to take a ride?"

Before Smoke could answer, Skinner said, "Excuse me. Who is this man?"

"My friend Mr. Jensen."

"He doesn't hold any official rank or position? He's not one of your deputies?"

"I'm just a rancher," Smoke drawled.

Skinner shook his head. "Then I'm not sure you're included in the invitation, mister."

"Smoke Jensen is one of the leading citizens in these parts," Monte said, his voice cool again, "and he has my complete trust. Anything your commander can say to me, he can say with Smoke there."

"Smoke Jensen, eh?" Recognition of the name flared in Skinner's eyes for a second. Smoke didn't know why a cavalryman would have heard of him, but Skinner obviously had. His broad shoulders rose and fell. "Well, the colonel didn't say I *couldn't* bring anybody else back with me. If you want to come along, Jensen, I suppose that's all right."

Smoke would have been fine with it if Monte hadn't roped him in on this army business, whatever it was, but after Skinner's reaction, he figured he wanted to find out more. The quickest way to get Smoke Jensen to do something was to tell him he couldn't. Maybe that was a little contrary of him, but he didn't care.

"I'll fetch Drifter and let Sally know where I'm going," he told Monte.

"Who's Drifter?" asked Skinner. "I'm not sure about letting anybody else tag along."

"Don't worry, Captain. Drifter's my horse. He's usually pretty discreet."

Skinner's jaw tightened at that mild gibe. He jerked his head in a nod and said, "Fine. As long as we can get going pretty soon. I don't like to keep the colonel waiting."

"I'll get my horse from the livery stable," Monte said.

Smoke found Sally inside the mercantile and told her what was going on.

"The army?" she said in surprise. "What's the army doing here?"

"I reckon I'll find out, assuming that colonel doesn't kick me out of his meeting with Monte," Smoke said. "Do you mind waiting for me here in town when you're finished getting the supplies?"

Sally frowned. "I've made the trip back out to the ranch by myself before, Smoke, you know that. *And* there's a Winchester in the buckboard if I happened to run into any trouble."

Smoke had given her lessons with the rifle and knew she was a crack shot as well as cool under fire, but he said, "I know that, and I know you can take care of yourself, but until I find out what's going on, I think I'd rather you were here in town, around other folks."

For a second, she looked as if she were going to argue, but then she said, "All right, Smoke, if that's the way you want it." She smiled. "This is a good excuse to go over to the bakery and have a piece of pie."

Smoke returned the smile and said, "For some reason, I've got a hunch I'd rather be having some pie with you, instead of listening to whatever that army fella has to say."

By the time he got back to the sheriff's office, Captain Skinner was mounted and Monte was approaching on horseback from the direction of Patterson's Livery. The three men fell in alongside each other and rode east along Center Street, heading out of town.

Skinner had said that the camp was a short distance from the settlement. Smoke estimated they had covered about half a mile when they came in sight of a large meadow bordered by trees on three sides. Several dozen tents had been pitched in the meadow, and at least fifty horses were tied to ropes strung between trees on the western side. Blue-uniformed troopers moved around, busy with the tasks of setting up the camp.

"Looks like you've got a pretty good-sized bunch here, Captain," Smoke commented to Skinner. "Not enough to be what I'd consider a brigade, though."

"This is just part of the outfit," Skinner said. He pointed to the largest tent, which was four times the size of the others. "That's our headquarters and Colonel Talbot's living quarters."

They dismounted in front of the big tent. A couple of troopers ran up. Skinner told Smoke and Monte that the men would take care of their horses. As Smoke handed over his reins, he unobtrusively studied the soldier who took them.

The man was lean and could have used a shave. His uniform was a little wrinkled, too. Although Smoke wasn't familiar with army regulations, it appeared that this Colonel Talbot wasn't a stickler about such things.

Skinner led them into the tent, which was divided into two sections by a canvas partition. The front part was larger and had several folding tables set up in it. Smoke assumed the rear section was where the commanding officer's quarters were.

One of the tables had a large map spread out on it, and a man bent over it, resting his hands on the table as he studied the map. He glanced up when Skinner and the two civilians entered, then straightened and regarded them with interest.

The colonel was medium-sized but had a vitality about him that made him seem bigger at first glance. He was hatless. His dark, curly hair was cut fairly short to his head. A thin mustache adorned his upper lip. Smoke estimated his age around thirty, but as they came closer and he saw the fine lines around the officer's eyes and mouth, he revised that. Colonel Talbot was closer to forty, Smoke judged, but still a handsome man.

Skinner came to attention and saluted. Talbot returned it. Both salutes were crisp.

"I've brought back the sheriff from Big Rock, Colonel, like you ordered," Skinner said. He nodded toward Monte. "This is Sheriff Carson."

Talbot stepped around the table, smiled, and extended his hand since he was greeting a civilian. "Sheriff Carson, it's my pleasure to meet you," he said. "I'm Colonel Lamar Talbot." The officer glanced curiously at Smoke as he and Monte shook hands. "And this is one of your deputies, perhaps?"

"Nope, this is Smoke Jensen, one of the leading citizens in the valley and also one of the founders of Big Rock." Monte chuckled. "Some would say *the* founder of Big Rock, but Smoke would argue with you about that."

"A modest man, eh?" Talbot shook hands with Smoke, as well. "Thank you for coming out here with the sheriff, Mr. Jensen. We're going to need the support of the citizens if we're to carry out our mission, and it sounds as if you're one of the men who commands their attention."

"Just a fella trying to get along," Smoke said as he returned Talbot's strong handclasp. "And I admit, I'm more than a mite curious about this mission you just mentioned."

"Of course. It's really very simple." Now that he had shaken hands with the two visitors, Talbot stood ramrod straight and clasped his hands together behind his back. "My men and I are here to see to it that every man, woman, and child in this valley isn't slaughtered by filthy savages."

Chapter 6

For a moment after Colonel Talbot made that surprising statement, all Smoke and Monte could do was stare at the officer. Then Monte burst out, "What in blazes are you talking about?"

Talbot's face stiffened. Clearly, he didn't like being talked to that way, and he didn't respond immediately.

Smoke said, "We haven't heard anything about an Indian threat around here, Colonel. From the sound of it, that's what you're talking about."

Talbot relaxed slightly. "Indeed it is, Mr. Jensen."

Grudgingly, Monte said, "Begging your pardon, Colonel, but that was just about the last thing I expected to hear. There hasn't been any Indian trouble around here for quite a while."

"That's because you've been fortunate, Sheriff," Talbot said. "Other people haven't been as lucky . . . such as the more than one hundred and twenty innocent souls murdered by the Cheyenne in the past month or so."

"A hundred and twenty?" Monte let out a low whistle. "I hadn't heard anything about it."

"Neither have I," said Smoke.

"The incidents have been scattered," Talbot admitted with a shrug, "but we're convinced that all the attacks are the work of the same group of renegades. Have you ever heard of a Cheyenne war chief called Black Drum?"

Smoke and Monte glanced at each other. Smoke shook his head, and Monte replied to Talbot's question, "First time I've heard tell of him, Colonel. He's the leader of this group of renegades?"

"That's right." Talbot somehow seemed to know. "He and some of his followers left the reservation in Indian Territory a while back, killing several people at the local agency when they did so. Since then, Black Drum appears to have attracted more renegades. It's thought that now his force may even exceed a hundred men. They practically wiped out a town in eastern Colorado not long ago."

"What town?" Smoke asked.

"A place called Wicker's Wells."

Smoke nodded slowly. "I've been there. Last time I passed through, there wasn't anything there except a trading post, as I recall."

"The settlement had grown some," Talbot said. "But it won't anymore. Black Drum and his men burned it to the ground and killed all but a handful of the citizens." He paused. "I don't want that happening to Big Rock."

"Believe me, I don't, either!" Monte replied fervently. "But I don't think even a hundred renegades would attack a place the size of Big Rock."

"You might be surprised. This Black Drum appears to be something of a madman. There's no telling what he might attempt. And as for the ranches in this area . . ."

Monte rubbed his chin and sighed. "Yeah, you're right about that, Colonel. A war party of that size wouldn't have any trouble wiping out any of the ranches in these parts."

Smoke asked, "Do you know for sure that those renegades are headed in this direction, Colonel?"

"I don't know that Big Rock is specifically their target,

Mr. Jensen. But if they continue following the path they have been, then they are headed straight for you." A grim smile curved Talbot's lips. "But I intend to be here waiting for the red devil when he arrives."

"I can see why you wanted to talk to me about this, Colonel," Monte said, nodding. "And I surely do appreciate the warning. I'd better start spreading the word through the area for folks to be on the lookout for anything suspicious. Like you said, those renegades probably won't just hit the town first thing."

Smoke said, "Maybe it would be a good idea to hold off on that right now, Monte. If you tell everybody that a Cheyenne war party is on the way, they're liable to panic. You probably have some scouts attached to your unit, Colonel. Give me a few days, and I'll go out with them and try to make sure whether that fella Black Drum is even around here—"

Talbot interrupted with a curt shake of his head. "With all due respect, Mr. Jensen, we don't need any help from civilians. I'm confident in the information I've received, and I think alerting the people who live in the settlement and the valley is precisely what needs to be done. For one thing, it won't take long for news of our presence to get around, and I'd rather people know why we're here, rather than wondering about it."

"That makes sense, I suppose," Monte said.

"For another thing," Talbot continued, "we may need to call on the settlers for assistance on various matters, and it's best they know that by helping us, they're also helping themselves."

"I thought you just said you *didn't* need any help from civilians, Colonel," Smoke pointed out.

Captain Skinner spoke up, growling, "It's not the same thing, Jensen." He had been glaring at Smoke and Monte most of the way through the conversation.

Talbot lifted a hand and said, "That's enough, Captain." He turned his attention back to Smoke. "But Captain Skinner is correct, it's not the same thing. I welcome logistical support from the civilian population. I don't require military support from them in the field."

"At least not now," Smoke said.

Talbot shrugged. "We can't predict the future, can we? To a certain extent, that's up to Black Drum. And who can predict what a crazed, bloodthirsty savage will do?"

Smoke and Monte couldn't argue with that statement. Monte said, "All right, Colonel, you can count on us. I'll let folks in town know what's going on."

"And I'll send word to the other ranches in the valley," Smoke added. "I can have my friend Pearlie ride around and alert all of them."

"Pearlie?" Skinner repeated. "You mean Pearlie Fontaine?"

Smoke looked at the captain with new interest. "That's right. Are you acquainted with Pearlie, Captain?"

Skinner shook his head and looked like he wished he hadn't said anything. "No, I, ah, I've just heard of him, that's all. I thought he was some sort of hired gun, not a ranch hand."

"I'd say that he's more than just a ranch hand, and he's put his past behind him. Sometimes men do that."

"Yeah, sure," Skinner said. "I was just a little surprised, that's all."

Talbot smiled and said, "It sounds as if we'll have plenty of good men on our side if trouble does come to this valley, gentlemen. I'm very glad I can count on you for your help."

"Yes, sir, you just let us know what you need," Monte said.

Talbot shook hands with both of them again, then said, "Captain, if you'll show our visitors back to town—"

"That's all right," Smoke said. "We know the way."

He nodded to Skinner as he and Monte left the tent. The troopers who had been given the job of looking after their horses were right outside, holding the reins of the two mounts. Smoke and Monte swung up in their saddles and rode back toward Big Rock.

"What do you think, Smoke?" asked Monte. "Are we going to have Indian trouble?"

"I don't know," Smoke replied with a musing tone in his voice. "But my gut's telling me that there's trouble of some sort on the way."

Captain Adam Skinner stood holding the canvas flap of the headquarters tent entrance as he watched Jensen and Carson ride away. When they were out of sight, Skinner let the flap fall closed and turned back to where Talbot was now sitting with his feet propped up on the table.

The colonel's black boots were polished to a high shine. His uniform was crisp, from the gold leaves pinned to his collar to the toes of those boots. He was something of a dandy, but Skinner didn't care about that.

Lamar Talbot was also the most dangerous man he knew.

Talbot reached inside his jacket and took a cigar from his shirt pocket. He scratched a match to life on the edge of the table and lit the cheroot, then puffed on it for a second before he said, "You look worried about something, Adam. Spit it out."

Skinner took off his hat and tossed it on one of the tables. He said, "It was bad enough when I found out that Monte Carson's the law in Big Rock. I wasn't expecting that. But to have Smoke Jensen and Pearlie Fontaine around, too . . ."

"They have reputations as gunfighters, I take it?"

Skinner grunted. "Carson and Fontaine are gunfighters, or at least they used to be. Jensen, though . . . Smoke Jensen is more than that, Colonel. Some claim he's the fastest draw and deadliest shot west of the Mississippi . . . or east of it, for that matter." Skinner scratched his heavy jaw and went on, "I've heard that he once walked into a town where nineteen men were waiting to kill him. When he walked back out, all nineteen of those men were dead. And *they* were professionals, too."

Talbot stared at him for a second, then said, "That's absurd. No man could do such a thing."

"I've heard about it enough times, from enough different people, that it seems pretty likely to be true," Skinner responded with a shrug. "And that's just the start of it when it comes to Jensen. He dropped out of sight for a while and I figured there was a good chance he was dead, but I guess he was here, lying low and starting that ranch he claims to have."

Talbot puffed on the cigar as he frowned in thought. After a moment, he said, "I'm not pleased that we have to deal with these potential obstacles, Adam, but at the same time, I'm not going to allow them to scare me off. We came here to do a job, and we're going to do it. I remain convinced that Black Drum and his renegades are on their way to this area, and when they get here, we're going to deal with them." An added edge of venom entered his voice as he went on, "I don't want a single one of those filthy savages left alive."

"And in the meantime?" asked Skinner.

"In the meantime," Talbot drawled, "I don't think it would be out of line for the settlers in this valley to show us their appreciation for what we're going to do."

Chapter 7

"Indians?" Sally said as she kept the buckboard rolling along the trail to the Sugarloaf.

Smoke rode alongside on Drifter and had just filled her in on the conversation he and Monte Carson had had with Colonel Lamar Talbot.

Sally continued, "There's never been any real trouble around here from Indians, has there?"

"Not in the time you and I have lived here," Smoke replied, "but that doesn't mean it's always been that way. Or that dangers like that can't pop up again. I haven't fought Indians all that much in my life, not like Preacher has, but it was after a skirmish that he and my pa and I had with some Pawnee that he started calling me Smoke."

A little shudder ran through Sally as she handled the reins. "From what that Colonel Talbot said, that chief called Black Drum sounds like a lunatic."

"The way we look at it, a lot about the Indians' way of life does seem a mite loco," Smoke admitted. "But you have to remember, they feel the same way about us. There's been plenty of bad things done on both sides. Slaughtering innocent folks is never acceptable, though. If the colonel's right about Black Drum, he's got to be stopped, and it's probably going to take the army to do that. People are still too scattered here in the valley. The folks who live in Big Rock might be safe, but not the ones who have ranches."

"Ranches like the Sugarloaf," Sally said.

Smoke nodded slowly. "That's right. I was wondering what you'd think about maybe moving into town for a while, just until we have a better idea just how real this threat is."

"Are *you* going to move into town, too?" she shot back.

"Well, I can't just leave the Sugarloaf—"

"That's what I thought. There's a ranch to run, and you and Pearlie wouldn't even think about abandoning it, would you?"

"After all the work that's gone into getting it started?" Smoke shook his head. "I don't reckon I could do that."

"Well, neither can I. The Sugarloaf is my home just as much as it is yours. I have just as much stake in defending it as you do."

"Pearlie and I will have to be away from the ranch house a lot of the time, though. We won't be there in case there's trouble."

"If there's trouble, I'll deal with it," Sally said.

Smoke wished it were that simple. He believed she was sincere in thinking that she could take care of herself and defend the ranch. Sally had never lacked for courage, and she was highly capable, too.

But she would stand no chance against a Cheyenne war party. She might be able to hold them off for a while, but it wouldn't take them long to kill or capture her and lay waste to the place.

He saw the stubborn set to her jaw and knew he'd be wasting time arguing with her right now. Maybe he could hire a few more hands to help run the ranch, he told himself. That way, it was less likely Sally would be there by herself.

But would Sally and two or three cowhands really fare that much better against a hundred renegades? The outcome wouldn't be any different in the end, Smoke knew.

Maybe Black Drum wouldn't come this direction, after all.

From everything Preacher had told him, it was almost impossible to predict what an Indian would do. They were "notional critters," as the old mountain man would put it.

And if the renegades *did* try to raid the valley, maybe Colonel Talbot and his troopers would stop them. Smoke wished the colonel had agreed to let him help get a better handle on the situation, but he supposed he'd have to trust Talbot's judgment . . . for now.

In the end, though, Smoke knew it might come down to his own efforts to defend himself and his wife and friends and the ranch . . . and he was prepared to take whatever steps he had to in order to do that.

Haywood Arden, the editor and publisher of the *Big Rock Bulletin*, put out a special edition of the newspaper the next day, after talking to Monte Carson.

ARMY ARRIVES IN BIG ROCK
CAVALRY TO MAKE TOWN THEIR HEADQUARTERS
WHILE DEALING WITH POTENTIAL INDIAN THREAT

Those headlines were enough to start the whole settlement buzzing with excitement . . . and more than a little fear. Most of the citizens had never fought Indians. The ones who had come from the east had never even lived somewhere that such a thing was possible. But enough people in town *had* lived through such clashes, and the stories they told about previous battles and atrocities were enough to make everyone's blood run cold.

As if that weren't enough, Arden's story, which quoted Colonel Lamar Talbot, commander of the First Colorado Rifle Brigade, just increased the atmosphere of fear and foreboding even more with its description of the blood-soaked raids Black Drum and his renegades had carried out already.

Don Baker, owner and proprietor of the Big Rock Mercantile, was in his store, standing behind the counter at the back of the room, with the special edition of the *Bulletin* in his hands and a worried frown on his face, when the bell over the front door jingled. Baker looked up and saw two blue-uniformed cavalrymen entering the store. He folded the paper, dropped it on the counter, and smiled.

"Hello, gentlemen," he greeted the troopers. "What can I do for you?"

The soldier in the lead, who had the three stripes of a sergeant on the sleeve of his blue shirt, looked around. The store was empty at the moment except for him and his companion and Baker. He hooked his thumbs in his waistband and said, "I'm Sergeant Rafferty from the First Colorado Rifles. We're gonna need some supplies."

"Then you've come to the right place," Baker said. A large, jovial man, he waved a hand at their surroundings. "I carry just about anything a body might need. What can I get for you?"

Sergeant Rafferty reached into his shirt pocket and pulled out a folded piece of paper. "I've got a list . . ."

He unfolded it and spread it out on the counter so Baker could read it. As the storekeeper studied the list, his smile faltered.

"That's quite a bit," he said.

"Fifty men eat a lot," Rafferty replied.

"This would just about clean me out on a few items. There are a couple of other stores here in town. Maybe I could provide some of what you need, and the others—"

"It'd be simpler to get it all in one place," Rafferty interrupted him. "Those are my orders. We'll get to those other places later. I reckon there's a good chance we'll be around here for a while."

"I see." Baker wanted to cooperate, so he managed to get that smile back on his face. "All right, I suppose I can accommodate you, Sergeant. It'll take me a while to put together an order of this size, though. My clerk is gone to lunch. When he gets back to help me, things'll go a little quicker."

"Take however much time you need," said Rafferty. "We've got a wagon parked right outside. You can load the stuff on there."

Baker considered asking the troopers if they could stay around to help with the loading, but before he could frame the question, the sergeant went on, "We'll check back later. C'mon, Hemphill."

The two soldiers turned to walk out. Baker let his expression lapse into one of dismay as soon as they weren't looking at him anymore. This order would wipe out all his flour, sugar, coffee, beans, salt, and other provisions. Until he could re-stock, he wouldn't be able to do enough business to justify opening the doors every morning.

But the army needed these supplies, he told himself, and the army was there to protect him and the other citizens of Big Rock from the savages. So he supposed it was a worthwhile sacrifice to make. It would only be a temporary inconvenience, Baker told himself.

A couple of women came into the store just before the two soldiers reached the entrance. Rafferty held up a hand toward them, palm out, and said, "Store's closed right now. The clerk's working on an order for us."

Baker heard the sergeant clearly, and anger flared inside him at the words. First of all, Rafferty had no right to declare that the mercantile was closed. That was mighty high-handed of him. Secondly—and Baker knew it was a mite vain—he didn't appreciate being referred to as a clerk when he owned the business.

One of the women looked past the troopers at him and said, "Is that true, Mr. Baker?"

Before Baker could answer, the other soldier—Hemphill,

Sergeant Rafferty had called him—said, "You hadn't ought to be questionin' a military order, lady. We're in charge around here now."

Boldly, he ran his gaze over the women, both of whom were in their thirties and fairly attractive.

"That's enough, Hemphill," Rafferty snapped.

Hemphill didn't say anything else, but he continued leering as he looked at the two women.

Baker said quickly, "If you'll come back in a little while, ladies, I'll be glad to help you."

Assuming that he still had anything in stock they wanted to buy after filling the army's order, he added to himself.

"Well . . . all right," the woman who had spoken said. She took her friend's arm and they hurried out, with Hemphill still watching them lecherously.

Rafferty jerked his head at his subordinate, and they both left, too. Baker wasn't sad to see them go, although he knew they would be back.

He supposed that a little rudeness was a small price to pay to have the army here to protect the town, he thought with a sigh as he set about gathering the items on Sergeant Rafferty's list.

Louis Longmont sat at his private table in his saloon, a half-full cup of coffee in front of him, a cigar smoldering in an ashtray, and an open book in his lap: *Twenty Thousand Leagues Under the Sea*, one of the latest in the Voyages Extraordinaires by Mssr. Jules Verne, in the original French. It was quite exciting, and one of the characters, the stalwart sailor Ned Land, even reminded Louis a bit of his friend Smoke Jensen.

Louis had just taken a sip of coffee and replaced the cup on its saucer when two soldiers swaggered into the saloon. Like everyone else in Big Rock, he knew about the arrival of the First Colorado Rifles, having read the story in the special edition of the *Bulletin*. These two troopers were the first he had actually laid eyes on, however.

Louis used the ribbon attached to the book to mark his place, then set the volume down and rose gracefully to his feet. The troopers had paused just inside the batwings to look around the room. The dozen or so customers were interested in the newcomers, too. The low hum of talk in the room had tapered off as the soldiers walked in.

"Gentleman, welcome," Louis said in his resonant voice as he stepped around the table. He gestured toward the bar. "Please, join me."

One of the troopers was a sergeant, the other a private, Louis saw as they walked over to the bar and the saloon resumed some of its normal midday chatter.

"My name is Louis Longmont," he went on as they joined him in front of the hardwood. "I'm the owner of this establishment."

"Sergeant Rafferty," the shorter man said in a rather sullen tone. He jerked his head at the other soldier. "This is Private Hemphill."

"I'm pleased to make your acquaintance," Louis said. He was as comfortable with this non-commissioned officer and enlisted man as he would have been with a general . . . or a president or a prime minister, for that matter. "I hope you'll have a drink with me. On the house, of course."

The rawboned, lantern-jawed Private Hemphill grinned and said, "We ain't gonna turn down a free drink, are we, Sarge?"

"We're obliged to you," Rafferty said to Louis without answering Hemphill's question directly. "Better make it beer."

"Aw, Sarge," Hemphill began. "I was hopin'—"

"I know what you were hoping," Rafferty broke in. "The colonel won't mind us having a drink, but we've got a job to do and getting drunk on whiskey will just make it harder. You don't want to make the colonel or Captain Skinner mad at us, do you?"

Hemphill rolled his eyes and said, "You're damn right I don't. I reckon beer's all right, Sarge." He looked at Louis and added without much grace or sincerity, "Obliged, mister."

Louis motioned to the bartender, who drew the two beers and placed the foaming mugs in front of the troopers. "Anything for you, boss?" he asked Louis.

"No, I'm fine." Louis turned his attention to the soldiers and went on, "What brings you two gentlemen into town this morning? Have there been any sightings of those Cheyenne and Arapaho renegades?"

"Not yet," said Rafferty. "We just came in to pick up some supplies."

"I see. Well, I know that everyone in town is relieved that you're camped nearby, and if you need anything, we're certainly willing to help."

"That's good," Hemphill said with a smirk, "since we're gonna be takin' what we need, anyway."

"Shut up and drink your beer," Rafferty snapped.

Something was off about these two, Louis thought. He hadn't been around that many soldiers, but he had spent considerable time in the company of numerous gunmen, hard cases, and outlaws. Other than the blue uniforms, that was the way Rafferty and Hemphill struck him.

He supposed not every outfit could be crisp and disciplined, however. A lot of that came from the top down. Louis hadn't met the commander, Colonel Talbot, or his second-in-command, Captain Skinner, and didn't know anything about either man. They might just be lax on discipline.

Louis hoped that wouldn't make any difference when it came time to fight the renegades.

The two troopers drank their beers. When Hemphill thumped his empty mug on the bar, he belched and dragged the back of his other hand across his mouth.

"How about another one, Sarge?" he suggested. "I reckon

this fella could be talked into givin' it to us on the house again."

"Forget it," Rafferty said. "We need to get back over to the mercantile and see how that clerk's coming along on our order."

He looked at Louis and gave him a curt nod, then turned toward the door and prodded Hemphill along with him.

At one of the tables, the poker game that had been going on when the two troopers came in had resumed, and as a hand ended and one of the players raked in the pot, another man, a cowboy from one of the local spreads, exclaimed, "Dadblast it, Hector, that just about cleans me out! All I got left is enough money for one drink."

Clearly incensed about losing, he stood up abruptly, swung around, and took a step toward the bar, evidently intent on buying that one drink he could still afford.

Instead, he ran smack-dab into Private Hemphill. The collision staggered Hemphill, while the cowboy bounced off, took an unsteady step backward, and might have fallen if he hadn't caught himself with one hand on the edge of the table.

As he recovered his balance and straightened, he said, "Son of a gun, mister, I'm sorry—"

That was as far as he got before Hemphill stepped in and slammed a brutal right-hand punch into his midsection. Taken completely by surprise, the cowboy doubled over as his eyes widened from the pain. Hemphill hit him again, this time a looping left that crashed into the cowboy's jaw and drove him to the floor.

Those two blows had been struck in little more than the blink of an eye, and everybody in the saloon was so taken aback by the sudden violence that they didn't move when Hemphill unsnapped the flap of his holstered revolver, pulled out the gun, and aimed it at the hapless cowboy as he eared back the hammer.

Chapter 8

Not surprisingly, Louis Longmont was the first to act. Even though he had given up his gunfighting ways, he hadn't lost any of his speed. He still practiced regularly to make sure that he didn't, because a man who had lived the life he had, never knew when some enemy from the past might show up.

His hand flashed under his coat and drew a .32 caliber Smith & Wesson from the shoulder holster under his left arm. The gun came level as he snapped, "Hold your fire, Private!"

Sergeant Rafferty looked over his shoulder and reached for his own holster. "Put that gun down, mister," he said. "You can't draw on us like that."

"Talk to your trooper, Sergeant," Louis said. "If he murders that man, I'll kill him."

Hemphill seemed to have gotten control of the insane rage that had gripped him for a moment. He didn't lower the gun, but he cast a nervous glance over his shoulder and said, "Sarge . . . ?"

Rafferty's narrowed eyes went back and forth between Louis and Hemphill. He must have seen how calm Louis was and how steady the gun in the gambler's hand was, and realized what that composure meant. If Hemphill opened the ball, Louis could kill him *and* kill Rafferty before the sergeant ever got his gun out of the holster.

"Damn it!" Rafferty burst out. "Put that weapon away, you idiot!"

"Carefully," warned Louis.

Hemphill gently lowered the hammer on his revolver and slid the gun back into its holster. He stepped back, holding both hands up in plain sight.

Rafferty moved his hand away from his gun. He hadn't gotten around to unsnapping the holster flap before Louis's cold, dangerous voice had stopped him.

"All right, mister," Rafferty said. "It's over. You can put that gun down."

"Once the two of you are gone," Louis said. "And you're not welcome in here anymore. Don't come back."

"You can't do that."

"I believe I can."

The sergeant's face was flushed dark red with anger. "I'm going to report this incident to the colonel," he said. "He'll have a talk with your sheriff. You're going to be sorry you drew a gun on us."

"I'm sorry I bought you a beer," Louis drawled. "And I'll be talking to Sheriff Carson as well. It's possible that Mr. Dutton there will want to have your man charged with assault for attacking him like that."

The young cowboy, whose name was Bob Dutton, still lay on the floor, but he had pushed himself up on an elbow and was shaking his head groggily. He must have understood at least some of what Louis said, because he raised his other arm and shook his head.

"No . . . no charges," he said. "I just want to . . . get back to the ranch."

"Are you sure, Bob?" asked Louis.

"Y-yeah, Mr. Longmont. I'm sure."

"Very well, then. But I'm still going to make sure the sheriff knows *exactly* what happened here."

"Go ahead," Rafferty said, glaring. "It won't matter. We're in charge here now." He gripped Hemphill's arm and practically shoved the trooper toward the batwings. "Go on. Let's get out of here."

Louis waited until they were gone before he slipped the .32 back in its holster. The men who had been playing poker with Bob Dutton gathered around him and helped him to his feet. Louis went over to the table and asked, "Are you all right, Bob? Do you need to see the doctor?"

Dutton rubbed his belly where he'd been punched, grimaced, and then took hold of his chin and moved his jaw back and forth to check it.

"Don't seem like anything's broken," he said. "I reckon I'll be all right, Mr. Longmont. What made that fella go loco? Sure, we bumped together pretty hard, but not hard enough to make him act like that."

"I don't know," Louis replied honestly. "He struck me as the sort of man who runs roughshod over people simply because he can."

"But that ain't good, if that's the sort of fella we're supposed to count on to protect us from the Injuns."

"No," Louis said. "No, it's not."

Don Baker grunted as he set a heavy sack of flour inside the wagon parked in front of the Big Rock Mercantile. Ike Hairston, his clerk, lowered a sack of beans next to the flour and said, "I think that's the last of it, Mr. Baker."

Filling the order that the troopers had left with him had gone faster once Ike returned from lunch. Even so, Baker had had to turn away a few customers who had shown up while they were busy with the task. Doing that went against the grain for Baker, as it would with any merchant.

But under the circumstances, with a huge war party of vicious renegades possibly threatening the settlement, Baker supposed it was best to take care of the army's needs first.

"Let me go check the list the sergeant gave me to make sure, Ike," Baker said. Both men went back into the store. Baker walked behind the counter and studied the paper that still lay there. He nodded as he moved the tip of his right index finger down the list, mentally checking off each item. Nodding in satisfaction, he said, "Yep, that's it."

Just in time, too, because heavy footsteps coming through the open door announced the return of Sergeant Rafferty and Private Hemphill.

Baker noticed right away that both men were scowling. He had no idea what had displeased the troopers, but he hoped they would be happy to find that their order was loaded.

The storekeeper rested both hands on the counter, smiled, and said, "Got you all fixed up, Sergeant. I had everything you wanted in stock, and it's loaded on your wagon."

Rafferty grunted as he picked up the list and stuffed it back in his pocket. "Good." He jerked his head at the private. "Come on, Hemphill."

They turned and started back out.

"Uh, gentlemen, wait a minute," Baker called after them. He tried not to frown as he went around the counter and followed them up the aisle toward the door. "There's still a little matter of the bill."

"You'll have to send it to the War Department in Washington," Rafferty said. He looked annoyed that Baker had stopped them from leaving.

"Well, you never said anything about that—"

"I don't owe you any explanations," Rafferty snapped.

"But you do owe me for all those goods, or somebody does. You've cleaned out a lot of my inventory. I need the money for this merchandise so I can order more stock to replace it."

Rafferty shook his head and said, "That's not my problem.

Cap'n Skinner just ordered us to pick up these supplies, and that's what we're going to do. He didn't say anything about paying for them."

Baker stepped toward the men, lifted a hand, and said, "Wait, maybe you could at least sign a receipt to show what you're taking—"

Private Hemphill swung around. A snarl twisted his features. Taking Baker completely by surprise, he cracked his left fist against the storekeeper's jaw in a backhanded blow.

The vicious punch knocked Baker to the side. He stumbled hard against one of the shelves and knocked it over. The shelf and the cast-iron pots and pans stacked on it crashed to the floor.

Ike Hairston, who had been standing in front of the counter, rushed toward the troopers, crying, "Hey! You can't—"

Hemphill met him with a hard right to the face that caused blood to spurt from Ike's nose and splatter down on the canvas apron he wore. Ike's head rocked back from the punch. Hemphill hooked his right foot behind Ike's left ankle and jerked that leg out from under him. Ike sat down hard and looked stunned.

Hemphill stepped closer and drew his leg back, obviously getting ready to kick Ike in the face. Baker had regained his balance by now and yelled, "No!"

"Private Hemphill!" Rafferty's voice cracked out. "Stop that."

"I don't like these yokels mouthin' off at us, Sarge. They should be thankful we're here to save 'em from those damned dirty redskins!"

"Yeah, maybe we ought to just ride away and leave them to fend for themselves," said Rafferty. "But that's not up to us to decide. We just follow orders." He glared at Baker. "And our orders are to get those supplies, so that's what we're doing. You don't like it, mister, take it up with Washington."

"I'll take it up with your commanding officer," Baker said.

He was frightened of these two, he wasn't going to deny that, but at the same time, he believed in standing up for his rights.

Rafferty didn't seem impressed, though. He just chuckled humorlessly and said, "You do that, mister. You just do that." He gestured curtly. "Come on, Hemphill."

From where he sat on the floor with blood still running from his swollen nose, Ike asked, "Do you want me to go after the sheriff, Mr. Baker?"

Rafferty and Hemphill had started to walk out. The sergeant paused to say over his shoulder, "Your law's got no authority over us, kid. The sooner you realize that, the better."

"We'll just see about that," Baker said, but the words sounded hollow even to him.

The two troopers must have thought so, too, because they were laughing as they left the mercantile. A moment later, while Baker was helping Ike to his feet, he heard the loaded wagon rolling away outside.

"Mr. Baker, what are we gonna do?" Ike asked as he held his bandanna to his crimson-leaking nose. "We can't let those soldier boys get away with this. Why, it's just plumb stealin'!"

"I don't know if there's anything we *can* do, Ike," Baker said with a gloomy look on his face. "But I'm going to tell Monte Carson about this anyway and see what he says. First, though, we need to tend to you."

Ike waved his free hand and told the storekeeper, "Don't worry about me. I've been punched in the nose before. Just go talk to the sheriff."

Monte Carson leaned back in his chair across the table from Louis Longmont and shook his head.

"I'm sorry, Louis," he said. "If Bob Dutton doesn't want to press charges against that trooper, there's nothing I can do. They didn't cause any damage in here or assault anybody else, did they?"

"No, they didn't," Louis confirmed. "If they had tried, there might well have been shooting. I wouldn't have just stood by and let them get away with it."

Monte chuckled and said, "Knowing you, I don't reckon you would have, so I'm glad there wasn't any." Monte frowned in thought. "Something you said sort of puzzles me, though. That private drew a pistol and threatened Dutton with it?"

"That's right."

"I'm no expert on how the army does things, but I thought that enlisted men just carried rifles, not handguns."

Louis frowned, too, and said, "I believe that's right."

"Come to think of it, when Smoke and I rode out to their camp to talk to Colonel Talbot, I believe every man I saw was packing a six-shooter. That's a little odd, isn't it? Especially since they're the First Colorado Rifles."

"Obviously the name doesn't mean they're armed exclusively with long guns." Louis paused, then said, "Honestly, though, Monte, neither of those men impressed me as being very soldier-like. Up close, they seemed more like the sort of men you and I used to ride with."

"Hired gun-wolves, you mean," Monte said heavily.

"You and I *are* uniquely qualified to recognize the breed."

"Yeah, that's the truth. I don't know it means, though—"

Before Monte could speculate any further, both men looked toward the entrance, where the batwings had just been slapped aside as a man hurried into the saloon. His urgency drew the attention of the sheriff and the gambler. As the newcomer paused to look around, they recognized Don Baker, the owner and proprietor of the Big Rock Mercantile.

Baker saw them, too, and strode toward them. The store-keeper had a bruise on the left side of his jaw, Monte noted. That and the look on Baker's face were plenty to tell him that more trouble had broken out.

Monte stood up and said, "What is it, Don?"

"Two of those cavalry troopers came into my store a while ago," Baker replied. "They gave me a big order of supplies they wanted to pick up."

Louis had gotten to his feet as well. He said, "They came in here while they were waiting for you to fill the order, Don, so we know about that."

"Did they start trouble here, too?"

"They most certainly did."

"What did they do to you?" asked Monte.

"Refused to pay for the goods Ike and I loaded on the wagon," Baker said. "And when I objected, that private walloped me with no warning." He gestured toward the bruise on his jaw. "It gets worse, though. Ike tried to jump in and help me, and Private Hemphill knocked him down and bloodied his nose. It may even be broken. He was about to kick poor Ike in the face when Sergeant Rafferty stopped him."

"So Hemphill assaulted you and Ike both," Monte said. "Do you want me to go out to their camp and arrest him?"

"Well, I don't know . . ." Baker replied with a doubtful frown. "Rafferty implied that if the town gives them too much trouble, they'll just ride away and leave us to the Indians."

Louis said, "I don't think the army can disobey orders like that. They were sent here to protect us."

Monte rubbed his chin. "You say they refused to pay for the supplies, too?"

"Well . . . Sergeant Rafferty said I'd have to send the bill to the War Department in Washington."

"Did they make arrangements for you to do that *before* you loaded up all the goods?"

"Absolutely not," Baker replied. "I was expecting to get paid before they left. He wouldn't even sign a receipt showing what they were taking, so I don't have a bit of proof of what they drove off with."

"Then it's doubtful the War Department would pay such a

claim, even if you sent it to them," Louis said. "That sounds like theft to me."

"Did anybody witness the fight Private Hemphill had with you and Ike?" asked Monte.

Baker made a face but shook his head.

"So it would be your word against theirs, all the way around. Even so, I believe you, Don. Your word, and Ike's, is enough for me to ride out there and arrest them if that's what you want."

Baker sighed and shook his head. "No, no, the more I think about it, the more I figure you don't need to do that. Especially since it's likely nothing would ever come of it."

Louis said, "But that means letting those two get away with what they did."

"Yeah, but we need the army here," Baker said. "If that loco Cheyenne Black Drum is coming this way with his war party, I don't want the town left undefended."

"We defended ourselves fairly well against Tilden Franklin's hired killers, as I recall," Louis pointed out.

"Yeah, but a bunch of bloodthirsty Cheyenne and Arapaho . . . that's different."

"It's up to you, Don," Monte said. "I'm not afraid of those soldiers."

"Of course not. Neither am I. I just don't want to make a bad situation even worse."

Monte shrugged. "Fine. You'll know better next time, if they come looking for more supplies."

"They won't be able to get much from me," Baker said glumly. "They just about cleaned me out already."

"It might be a good idea to spread the word to the other merchants to be careful in their dealings with the troopers," Monte said. "I'll take care of that."

"Thanks, Sheriff." With his shoulders slumping in defeat, Baker turned and left the saloon.

Monte turned to Louis and said, "I don't like the way this is shaping up. It looks like those soldiers believe they can do whatever they want around here and get away with it."

"And so far they have," Louis said coolly.

"Don't you start giving me a rough time about this," Monte said. "They've got me caught between a rock and a hard place."

Louis nodded and said, "I know. I just can't help but wonder how hard a place it's going to be."

Chapter 9

In addition to raising cattle on the Sugarloaf, Smoke had one of the finest horse herds in this part of the state. Word had started to get around about that top-notch horseflesh, and men had begun visiting the ranch to buy saddle mounts for themselves or working cow ponies for their remudas.

Smoke was perched on the top rail of one of his corrals, watching Pearlie work with a stubborn bronc. The horse sunfished and swapped ends and crow-hopped as it tried to buck Pearlie off. He stuck in the saddle, though, every bit as stubborn as the horse. Even though he wore spurs, he didn't rake the rowels against the animal's flank or jerk hard on the bit. He wasn't trying to break the horse's spirit, just show it who was boss.

Pearlie had been working on gentling this particular mustang for several days, and each day the horse put up a little less of a fight. This patient approach would result in a better mount in the end.

A swift rataplan of hoofbeats made Smoke turn his head to look along the trail leading from Big Rock to the Sugarloaf. He spotted a single rider coming quickly toward the ranch headquarters. As the man came closer, Smoke recognized him as Bob Dutton.

The young cowboy had come to work at the Sugarloaf only a few days earlier, although Smoke had known him for a while. Dutton had ridden for several of the spreads in the valley and in other places before that. He tended not to stay in any one job for too long, not because he had trouble with the men he worked for but simply because he had the sort of restless nature that wouldn't let him stay still.

Most hombres who were plagued by that tendency were called shiftless or saddle tramps. In the time that Bob Dutton had worked on the Sugarloaf, though, Smoke had found him to be both capable and industrious. He was glad to have the youngster around for however long Dutton wanted to be part of his crew, which had expanded to four men in the past week, since Smoke had heard about the possible threat to the valley posed by Black Drum's war party.

Dutton reined his horse to a walk as he approached the corral. Smoke lifted a hand in greeting and called, "Howdy, Bob. Trouble somewhere on the range?"

Earlier, Smoke had sent Dutton over to the Sugarloaf's eastern pastures to check on some stock there.

The young cowboy brought his mount to a stop and thumbed his hat back on his head. "There are half a dozen riders headed this direction from town, Mr. Jensen," he reported. His mouth tightened and he frowned. "Soldiers."

Smoke knew that Dutton had gotten into a ruckus in town with one of the troopers. Dutton had been honest about that when he asked Smoke for a job. His previous employer, a stiff-necked rancher named Coleman, had fired him over that scrape, even though it sounded as if Dutton hadn't done anything wrong. Coleman didn't want to get on the bad side of the soldiers, though.

Smoke, on the other hand, trusted his instincts, and they told him Bob Dutton was all right. Given what had happened, it was no surprise that the youngster wasn't happy about the troopers visiting the Sugarloaf.

"Did you talk to them," Smoke asked, "or just see them?"

"I lit a shuck back here to headquarters as soon as I spotted them," Dutton replied. "I didn't figure I had anything to say to any of that bunch."

Smoke nodded. "Tend to your horse, then go over to the house and tell Mrs. Jensen I said to give you a cup of coffee. Don't worry, Bob, I'll handle the troopers."

Dutton swung down from his saddle and said, "Well, if they give you any trouble, Mr. Jensen, you just holler. I won't be far off."

Pearlie had dismounted as well. He tied the bronc's reins to the snubbing post in the center of the corral and said, "I don't reckon those soldier boys can come up with anything Smoke and me can't handle."

Smoke felt the same way. He looked along the trail and spotted the dust rising from the hooves of the approaching horses.

"Go ahead and do what I told you, Bob," he said quietly.

Dutton led his mount into the barn, then emerged a few minutes later and walked over to the ranch house. Sally must have heard the conversation and realized something was going on, because she had appeared in the doorway. Dutton spoke briefly to her, and they both went inside.

Smoke was glad the young cowboy was out of sight. He wasn't the sort to run away from trouble, but he wasn't going to provoke it unnecessarily, either.

By now, the visitors were close enough for him to make out the individual riders. Five of the men wore black, stiff-billed caps, but the man in the lead had a tan hat on his head with the brim pushed up a little in the front. Smoke recognized him by that headgear as Captain Adam Skinner, second-in-command of the cavalry unit.

Pearlie climbed over the corral fence and dropped lightly to his feet next to Smoke. He had buckled on the gun belt he had draped over the fence before he started gentling the feisty mustang. He checked the Colt, sliding it a little in and out of the holster in which it rode.

"You shouldn't need that," Smoke said.

"Shouldn't," Pearlie agreed. "But you never know."

That was the truth, thought Smoke. He hooked his thumbs in his own gun belt and waited for the cavalrymen to ride up.

When they did, Skinner lifted a hand in a signal for them to halt. The captain walked his own mount forward until he was about twenty feet from Smoke, then stopped. With a curt nod, he said, "Hello, Jensen."

"Captain," Smoke said. "What can I do for you?"

Skinner looked around, turning his head slowly from side to side. "Nice spread you've got here," he said.

"We're small but growing," Smoke allowed.

"I'm told you have some of the best horses in the state."

Smoke's shoulders, broad as an ax handle, rose and fell slightly. "I'd like to think so."

Skinner nodded toward the horse in the corral and said, "That one there looks like a fine piece of horseflesh."

"He is," Pearlie agreed. "He'll be even better once I get finished workin' with him."

"You're the bronc buster, eh?"

"I don't bust 'em. I make 'em better."

Skinner grunted, then said, "I need some horses that are already good saddle mounts. How many do you have on hand, Jensen?"

Smoke, having heard from Bob Dutton about the other trouble that had happened at the mercantile in Big Rock, asked coolly, "Are you looking to *buy*, Captain?"

Skinner's jaw tightened. "Like I said, I need horses. Seems to me like you ought to be willing to provide them, seeing as we're here risking our lives to protect you folks from those bloodthirsty heathens."

"You haven't done any protecting so far," Smoke pointed

out. "In fact, from what I've heard, the only trouble any of our citizens have had came from your men."

"You're talking about that scrape in town?" Skinner jerked a hand in a curt, slashing gesture. "That was just a misunderstanding."

"A misunderstanding with some bruises and a bloody nose involved."

Making a visible effort to control his temper, Skinner said, "Look, I didn't come here for an argument. I need a dozen good horses, and if you're not willing to provide them, I have no choice but to commandeer them for the army's use."

Smoke had to tighten the reins on his own temper now. He drew in a deep breath and then said, "Do you mean you're going to steal them, Captain?" His voice lowered a notch and became even flatter and more dangerous. "That would make you a horse thief, wouldn't it?"

Skinner was beyond angry now. His face flushed a deep red as he dismounted and flipped his reins to one of the troopers who brought his horse up alongside Skinner's mount.

"You've got no right to talk to me like that," Skinner rasped as he strode toward Smoke. "We can take whatever we need in order to carry out our orders."

"Not unless the area is under martial law, you can't," Smoke said. "And I don't recall hearing anything about that."

He still stood in a seemingly casual stance as he faced Skinner squarely over a distance of about ten feet, but in reality, every muscle in his body was taut and ready for action if need be.

Skinner stopped, scowled at him for a long moment, and then said, "We're commandeering a dozen horses for temporary use. When our mission here is completed, the animals will be returned to you."

Smoke could tell that Skinner didn't like making that statement. The captain didn't like anybody defying him, period.

So he wasn't going to care for what was about to happen next. Smoke shook his head and said, "I'm not going to comply with that *request*, Captain. I'm a civilian and not under your authority, unless martial law has been declared, like I said. You come back with a declaration like that from the governor, and I'll be glad to help you out."

Skinner's anger erupted. "Damn it, that was an order, not a request, and you can't refuse an order like that!"

"I just did," Smoke replied coolly.

"I have five men!"

"Are you going to order them to open fire on us illegally?" asked Smoke. "I'm not sure they'd want to do that."

Actually, he was convinced the troopers probably *would* do whatever Skinner told them to, whether the order was legal or not. They had the same lean, wolfish appearance as the other soldiers Smoke had seen. But he was still trying to head off trouble if he could.

"There are only two of you," Skinner pointed out.

"Three!" Bob Dutton called from the ranch house doorway, where he had appeared with a Henry rifle in his hands.

"Four!" Sally added from a window. She rested a Henry's octagonal barrel on the sill as it pointed toward the troopers. Smoke would have just as soon she had stayed out of this . . . but he wasn't the least bit surprised that she hadn't.

All the troopers sat tensely on their horses. None of them had drawn a gun, but clearly, they were ready to do so. On the ground, Pearlie had eased a little to one side, so he would have a clean shot at them if he had to slap leather. Although the civilians were outnumbered, the odds were close enough to even that the Henrys might be enough to tip the balance. The air was thick with tension, and Smoke knew they were one spark away from all hell breaking loose.

Then Skinner drew in a breath that made his nostrils flare and snapped, "At ease!"

The troopers relaxed—but only a little.

To Smoke, Skinner went on, "You haven't heard the end of this, Jensen. You won't get away with it."

"Like I said, bring me a declaration of martial law, and I'll cooperate however you want."

Snarling, Skinner started to turn back to his horse. He was reaching for the reins being held by one of the troopers when he paused abruptly and looked back at Smoke.

"Forget the army and martial law and everything else," he said. "I don't like you, Jensen. What say we settle this between ourselves, man to man?"

"You want to draw against me?" Smoke was surprised.

Skinner shook his head. "Hell, no. I've heard about you. I know you're supposed to be some sort of fancy gunfighter." The captain's eyes narrowed. "But how brave are you when you're not packing iron?"

"You figure to take me on hand to hand?"

"Unless you don't have the guts for it." Skinner let out an ugly laugh. "Call it a bet. A friendly wager. You and me, bare knuckles, no-holds-barred. You win, we'll ride away and not bother you anymore. I win, and we get those horses the colonel sent us after. For good, instead of them being commandeered temporarily."

Smoke considered the proposition. Skinner was an inch or two taller than him and probably twenty pounds heavier. It was hard to be sure because of the uniform he wore, but his burly frame seemed to be covered with thick slabs of muscle. He probably had a lot of experience when it came to brawling, or he wouldn't have issued such a challenge in the first place.

"How about it, Jensen?" Skinner prodded. "Are you man enough to take me on?"

Skinner's confidence bordering on arrogance grated on Smoke's nerves. His hands went to the buckle of his gun belt.

"All right, Captain," he said. "You've got a bet."

Quietly, Pearlie said, "Are you sure you want to do this, Smoke?"

"Yeah." Smoke grinned as he handed the coiled shell belt and holstered Colt to his friend. "Anyway, it's too late to back out now, isn't it?"

Skinner was taking off his gun, too. He handed it and his hat to one of the troopers, then started rolling up the sleeves of his blue uniform shirt while Smoke hung his hat on a fence post. He noted how heavily muscled Skinner's forearms were, just as he'd expected.

"No-holds-barred, you said?" Smoke asked as he and Skinner began circling each other warily.

"That's right," Skinner said, and then with no more warning than that, he launched a vicious kick aimed right at Smoke's groin.

Chapter 10

Smoke expected something dirty from Skinner, so he wasn't surprised. He twisted aside so the captain's boot just scraped along the outside of his left thigh.

With the same almost supernatural speed that made him one of the most feared gunmen on the frontier, Smoke grabbed Skinner's ankle and heaved up on the leg that was already in the air. Off-balance the way he was, Skinner had no chance of staying upright. He went over backward and crashed down heavily on his back.

Smoke could have rushed in while Skinner was stunned and broken some of the captain's ribs with a few well-placed kicks of his own. He could have stomped his boot heel on Skinner's throat and crushed the man's windpipe. He had no doubt that Skinner would have tried to do that if the tables had been turned.

Smoke Jensen wasn't that sort of man, however. He took a step back and waited for Skinner to recover.

"I've had enough if you have, Captain," he offered. He didn't expect Skinner to call off the fight, but he was willing to extend the opportunity.

Skinner rolled onto his side, pushed up on hands and knees, and stayed there for a moment, head hanging and back heaving as he tried to catch the breath that the hard landing had knocked out of him. He shook his head like a dog and then raised it to glare at Smoke.

"Not hardly," he growled as he climbed to his feet. "This fight's just getting started."

With that, he rushed Smoke, swinging wildly. Those round-house punches might have taken Smoke's head off if any of them had connected, but Smoke ducked under them, stepped in, and hammered a pair of hooks, right and left, into Skinner's midsection.

It was a little like punching a washboard, Smoke realized. Skinner's torso didn't have an ounce of fat on it. But even though the blows didn't seem to hurt him, the force of them knocked him back a couple of steps. That gave Smoke enough room to snap a straight right to Skinner's jaw.

Skinner's head rocked back. Smoke tried to press his advantage, then saw too late that his punch actually hadn't had as much effect as Skinner acted like it had. The captain was ready for him and slipped in a hard right that caught Smoke in the chest. It felt like somebody had swung a log on a chain and hit him with the end of it. He was the one gasping for air now as he stumbled back a step.

Skinner bored in, punching fast and hard. Smoke blocked the first two blows, but the third one got past him and landed like a stick of dynamite on his chin, slewing his head to the right. His knees went weak and he started to sag.

Smoke turned that to his advantage and let himself fall as Skinner swung another wild punch above his head. He went forward in a diving tackle that caught Skinner around the knees. Skinner went down in a tangled heap as Smoke rolled to his right.

With a shake of his head to clear the cobwebs from his brain, Smoke pushed up and saw Skinner sprawled on the ground a few feet away. As Skinner rolled onto his back, Smoke leaped and landed on top of him. He dug a knee into the captain's belly to pin Skinner to the ground. Then he slammed a right and a left into Skinner's face before the man could get his hands up to block them.

Blood from Skinner's mouth made a crimson smear across the bottom half of his face. He looked pretty groggy, as if he were on the verge of passing out. He must have realized that his situation was desperate, because he suddenly bucked wildly, just like that bronc had tried to get Pearlie off its back earlier.

Smoke tried to hold on, but Skinner threw him off. At the same time, Skinner lifted his right elbow and caught Smoke under the jaw with it. That made the world spin crazily for Smoke again. He hit the ground on his left shoulder and rolled, vaguely aware that the other soldiers were yelling encouragement to Skinner now. They thought their captain was about to win.

Skinner scrambled up and tried to leap on Smoke, the same way Smoke had jumped on him a few moments earlier. Smoke was able to jerk his left knee up, though, and he met Skinner's attack with a kick that sunk his boot heel into the cavalryman's belly. Skinner doubled over and collapsed, curling up around the pain in his midsection. Smoke scooted away a few feet and got up on one knee, where he remained, huffing and puffing.

Skinner was one hell of a brawler. He and Smoke were just about evenly matched. Just as Smoke had met few men who could even come close to matching his speed with a gun, he hadn't encountered many who could hold their own with him in a hand-to-hand battle like this.

Skinner still wasn't ready to admit defeat. Uttering curses, he got a hand on the ground and pushed himself up. He climbed unsteadily to his feet. He was hunched over now, obviously still hurting from the kick to the belly. But he shuffled forward, hands clenching into fists.

"I'm gonna beat you down, Jensen," he panted. "Then I'm gonna tear you limb from limb and stomp the pieces!"

"Come on," Smoke said, back on his feet now, too. From the corner of his eye, he saw Sally and Bob Dutton watching anxiously from the ranch house. A glance in the other direction told him that Pearlie was watching the fight, too, but the former gunman was also keeping an eye on those troopers. Pearlie wouldn't let his guard down.

With a sudden bellow of rage, Skinner straightened and charged. Smoke could tell that the wild punch the captain threw was just a feint, though. Skinner expected him to move away from it, and Skinner's other fist was already lifting in an uppercut. Smoke swayed toward it to make Skinner believe he had bitten on the feint, then abruptly leaned back. Skinner's punch whistled past, missing his chin by mere inches.

Smoke hooked a left to Skinner's wide-open solar plexus. That washboard middle was a little weaker now. Skinner gasped and dropped his arms. Smoke whipped a roundhouse right at his jaw. The blow landed cleanly and snapped Skinner's head to the side. The captain's eyes rolled up in their sockets. Smoke stepped back and got out of the way as Skinner toppled face-first to the ground, unconscious.

The other soldiers weren't yelling now. They stared in silent, dumbfounded amazement instead. It was quite possible, Smoke thought, that they had never seen Skinner defeated before.

The captain was beaten now, though. He was out cold. In fact, Smoke thought for a second that he might have killed the man, until he saw Skinner's back moving up and down.

Smoke stood there, breathing hard himself, and carefully flexed both hands. They hurt, but all the joints and muscles worked. He would need to soak them in cold water to keep the swelling down. He had some horse liniment that would help, too.

Even so, it was sort of a stupid thing he had done, he told himself. He was lucky he hadn't broken a knuckle or two, pounding on Skinner like that. A man who depended on his hands to draw and fire a gun like Smoke did had no business taking chances with them like that.

He had never been one to back down from a fight, though, especially against somebody as obnoxious as Captain Adam Skinner.

Pearlie stepped forward and said, "You all right, Smoke?"

"Yeah, I'm fine."

Pearlie nodded and turned to the troopers. "Some of you boys pick up the cap'n and put him on his horse. Then you can go back to the colonel and tell him you didn't get those horses you came after. And when you tell him about this little fracas, you be sure he understands it was Skinner's idea . . . *and* that it was a fair fight. If I hear any different, I ain't gonna take it kindly."

One of the troopers sneered and said, "You act like you're a big man, Fontaine, but you ain't."

"Do we know each other?" Pearlie snapped.

"No, but I know who you are." The man jerked a hand at the others. "Get the cap'n."

While they were doing that, Sally emerged from the house and started toward Smoke. She still carried the Henry rifle. Smoke held up a hand to stop her before she had taken more than a couple of steps.

"I'm all right," he called to her. "Stay back for now."

She hesitated, obviously torn between the urge to rush to his side and her desire to do what he wanted. Then she nodded and stayed where she was, the Henry held at a slant in front of her. Bob Dutton was in the doorway behind her, his rifle at the ready, too.

The troopers lifted Skinner onto his saddle. He was big enough that it took three of them and considerable grunting and heaving before he was sitting upright. He had regained just enough consciousness to sit there shaking his head groggily. One man held him while two more moved their horses up close enough alongside to grasp his arms and keep him from toppling off his mount.

"Now git!" Pearlie ordered.

The troopers rode away, several of them glancing back balefully over their shoulders. Once they had put some distance between themselves and the civilians, Sally hurried over to Smoke and laid a hand on his arm.

"Are you really all right?" she asked.

"Yeah," he assured her. "My hands ache some, but I've bounced them off plenty of jackasses like that in the past. They'll be fine by tomorrow." He shrugged. "Well enough, anyway."

She knew what he meant: well enough to handle a gun if he needed to.

Pearlie raked a thumbnail along his jawline and frowned. "I reckon that Cap'n Skinner was right about one thing, Smoke. It's mighty likely you *ain't* heard the end of this."

"Probably not," Smoke agreed. "Colonel Talbot won't like it that he didn't get the horses he sent Skinner after, and I've got a hunch he'll be upset about Skinner getting whipped, too."

"Smoke," Sally said as her hand tightened on his arm, "are we in more danger from the army than we are from the Indians they're supposed to protect us from?"

"I wish I knew," he told her. "I really do."

Chapter 11

Hank Coleman was a medium-sized man with iron-gray hair and a neatly trimmed mustache of the same shade. He had been one of the first settlers in this valley and had a nice-sized cattle spread, the Triangle EC, after the initials of his late wife Edith. Coleman was known to be a hard taskmaster for the men who worked for him, but nobody had ever accused him of not being a straight shooter. He always said what he meant and meant what he said.

Right now, he meant every word of it as he yelled, "Get back to the ranch! Get back to the ranch!"

He leaned far forward over his horse's neck, dug in his spurs, and slashed with the reins, trying to get every ounce of speed possible out of the cow pony.

Ten yards in front of Coleman, riding every bit as hard as he was, were three of his ranch hands: Hal Abrams, Oscar Nickerson, and Sam Bentley. The four men had been exploring an area of rough breaks at the very eastern edge of Coleman's range, hazing out some cattle who had drifted up in there.

Nickerson had been trying to get in front of a particular stubborn steer when his horse had stumbled and nearly thrown him. That misstep had saved the cowboy's life, because at that moment, an arrow had come flying from behind him and struck Nickerson's hat, knocking it right off his head. If that stumble hadn't caused him to lurch forward in the saddle, though, the arrow would have hit him in the back of the neck and probably come out the front of his throat.

Nickerson's startled yell had drawn the attention of Hank Coleman, riding nearby, and Coleman had shouted at the top of his lungs, "Indians!"

With everyone in the valley keyed up because of the threat from Black Drum's renegades, that single shouted word was enough to send all four men racing hellbent-for-leather away from there.

Moments later, a group of mounted warriors burst out of some brush and charged after them, whooping with blood-thirsty anticipation.

Those savages were fifty yards behind Coleman now, and it was still a mile or more back to the ranch house. If they could make it to that sturdy structure, they might be able to fort up and hold off the war party.

If they were caught before then, however, they wouldn't stand a chance.

Coleman twisted in the saddle, thrust out his right arm, and triggered the gun in that hand. He fired four shots, not expecting to hit anything at that range, especially from the back of a galloping horse. He just wanted to discourage the warriors and slow them down a little if he could.

To his shock, one of the Indians screeched, threw his arms in the air, and pitched off the back of his pony to land in a limp, rolling sprawl. Blind luck had guided that bullet, Coleman knew, but he felt a swift surge of satisfaction anyway.

No matter what happened from here on out, he had sent at least one of the red devils back to the hell he'd come from, he told himself. That was something to cling to.

A few of the pursuers fired arrows after the fleeing men, but the shafts fell short. Coleman heard a boom and glanced back again to see a puff of powder smoke from the war party. More spurts of smoke became visible as a few shots were fired. None of them found their targets. The horses carrying Coleman and the three cowboys never broke stride.

Those Indians might have picked up some rifles from white men they had killed, but that didn't mean they were any good with the weapons.

Luckily, the horses on which Coleman and his men were mounted were relatively fresh. They were running easily, with long, smooth strides, and when Coleman looked back over his shoulder again, he saw that the war party hadn't gained on them. He began to have some real hope that they would make it to the ranch headquarters before the Indians caught them. That house was built to be defended.

Maybe they wouldn't die today after all, thought Coleman.

On the Sugarloaf, Bob Dutton let out a vehement, "Dad-blast it!"

"What's wrong, kid?" asked Pearlie. They were in the partially completed bunkhouse, which Smoke and Pearlie had started working on a while back. The frame was up, including the roof joists, and one wall and part of another had been completed. The crew pitched their bedrolls in the barn for the time being but would move in here when the bunkhouse was finished.

"I think I left my harmonica over at Mr. Coleman's place," Dutton said. He tapped his hand against his shirt pocket, then checked the pockets in his denim trousers. "It's sure enough gone."

"And here I thought something was actually wrong," Pearlie said with a grin.

"But you don't know those fellas over there, Mr. Fontaine! They'll keep that harmonica, and there ain't a one of 'em who can play worth a lick."

Pearlie looked like he didn't know whether to laugh or be annoyed. He and Dutton had been nailing up some wall boards when the young cowboy started acting bothered.

"First of all, I told you to call me Pearlie, not Mr. Fontaine. I ain't *that* much older than you, kid. As for that harmonica of yours, they ain't that expensive. You can pick up another one the next time you go to town. Shoot, I'll even pay for it. Consider it a present."

Dutton shook his head and said, "It's not the cost of it, Mr. Fon—I mean, Pearlie. That harmonica's got some special meanin' to me. My pa gave it to me when I was a boy."

Pearlie frowned. Like a lot of rugged frontiersmen, he had a deeply sentimental streak, whether he would admit it or not.

"Look, I can work on this by myself," he told Dutton. "If you want to ride over to Coleman's ranch and see if you can get that mouth organ back, I reckon it'd be all right."

"You think so? I don't like to neglect my chores—"

"I just said it'd be all right, didn't I?"

"Maybe I ought to hunt up Mr. Jensen and ask him . . ."

"Smoke's out on the range somewhere with the other boys," Pearlie said. He was starting to sound a little annoyed. "No need for you to go and bother him. *I'm* the foreman around here, and if I say it's all right for one of the hands to take a little time off, then he ain't gonna argue with me."

Dutton wasn't sure that Pearlie had quite as much authority as he claimed to, but that was between Pearlie and Smoke. And Dutton surely hated to think about losing that old harmonica for good.

"All right," he said. "I won't dawdle around, though. I'll get over to the Triangle EC and back as fast as I can."

Pearlie nodded and said, "That's fine. Don't reckon you'd want to hang around there any longer than you have to, considerin' how Hank Coleman fired you for somethin' that wasn't even your fault."

"Yeah, there's that," Dutton admitted. "I might not even have to see him, though. He's like Mr. Jensen, usually out on the range somewhere workin'." He frowned. "If I leave, though, then you'll be holdin' down the fort here all by your lonesome."

"I've done that plenty of times before."

"Yeah, but that was before the Injuns were stirrin' up so much trouble, not to mention those blasted cavalrymen."

Several days had passed since the brutal battle between Smoke and Captain Adam Skinner. They had seen no sign of the troopers since then. If Colonel Talbot had taken offense at Smoke's refusal to turn over a dozen horses, he hadn't done anything about it . . . yet.

"Smoke and the other boys weren't goin' so far out on the range that they wouldn't hear shots if any trouble crops up," Pearlie pointed out. "And if they hear gunfire, they'll light a shuck back here mighty quick-like. Just go ahead and get your blasted harmonica, boy, before I change my mind."

Dutton grinned and nodded. "All right, Pearlie. Thanks."

He left the unfinished bunkhouse and hurried toward the barn to slap his saddle on his horse.

As he rode away from the Sugarloaf, Dutton thought about how lucky he'd been to land a place on Smoke Jensen's spread. Smoke was probably the most admired man in the valley, although some folks clung stubbornly to the belief that he was an outlaw and a hired killer. Several years earlier, a lot of phony wanted posters with Smoke's name and likeness had floated around the frontier, and that was why he'd kept quiet about his true identity when he and Sally first settled in this lush Colorado valley.

These days, Smoke was using his real name again, and he'd done his best to put that notorious past behind him. The war against Tilden Franklin and the founding of Big Rock had gone a long way toward accomplishing that. Dutton knew these things because he had talked to Pearlie and some of the other cowboys about them. He wasn't going to bring up the subject with Smoke himself, but he was proud to be working for him.

The miles fell behind Dutton without him really thinking about it. Between musing about Smoke and just enjoying a pretty day, he wasn't aware of how close he was to the headquarters of the Triangle EC until he suddenly recognized some landmarks: a cluster of three trees beside the trail, a rocky knob jutting up, a ford where a shallow creek crossed his path. Another half mile over the next ridge, and he would reach his destination.

His horse had just splashed through that stream when Bob Dutton heard the ominous sound of gunshots hammering through the clean, high country air.

Hank Coleman saw the sturdy ranch house ahead, no more than two hundred yards away. He glanced over his shoulder. The Indians were forty yards back. Way too close for comfort. But Coleman and his three ranch hands raced on, all their attention focused on reaching that shelter.

It was a miracle none of their horses had taken a misstep and fallen, and miraculous as well that none of the arrows flying around them had found its target.

That lucky streak came to an abrupt, tragic end as an arrow thumped solidly into Hal Abrams's back, right between his shoulder blades. The cowboy yelled in pain and slumped forward in his saddle. The arrowhead was buried deep in his body.

"Hal!" Oscar Nickerson shouted in alarm as he glanced over and saw that his friend was wounded. Abrams swayed far to the left. Nickerson was on his right. He made a grab for Abrams's arm to try to hold him in the saddle, but his reach came up short. Abrams toppled off the galloping horse and instantly was left behind.

Bloodthirsty screeches rose from the pursuers. As Coleman glanced back, he saw more arrows skewering Abrams's body. Poor Hal was done for.

But the rest of them were still alive, and they would fight to stay that way.

"Get in the house!" Coleman bellowed to Nickerson and Bentley. "Leave your horses and get in the house!"

He hated to abandon the mounts to the mercies of the war party, but there was nothing else they could do.

Coleman yanked his rifle from its saddle sheath. Nickerson and Bentley did likewise. They all left their saddles and landed running. Bentley tripped and went down, but he rolled and came up on his feet again almost immediately.

Even that slight delay was enough to cause a problem. An arrow struck him in the left calf, just above his boot. Bentley yelped as that leg started to buckle underneath him.

Unlike with Abrams, Nickerson was close enough this time to grab his wounded friend and hold him up. With Bentley limping and slowing them down, they ran for the ranch house's door, which was pulled up but not closed all the way. Nickerson rammed his shoulder against it and knocked it open. They practically tumbled through it into the cabin.

Coleman had turned to open fire on the renegades as he ran after the two cowboys. He cranked out four rounds from the Henry as fast as he could work the rifle's lever. He *felt* the arrows whipping closely past his head, and one of the shafts tugged at his shirt sleeve, but so far none of them had struck him.

One of the Indian ponies in the front rank of the charge went down. Whether the animal tripped or one of his bullets had found it, Coleman didn't know, nor did he care. What was important was that the mishap caused the rest of the renegades to either veer sharply to the sides or else pull up short to keep from trampling the warrior or piling up themselves. That blunted the attack and gave Coleman a chance to whirl around and dash into the ranch house, too.

There were no windows in the cabin, only a number of loopholes that defenders could use to fire through. Since Coleman had been one of the early settlers, he had come here when the valley was still full of dangers ranging from Indians to badmen to mountain lions and bears.

Oscar Nickerson already knelt at one of those loopholes and had thrust his rifle barrel through it. As Coleman kicked the door shut, Nickerson's weapon cracked wickedly, the report loud in the close confines of the cabin.

Sam Bentley leaned on his rifle, using it for a crutch as he dragged a chair from the table over to one of the other loopholes. He paused in what he was doing and asked Coleman, "Are you hit, boss?"

"Not yet," replied Coleman. "But what are you doing, Sam? You're hurt!"

"Just my leg," Bentley said. "As long as I'm careful how I sit, I can still shoot, by grab!"

That was true, Coleman supposed as he lowered a thick beam into brackets attached to the wall on either side of the door. And they needed all the firepower they could get right now. With the bar in place, the savages couldn't get in here. If he and the two cowboys could hold them off for a while, there was a chance the renegades would get tired of fighting and call off the attack. The shooting might attract help, too.

It would take a large, well-armed group to run off those Indians, though. From the glimpses Coleman had gotten of the war party, there were at least four or five dozen of them. Probably more. Enough to take on any of the ranch crews in the valley.

Coleman understood now why the army had sent those cavalry troopers here. A war party of that size could sweep the valley clean of settlers. Even Big Rock might not be safe. Black

Drum might have enough warriors to overrun the town and burn it to the ground, killing every man, woman, and child in the process.

Coleman couldn't worry about that now. It was him and his two companions against that ravening horde. Coleman dropped to a knee, slid his Henry's barrel through a loophole, and searched for a target. After a moment, he squeezed off a shot and was rewarded by the sight of an Indian falling from his pony as the war party milled around.

Then, whooping, the savages turned and retreated, heading away from the ranch house as quickly as they had charged it.

Nickerson saw that through his loophole and exclaimed in surprise. "Look at that, boss!" he said. "We've already run the varmints off!"

"Don't count on that," Coleman said grimly as he fished several cartridges out of his pocket and began thumbing them through the Henry's loading gate to replace the ones he'd already fired. "We haven't hurt 'em bad enough yet to make them quit. They're up to something."

"Look at 'em just sittin' out there," Bentley said. The pain from his wound made his voice sound strained. "They're still in rifle range, Mr. Coleman. Should we try to pick some of 'em off?"

"Save your ammunition," Coleman advised. "You're liable to need it even more later."

Somebody had to be close enough to ride to their help, he told himself as he watched the war party's ranks swell more and more. Otherwise, he and his two companions would have no chance. Sooner or later, they would run out of ammunition, or the Indians would set the ranch house on fire, or they would flush out the defenders some other way.

But no matter what happened, Coleman thought as he sleeved sweat off his forehead, they would fight to the end and sell their lives as dearly as possible.

Chapter 12

Bob Dutton could tell the shots came from the direction of the Triangle EC headquarters. He charged up the ridge, his horse lunging underneath him. When he reached the top, he reined the animal to a halt and peered anxiously across the landscape in front of him.

A little more than a quarter of a mile away, he could see the open area where the ranch house, the barn, the corrals, and the bunkhouse sat. Coleman's ranch house was the original cabin he had built when he and his wife came here. If they had ever had children, he probably would have expanded it, maybe even built a completely new house for his family, but Edith Coleman had died of a fever within a year of settling here.

Dutton had never known Coleman himself to talk about that, but he'd heard the story from some of the other hands who had been around the valley for a long time. It made him a little more understanding of why Coleman was usually such a crotchety old cuss.

Puffs of smoke came from the ranch house, seemingly spurting out from the structure's front wall in three places. Dutton had been in that building and knew it had rifle loopholes instead of windows so it would be easier to defend. Three men were firing from in there.

Dutton's eyes widened as he saw the targets, too. Dozens of mounted Indians swept toward the ranch house. When a couple of them fell from their ponies, evidently wounded or killed, the war party broke off its charge and retreated.

That made Dutton feel better for a second, but then his spirits sank again as he noticed the bodies of a man and a horse lying in front of the ranch house. He had a pair of field glasses in his saddlebags. He dug them out and lifted the lenses to his eyes.

It took Dutton a moment to focus in on the fallen man, but when he did, he caught his breath as he recognized Hal Abrams. The cowboy's head was twisted so Dutton could see part of his face. Agony was etched on Abrams's features. At least half a dozen arrows protruded from his body. He was dead, no question about that. So was his horse.

Dutton had always gotten along well with Abrams. With all the hands here on the Triangle EC, for that matter. Mingled grief and anger welled up inside him. He lowered the field glasses and reached for the butt of the rifle that stuck up from the scabbard strapped to his saddle.

He paused with his fingers wrapped around the smooth wooden stock. There were more than fifty Indians down there. He couldn't do much damage to them by himself, and more than likely, if he opened fire on them some members of the war party would break off and come after him. He would have to flee, and he might not get away.

He could do more good for the three men holed up in the ranch house if he raced back to the Sugarloaf and got Smoke, Pearlie, and the rest of the crew to help him. That might be enough to drive off the savages.

Dutton's stomach twisted in knots, though, because no matter how he looked at the situation, it felt to him as if he were running out. Abandoning his friends who rode for the Triangle EC. The decision might make sense, but it sure stuck in his craw.

With every second that ticked past, the chances of him being able to help the men trapped down there shrank a little more. With a grimace and a heartfelt curse, Dutton yanked his horse around and kicked it into a gallop back toward the Sugarloaf.

Bob Dutton never saw the trio of Indians approaching the ranch house from the rear, and neither did the men inside. Each of the warriors carried an armload of brush. When they reached the back wall, they put the brush down. Two of them formed a stirrup with their hands and lifted the third man high enough for him to pull himself onto the roof. He reached back down for the bundles of broken branches and dried grass as his companions handed them up to him.

He went to the chimney and dropped two of the highly combustible bundles down into the fireplace, holding off on the last one until he had set it on fire using flint and steel. Then he dropped it down onto the waiting fuel and whipped off a blanket that had been tied around his waist. He spread it over the opening at the top of the chimney and held it down.

Startled shouts came from the men inside. They might be able to put out the fire, but even if they did, smoke would be clogging the air and stinging their eyes, noses, and throats already. And the two warriors below were making up more bundles and tossing them onto the roof.

Guns blasted inside the cabin, but the Cheyenne warrior who crouched beside the chimney, holding the blanket in place, wasn't worried. The slabs of wood that formed the roof were too thick for bullets to penetrate. The roof had been built sturdy, just like the rest of the place.

That extra effort was going to be the deaths of those white men now.

With such a thick haze of powder smoke floating in the air, Hank Coleman didn't notice the added smoke right away. Nor did his ears, assaulted by the thunderous reports of gunshots in the close confines of this one-room cabin, register the crackling of flames until he, Nickerson, and Bentley all paused to reload at the same time.

Then, even though the din still echoed in his head, Coleman realized something was burning.

He jerked his head around, saw the blaze leaping and capering in the stone fireplace, and instantly realized what was going on. The Indians were trying to smoke them out! That meant at least one of the red devils was on the roof.

"Up there!" he shouted at Nickerson and Bentley. "They're on the roof!"

He pointed his Henry up and triggered it. Splinters flew where the bullet struck the ceiling, but he couldn't tell if it penetrated and went on through the roof. Coleman levered the rifle and fired again.

Nickerson and Bentley followed suit. Chunks of wood from the ceiling rained down around them, but it was impossible to know if they were doing any good. Anyway, Coleman realized, the real danger was already in here with them.

"Sam, Oscar, watch that war party!" he said. "I'll put that fire out!"

Thick clouds of gray smoke filled the room, making it hard for Coleman to see as he stumbled over to the table. He had left a bucket of water sitting there earlier in the day, so it would be ready when he got back to prepare supper that evening. He had a pretty good idea where it was, but with the smoke obscuring his vision, when he reached for it, his hand banged hard against the bucket and it started to tip over.

Coleman grabbed for it desperately as some of the water sloshed out of it. He caught the bucket in time to keep it from tipping over completely, but when he picked it up, he could tell that half of the water had spilled. He would just have to hope enough was left to put out that fire.

He could see the flames through the smoke, but barely.

When he got close, he felt the heat from the fire and flung the water onto it. With a loud sizzle, most of the flames were extinguished.

But the smoke they had given off was trapped in here. The Indians had blocked the chimney somehow. There was nowhere for the smoke to go except out through the rifle loopholes, and the air would take forever to clear that way.

Suddenly, Coleman felt a draft. The chimney wasn't covered anymore. But before he had a chance to feel any hope at that development, a blazing bundle of sticks and brush landed in the fireplace, followed by more brush that caught fire instantly and started pouring out more smoke. It backed up and billowed out into the room.

Nickerson and Bentley were coughing by now. So was Coleman, loud, wracking coughs that shook him to his core. Every breath was torment, too, as more of the smoke invaded his lungs and clawed at his eyes, nose, and throat.

"Boss!" Nickerson yelled. "Boss, we gotta get out of here!"

"Those redskins are waiting out there!"

"Maybe so, but if we stay in here, we'll choke to death!"

Nickerson was right about that. They might be able to grab the blankets off Coleman's bunk and use them to beat out the flames, but that would take a while and there was a good chance the blankets would just catch on fire, too. Even if they succeeded, there was already too much smoke in here for a man to endure it for very long.

Bentley said, "I'd rather take the fight to them, Mr. Coleman. Let me go out first. I'll go a-shootin', and that might give you and Oscar enough time to look around and see if our horses are still close enough to grab."

Heavy coughs punctuated the cowboy's words, as they did Coleman's when he replied, "But, Sam, you'll never make it—"

"With this wounded leg, I couldn't run and jump on a horse anyway . . . Lemme do this . . . Mr. Coleman. At least you and Oscar . . . might have a chance . . . !"

Coleman figured the odds were very much against that, but he appreciated what Bentley was trying to do.

"Thanks, Sam," he said. "Both of you . . . get ready."

They moved to the door, Bentley standing closest to it. Coleman could tell he was stiffening his wounded leg, forcing it to hold his weight and move through sheer willpower.

Coleman went to one end of the bar across the door, Nickerson to the other. They grasped the beam. Coleman said, "Ready, Sam?"

"I got a full magazine in this Henry," said Bentley, "and a full wheel in my six-gun, to boot. Let 'er rip!"

Coleman and Nickerson lifted the bar out of its brackets and tossed it up and over Bentley's head to clatter to the floor next to the table. Nickerson grabbed the door latch and threw it open. Bentley charged out of the cabin, the rifle in his hands spitting flame and death.

The other two men came out after him, emerging from the smoke into cleaner air. Coleman dragged in lungfuls of it as he brought his rifle to his shoulder and angled right. Nickerson went left. Both men opened fire. Coleman wasn't trying to aim, though, because his eyes searched frantically for the horses they had abandoned a while earlier.

He had known before they ever made this breakout how slim the chances were that the mounts would still be close by. He didn't see them anywhere. Tears streamed from his smoke-tortured eyes, but his vision was clear enough to know that the desperate gamble wasn't going to pay off. He screamed curses at the wall of savages thundering toward them.

Bentley stumbled and went down, but it wasn't because of his wounded leg. He fell because of the three arrows that had sprouted from his chest.

A few feet away, Nickerson staggered, dropped his rifle, and pawed at the shaft of the arrow lodged in his throat. He managed to get hold of it and rip it out, but that just made a crimson flood explode over his chest. He tried to draw the revolver holstered at his waist, but he collapsed before he could clear leather.

That left just Hank Coleman on his feet. He felt the impacts shiver through him as arrows struck his torso, but he kept shooting until the Henry's hammer fell with an impotent click. He staggered, threw the empty rifle away, and hauled out his Colt. He emptied it as well, not knowing if he hit anything and not caring, either. Fighting was what mattered. Not giving up as long as there was breath in his body.

Finally, he realized that the Colt's hammer was clicking uselessly, too, as he pulled back the hammer and squeezed the trigger again and again. He lowered the gun, swaying but still on his feet somehow even though agony filled every inch of his body. He looked down and saw that he had four . . . no, five . . . arrows embedded in him.

And the renegades were all around him.

One of them stepped forward and came toward him, a tall, brawny, ugly varmint with a little drum hanging from a sling around his neck. The Indian carried a tomahawk. He raised it as he came to a stop in front of Coleman.

The rancher worked up a gobbet of spit and blood and spat it at the warrior's feet. "Do your worst, you heathen," he rasped. "I'm coming to you, E—"

He died with his wife's name on his lips.

Smoke and the other two Sugarloaf hands had ridden in by the time Bob Dutton reached the ranch headquarters. The three of them, along with Pearlie, hurried out of the barn as they heard the swift rataplan of the approaching horse's hoofbeats.

Out here, folks didn't generally ride that fast unless there was bad trouble.

Pearlie had told Smoke about Dutton paying a visit to the Triangle EC to retrieve the harmonica he had left at the other ranch. That was fine with Smoke. He expected a good day's work from his men, but he wasn't a slave driver, either. As long as Dutton got his assigned tasks done, Smoke didn't care what else he did.

Dutton had had time to get to Hank Coleman's spread and back, but just barely. And as he raced up and hauled back on his reins, he didn't look like a man who had gotten what he went after.

"Indians!" he cried. "Dozens of 'em! Maybe a hundred!"

"Slow down, son," Smoke told him, even though he wasn't that much older than Dutton. He needed Dutton to calm down, though. "Where did you see these Indians?"

"At . . . at Mr. Coleman's place." Dutton breathed hard as he leaned on his saddle horn. "They were shootin'. They'd already killed Hal Abrams!"

"Where was Coleman?" Pearlie asked.

"Looked like three men were holed up in the old cabin where Mr. Coleman lives. That'd be him and the other two hands, Oscar Nickerson and Sam Bentley, I reckon. Nobody else it could be. We have to help them!"

"You said there may have been as many as a hundred Indians?" asked Smoke.

"Yeah. More than I ever saw in one place before, that's for sure!"

Smoke and Pearlie looked at each other. With odds like those, and considering how long it would have taken Bob Dutton to ride back to the Sugarloaf, it was unlikely any of the Triangle EC's defenders were still alive. The savages would have overrun them by now.

But Hank Coleman's old cabin was built strong and had come through Indian attacks in the past, so there was a slim chance the men inside it might have been able to hold off Black Drum's war party.

And there was no doubt in Smoke's mind that it was Black

Drum and his renegades who were attacking the other ranch. After hearing so much about the threat he represented, Black Drum finally had shown up in the valley.

"Pearlie, you and I will go with Bob back to Coleman's spread," Smoke said, reaching a decision quickly, as always. He looked at the other two hands, Max Collier and Jed Hightower. "Max, throw Bob's saddle on a fresh horse while Bob catches his breath."

"We're not coming with you, Smoke?" asked Hightower.

Smoke shook his head. "I'm not leaving Mrs. Jensen here by herself, not with that war party already on the rampage here in the valley. You two boys stick close and keep your eyes open. Keep your rifles handy, too."

"You can count on us, Smoke," Hightower said, even though he looked like he wished he and Collier were coming along to the Triangle EC.

Sally had heard the urgent hoofbeats, too. She stood at the front door of the ranch house, waiting as Smoke came over to her while Pearlie saddled horses for the two of them.

"I overheard some of that," she said. "Mr. Coleman's ranch is under attack?"

"That's what it sounds like, and I don't hardly see how Bob could have gotten something like that wrong."

"And you're going to help."

"Hank Coleman would try to help us, if the tables were turned."

She shook her head and said, "I'm not so sure about that. He never seems very friendly."

"That doesn't mean he'd turn his back on his neighbors in times of trouble."

"And I know you never would, either." She laid a hand on his arm. "I wouldn't want you to, Smoke. Just be careful, that's all I ask."

"There were only a hundred Indians, Bob said," Smoke told her with a smile. "We've got 'em outnumbered."

Then he winced a little as the look on her face told him that his feeble effort at humor wasn't appreciated right now. She was right. He was a fighter, not a joker.

And a few moments later, after a quick kiss, he swung up into the saddle and led Pearlie and Dutton at a swift pace toward Hank Coleman's ranch . . .

All the time knowing in his heart that they were probably too late.

Chapter 13

A column of black smoke rising into the sky seemed to be grim confirmation of Smoke's hunch as the men approached the Triangle EC a while later.

"Oh, hell," Bob Dutton groaned. "Do you fellas see that?"

"I reckon we all do," replied Pearlie. "It don't look good, neither."

"Let's just wait until we see what we find before jumping to any conclusions," Smoke advised, even though he agreed with the sentiment Pearlie and Dutton obviously felt as well.

They reached the crest of the same ridge where Dutton had observed the battle earlier. Every building on the place was on fire, and they looked like they had been burning for a while. The roofs of the cabin and the barn had collapsed already. Flames still leaped high inside the ruined structures.

Five bodies were sprawled on the ground in front of the burning cabin: four men and one horse. Dutton choked back a sob and said, "They didn't make it. None of 'em made it."

Quietly, Smoke asked, "Pearlie, do you see any signs of that war party hanging around?"

"Nope. Looks to me like they lit a shuck, Smoke."

"That's the way it looks to me, too," Smoke said. He nudged his horse into motion and rode down the slope, not hurrying now. There was no reason to rush.

The bodies of the four men were covered with wounds, so many that it looked like someone had thrown buckets of blood on them. The renegades had retrieved their arrows, however, so none of the shafts were left in the corpses.

In addition, Hank Coleman's skull was split open. Someone had brained him with a tomahawk, Smoke guessed. He wondered if Black Drum himself had struck the fatal blow. The bodies had been stripped and mutilated, too. Smoke figured that degradation had occurred after the men were dead.

He hoped that was the case, anyway.

While Smoke and Dutton checked the bodies for any signs of life—futile, as they both knew, but it had to be done—Pearlie rode around the area. He loped back over to rejoin the other two and reported, "There are quite a few splashes of blood here and there, Smoke. These fellas put some hurtin' on that bunch before they crossed the divide."

"The renegades took all their dead and wounded with them?"

"Yeah. The spilled blood's all I found."

"Could you tell which direction they went when they left?"

Pearlie pointed. "Northwest. I'd say less than an hour ago."

Smoke considered that. The Sugarloaf was just slightly south of due west from here. The route Black Drum and his renegades had taken would send them well north of Smoke's ranch. But there was no guarantee the war party would continue to follow that course. They might angle back south again.

Whatever he did next would be a gamble, Smoke told himself. As much as he wanted to get back to the Sugarloaf and make sure Sally was safe, there were other things to think about.

"There's another spread northwest of here," he said. "Some folks named Bagby own it, I think. I'm not sure I've ever met them."

"Amos Bagby," Pearlie said. "I ran into him once in town.

Has a couple of grown boys, but I don't recollect their names." His voice grew more solemn as he went on, "Those Bagby boys got wives and kids, Smoke."

Smoke nodded. "Bob, you rode for the Triangle EC not long ago. Why don't you stay here and give these men a decent burial? Pearlie and I will go after Black Drum."

"Just the two of you against that giant war party?" asked Dutton, as if he couldn't believe what he'd just heard.

"We're not necessarily going to tackle them ourselves, but if they haven't attacked the Bagby spread yet, maybe we'll have a chance to warn those folks. And if they don't head that way but turn back toward the Sugarloaf instead, we'll see their tracks and know about it."

Pearlie added, "When you get finished layin' these fellas to rest, you ought to head for the Sugarloaf your own self."

"Yeah, I reckon I can understand that, just in case there's trouble there," Dutton said. He sighed and shook his head. "We're gonna be spread mighty thin if we have to fight that big war party."

"That's why the army's here in the valley," Smoke said, but at the same time, everything he had seen and heard so far about the First Colorado Rifles didn't fill him with a great deal of confidence.

For now, he and Pearlie took up the trail of the renegades, while Dutton remained behind at the Triangle EC, searching for something he could use to scrape out graves for the fallen men.

Dutton knew there had been a couple of shovels in a tool shed behind the barn the last time he was here. He circled the still-burning structure, making a face as the smoke stung his nose and eyes, and saw that part of the shed had burned, too.

But a couple of walls were still standing, and although they were smoldering, no flames came from them. Dutton held his bandanna over his mouth and nose to give him a little protection from the smoke and approached the ruins carefully. A lot of heat still rose from where the shed's roof had fallen in.

He looked through the rubble, spotted a shovel blade, and went back to his horse to fetch a rope. He was a good hand with a lasso and dabbed a loop over the shovel blade with only a couple of tosses. He pulled it out of the ashes, then took hold of it with the bandanna. It was still hot enough to make him wince as he let it drop on the ground.

Flames had blackened the shovel's blade but not really damaged it. The handle was charred but appeared to be intact. Dutton let the tool lie there, out of the fire, and cool off while he walked around and decided where to dig the graves. There was a nice grassy area back of the ranch house that had some shade at times, but it wasn't close enough to the trees for roots to be a problem when he started digging.

Dutton's eyes roamed constantly on the surroundings. He was keenly aware that he was alone here. The chances of the Cheyenne renegades doubling back were pretty slim, but he couldn't rule it out completely. If he saw anything suspicious, he would have to jump on his horse and get out of here in a hurry, whether he had completed his grim task or not.

When he checked the shovel again, it had cooled off enough for him to pick it up. He carried it to the place he had picked out and got to work.

Nothing happened while Dutton was digging the graves except that he got hot and sweat soaked his shirt. By the time he got the four holes scooped out of the earth, the fires had burned down enough for him to carefully explore around the edges of what was left of the cabin and the bunkhouse. He was looking for blankets in which to wrap the bodies. He found a few scraps that hadn't burned and reached into the ashes with the shovel to drag them out. As far as burial shrouds went, they were woefully inadequate, but they were all he had.

He buried Hank Coleman first, then the three cowboys. As he approached the last of the bodies, that of Oscar Nickerson, he averted his eyes from the mutilation that almost rendered Nickerson unrecognizable.

When he did that, he saw the sun reflect off something lying on the ground several yards away. Giving in to his curiosity, he stepped over to the spot and looked down.

His harmonica was lying there, and as he stared at it, Dutton realized that it must have been in Nickerson's shirt pocket. One of the savages had found it while looting the body and cast it aside as something worthless. That was the only explanation that made sense.

"So you're the one who had it, Oscar. You . . . you know you couldn't play it. Every time you tried, you sounded like . . . like a lovesick calf!"

Dutton bent and picked up the harmonica. Emotion made him close his hand tightly around it for a moment. Then, with a shudder, he got control of himself. He slipped the harmonica into his pocket and went back to work.

When he had the dirt mounded on all four graves, he stepped back and stuck the shovel in the ground so the handle stood straight up. That was all he had to use for a marker right now, but he promised himself he would ride back over here as soon as he had a chance and put up some proper markers for the four men. He was sure Smoke and Pearlie would be happy to help him do that.

Thinking of Smoke and Pearlie reminded him that he needed to get back to the Sugarloaf. But before he left . . .

He took the harmonica from his pocket and tapped it against his other hand to get any dirt or debris out of it. Then, cradling the instrument in both hands, he lifted it to his lips and began to play. The strains of "Amazing Grace" lifted into the air above the devastated ranch headquarters and the four graves. Dutton played the hymn all the way through, then mounted up and rode away.

* * *

Amos Bagby was a tall, rawboned man with a tuft of gray beard that made him look like a billy goat. He knew that but would still get annoyed with anybody who pointed out the resemblance. His sons Martin and Richard were too smart to do such a thing, but every now and then one of the grandkids would go *"Baaaa!"* behind his back.

That annoyed him, but he couldn't stay mad at the little varmints.

Martin and his wife, Elise, had two boys and a girl. Richard and his wife, Dorothy, had two girls. It was a mighty fine family he had here, Amos Bagby often thought, and a fine, growing spread as well. Moving to Colorado and starting the ranch had been a good thing.

Right now, however, he hoped settling here wouldn't get them all killed.

Bagby's son Martin gripped the shoulders of *his* oldest son, young Marty, and asked, "Are you *sure* you saw Indians?"

The red-headed ten-year-old bobbed his head and said, "I'm sure, Pa, sure as I can be!" The youngster's eyes were wide. "I was down by the creek and I looked up on the hill on the other side, and there they was, big as life, a-lookin' down at me! I figured they were gonna shoot me with arrows and then scalp me, but then they sorta just faded back out of sight and were gone."

Elise, Martin's wife and young Marty's mother, pressed a hand to the bosom of her dress and said, "They . . . they must have been tame Indians." She looked around at the others gathered in front of the ranch house. "Don't you think so? There are some tame Indians around here, aren't there?"

"A few," Amos Bagby admitted. "But I don't reckon any of 'em would have any reason to be skulkin' around our spread. I expect that since the cavalry arrived and got everybody stirred up, any redskins who *ain't* hostile have been layin' pretty low, just so's nobody will mistake 'em for renegades."

Bagby and his sons had been working in the barn when young Marty came running in, yelling about Indians. The women and the other kids, drawn by the commotion, had come out of the house and they had all congregated to listen to young Marty's breathless tale. At first, Martin had accused the boy of making up the story, but it quickly became obvious that young Marty was sincere.

Bagby's younger son, Richard, looked at him and asked, "What do you think, Pa? You reckon it's that war party we've heard so much about?"

"Scouts from it, more than likely," said Bagby, "if there was only two of them."

"That's all I saw, Grandpa, I swear it," young Marty piped up.

"They'll hurry and fetch the rest o' their bloodthirsty friends, though," Bagby went on. "Bloodthirsty fiends, I should say." He looked around, the need for urgency welling up inside him. "Elise, Dorothy, get all those young'uns inside. Close all the shutters over the windows and bar the back door."

Even though this area had a reputation for not being plagued by hostiles when they moved here, Bagby had fought Indians back in Kansas and knew how important it was to have a place that could be defended. Just because there was no trouble in a place didn't mean it would always be like that. So the house had thick log walls and sturdy shutters.

"Martin, you'll be in the house, too," Bagby went on. "You and Elise and Dorothy will be at the front windows with rifles." He paused. "Young Marty, you'll have to cover the back. The girls will reload."

"Wait a minute," Elise said as she pulled her oldest son to her. "He's ten!"

"Yeah, but he can handle a rifle. I've seen him do it, hunting game."

"I'm a good shot!" young Marty declared.

"I hate to think about him having to kill a man," Elise said.

"I hate even worse to think about him and the rest of you bein' slaughtered by them savages," Bagby said, making his voice as harsh and blunt as possible. He wanted to get it through Elise's head—through *all* their heads—just how serious and dangerous this situation was.

Martin squeezed his son's shoulder. "Grandpa's right, Marty. We all have faith in you."

"Thanks, Pa. I won't let you down."

Richard said, "You told Martin to get in the house, Pa. What about me?"

"You and me will be in the barn," Bagby said as he nodded toward the large structure on the other side of the wide, open area in front of the house. "When those heathens attack the house, we'll hit 'em from behind and catch them in a crossfire. Now get movin', all of you!"

That actually wasn't a bad plan, he thought as he hurried into the house to get his rifle. Or at least, it wouldn't have been if the odds had been anywhere close to even.

But judging from the rumors they had heard, the odds would be more like ten to one, at the very least. He and his boys were good shots, but Martin and Richard had never been in a real fight before. He hoped they would be able to stay steady and cool-nerved. He didn't expect that of the women, but they might surprise him.

Their only chance—and it was a mighty slim one—was to do enough damage to the Indians that their war chief, Black Drum, might decide it was going to cost him too big a price to wipe out this ranch and its defenders.

Thinking about how unlikely that was, Bagby wished he had gone around and hugged all of his family while he still had the chance. But such a display of emotion from him might just unnerve them even more. Gripping his rifle tightly, he strode toward the barn. Richard hurried along behind him, struggling to keep up with his father's long-legged gait.

A group as large as the war party that rode away from the Triangle EC couldn't help but leave a trail that a skilled tracker could follow. The old mountain man called Preacher had taught Smoke his tracking skills, and while Smoke never reached the almost supernatural level of Preacher's talent, he could still follow a trail better than most. So there was no chance of Smoke and Pearlie being unable to track their quarry.

"You plan to jump them Injuns if we come up on 'em, Smoke?" Pearlie asked.

"Not until we're sure what they're going to do," Smoke replied. "Although if we get the chance to take care of a few stragglers, we sure might. I'm more interested in figuring out if they're headed for the Bagby spread or somewhere else, though."

"Speakin' of that . . ." Pearlie said as he slowed his mount. He came to a stop and pointed. "Look at those tracks."

Smoke reined to a halt as well and frowned as he studied the unshod hoofprints they had been following. After a moment, Smoke did something he hardly ever did. He cursed, uttering a heartfelt, "Damn."

It was clear from the tracks that the war party had split into two groups. One bunch headed on northwest, the way they had been going, toward Amos Bagby's ranch.

The trail left by the other group curved back toward the south . . . in the general direction of the Sugarloaf.

"We'd better light a shuck for home," Pearlie said. "That second bunch may not be headin' for the ranch, but they sure might be."

"Didn't you say that Bagby had women and children at his place?" Smoke asked.

"Yeah, but—"

"Collier and Hightower are at the Sugarloaf, and Sally's probably a better shot than either of them, when you get right down to it." Smoke looked around, thought swiftly about the logistics of the situation. "And we're closer to the Bagby place, I think. We can get there quicker and lend them a hand if there's trouble."

"But Smoke—" Pearlie began again.

"I know what I'm doing," Smoke interrupted. "Come on."

He kneed his horse into motion and rode after the part of the war party heading northwest. Pearlie grimaced and fell in alongside him.

Smoke knew what he was doing, all right. Several years earlier, he had left his first wife, Nicole, and their infant son Arthur alone at their isolated cabin. A gang of gun-wolves who wanted to kill Smoke had shown up, but it had been Nicole and Arthur who had died—along with a lot of the brutal beasts who had murdered them.

But vengeance never actually set anything right, Smoke had discovered on that bloody day and in the days that followed. The loss, the injustice that cried out for revenge was still there, even after that summons was answered. You could never get back what was lost.

And now he was risking Sally's life so he could help some people he had never even met, simply because a small voice in the back of his mind told him it was the right thing to do. If anything happened to her . . .

Smoke forced that thought out of his head and rode on, his face set in grim, stony lines.

Chapter 14

Sally checked the fire under the kettle and then, satisfied with the way the grease was bubbling, carefully dropped in the rings of dough to fry them. Once they were ready, she would cover them with a sugary glaze she had concocted. Preacher had taught her how to cook what he called bear sign, but Sally had modified the recipe slightly. She was convinced her version was even better.

She would know one way or the other once Smoke, Pearlie, and the other men got back. Nobody appreciated a treat more than hardworking cowboys. If they praised her efforts, she could be sure that she'd succeeded.

A knock sounded on the ranch house door. Sally called, "Come in."

Max Collier stuck his head inside and said, "Just lettin' you know that everything's still peaceful out here, Miz Jensen."

"That's what I assumed, since I hadn't heard any gunshots," she told him. "But I appreciate you letting me know for sure, Max."

"Yes'm. You can't always figure that things are all right just because it's quiet, though. Why, some of those renegades could've snuck up on me and Jed and cut our throats—"

He stopped short, as if he'd just realized that his words

weren't all that reassuring. Making a face, he went on, "I, uh, I mean . . ."

"Never mind, Max," Sally said with a smile. "It's all right. I'm aware of the danger, I promise you."

She nodded toward the table, where a loaded rifle rested. A Colt lay on the counter where she had been mixing the dough for the bear sign a few minutes earlier. Another rifle hung on pegs near the door, and shotguns leaned in two corners of the room. Anybody who tried to start trouble on the Sugarloaf would get an unexpectedly hot welcome.

Collier tugged on his hat brim and said, "All right, ma'am. If you need anything, you just give us a holler. We'll be close by."

"Thank you, Max."

Collier shut the door and went back to whatever he had been doing. Sally checked a pot of beans simmering on the stove. They would be ready when Smoke and the others got back, as would the bear sign. Sally told herself it was just a matter of time until her husband returned, safe and sound and ready to sweep her into his arms for a big hug and a resounding kiss . . . the same way he had returned from all the other trouble he had ridden off to face during their eventful time together. Smoke always came back.

But what if someday he didn't?

Sally refused to allow herself to think about that. She hummed a little tune under her breath as she went about her work.

It helped drown out the little voice of worry in the back of her mind.

"Where the hell are they, Pa?" asked Richard Bagby as he and his father waited anxiously in the barn across from the ranch house. They were on either side of the big door, which was open just wide enough for them to peer out.

"Don't know," Amos Bagby replied. "Just because the

young'un seen those scouts, that's no guarantee the war party will show up here. You can't predict what a redskin will do . . . ever! And from what we've heard, that fella Black Drum is even crazier than most of 'em."

"So you think they might just ride on and leave us alone?" Richard sounded like he desperately wanted to believe that was a possibility.

"Might happen. Or it might n—"

Bagby stopped short as an arrow whipped through the opening and passed so close to him that he felt the feather fletching brush against his ear. It took him so much by surprise that for a long second he couldn't even grasp what had just happened.

But then his heart dropped like a stone, even as he lifted his rifle to his shoulder and called to his son, "Here they come!"

The arrow fired into the barn could mean only one thing: The Indians knew somebody was in here. Bagby's plan to catch the hostiles by surprise was ruined before it ever had a chance to work.

Since they had lost that element of surprise, he crowded forward to look out and saw a line of about twenty mounted warriors charging into the open area between the house and barn. Arrows flew toward both structures. Bagby heard them striking the door and the wall as he aimed and squeezed his rifle's trigger. The weapon cracked and bucked against his shoulder. He hoped to see one of the attackers fall, but that didn't happen. The raiders were moving so fast and their ponies' hooves were kicking up so much dust, it was hard to draw a bead on any of them.

A few feet away, Richard fired, too. Shots erupted from the house. The shutters over the windows were made with firing ports in them, little hinged doors that opened upward and could be hooked in place. Martin, Elise, and Dorothy raked the attackers with lead from in there. Amos Bagby felt a surge of pride as he heard the steady pounding of gunfire from his son and two daughters-in-law.

Richard seemed cool-headed so far, too, cranking off several rounds into the charging renegades. The lead scything into them blunted the charge. The warriors hauled back on the reins, and their ponies began to mill around. Bagby shot again, and this time the sight of a Cheyenne sagging forward as blood welled from the hole in his side was the welcome result.

The Indians retreated.

"They're leaving, Pa!" Richard said.

"Don't you believe that for a second," Bagby replied as he delved in a pocket for more cartridges to replace the ones he'd fired. "Black Drum was just feelin' us out, seein' where our defenses are and how strong they might be."

"But we killed two or three of them, looked like."

Bagby snorted. "Hell, you don't think Black Drum cares about that, do you? With all the slaughterin' he's been doing ever since he jumped the reservation, you can tell he doesn't care about anything except killin' white folks. If he has to sacrifice some of his warriors, he'll do it, as long as he gets what he wants. He's got a big enough bunch followin' him that he can afford to lose some of them."

The old rancher drew in a weary breath and sighed before he went on, "Besides, word of what he's been doing has likely spread to more than the settlers. Every malcontent redskin in these parts will have heard about Black Drum and want to throw in with him. Some of them back on the reservation have probably escaped already and are on their way to join him. The longer he gets away with all the killin', the stronger his bunch will get."

Richard gulped and said, "Pa, you make it sound like he's getting himself an army!"

"Pretty close to it, boy, pretty close to it." Bagby lifted his reloaded rifle. "And here they come again!"

* * *

Inside the house, young Marty Bagby stood at a shuttered rear window, peering wide-eyed through the little firing port. He shifted his head from side to side, changing the angle so he could widen the area he could see. The rifle in his hands was heavy enough to make his muscles quiver slightly. The rifle's weight was all it was, he told himself. He wasn't trembling because he was scared.

Well, not *too* scared, anyway.

He heard the shooting from the front room and wished he was up there with his ma and pa and Aunt Dorothy. Instead, he was back here in this bedroom with his sister Millie, who was a year younger than him. She had a second rifle already loaded, lying on a small table the two of them had pulled out from a wall. An open box of ammunition sat on the table, as well.

"You see anything, Marty?" she asked.

"Not a da—not a blasted thing," he said. He'd started to cuss and say he didn't see a damned thing, but he stopped because he knew his sister would tattle on him if he did. Still, it seemed like if he was old enough to handle a rifle and shoot Injuns, he ought to be able to swear now and then, like he knew his pa and uncle and grandpa did when none of the womenfolks were around.

Then he saw something move out yonder, in the trees behind the ranch house, and he forgot all about being tattled on as he said, "Oh, hell!"

"Is it an Indian?" asked Millie, her voice trembling.

"I think so." Marty laid his cheek against the rifle's smooth stock and squinted over the barrel as he rested it in the firing port. "I saw something out there in the woods—"

He had stuck the rifle out too far. Something grabbed the barrel and jerked. Marty felt it almost slip away from him. But as he tightened his grip on it and lurched forward along with the rifle, his finger pulled the trigger. The rifle went off with a thunderous roar.

Somebody screeched outside. Millie clapped her hands to her cheeks and screamed. Marty worked the rifle's lever, threw his weight against it so it angled toward whoever had hold of it, and pulled the trigger again. The varmint let go as another howl sounded.

Marty pulled the rifle back until just the muzzle protruded. He saw buckskin-clad shapes erupt from the woods as he jacked another round in the chamber.

"Stop that caterwaulin'!" he yelled at his sister without looking around. The rifle cracked and kicked again. His shoulder was starting to hurt already from the recoil, but he ignored the pain as he saw one of the attackers tumble to the ground and go head over heels. Marty thought for a second that the Indian might have just tripped, but when he didn't get up again, Marty had a pretty strong hunch that he'd hit him.

The firing port was about four inches square. That wasn't very big, but it was big enough for an arrow to come through it, even with the rifle barrel taking up part of the opening. Marty caught his breath as he spotted one of the missiles streaking straight toward him. Instinct made him jerk the rifle barrel up a little. The arrow struck it and clattered off instead of coming through the opening to hit him.

He had another round chambered already, so he let loose at an Indian who was lowering a bow. The warrior staggered and dropped the bow. Through the powder smoke that stung his eyes, Marty saw blood on the Indian's arm.

"That'll learn you!" he exclaimed as he worked the rifle's lever again.

"Marty!" The cry came from the doorway. He jerked his head around to look over his shoulder. His mother stood there, a terrified expression on her face.

"I'm fine, Ma," he told her. "Go on back up front and help

Pa. Millie, get ready to hand me that other rifle. We got Injuns to fight!"

Smoke and Pearlie heard the angry snarl of gunfire when they were still quite a distance from the Bagby ranch. Pearlie groaned and said, "Dadgummit! That's where this bunch was headed, all right."

"The shooting just started," Smoke called as he kneed his mount into a gallop. "Maybe we can get there before the Bagbys are overrun!"

The two men rode hard, up and down ridges and around hills. The shooting guided their course as they closed in on the Bagby spread. They came to a creek and turned to follow it along the smaller valley it had carved out within the wide expanse between mountain ranges.

Smoke spotted some buildings up ahead, set back a short distance from the creek. A hazy cloud of powder smoke hung over the ranch headquarters. A couple of hundred yards from the ranch house, a large group of mounted warriors milled around. The shooting had trailed off, so Smoke figured the renegades were regrouping after a failed charge and getting ready to attack again.

"Over there!" he told Pearlie as he pointed to a small, brush-covered knoll to the left. "Let's get up there and see if we can pick some of them off!"

They were still far enough away that it was unlikely anybody in the war party had spotted them. The renegades would have their attention focused on the buildings where they were trying to root out the defenders. Smoke and Pearlie rode rapidly behind some trees that screened them from the warriors' view as they approached the knoll.

They reached the top of the brushy knob and dropped from their saddles just as the Indians launched another assault.

Blood-curdling screeches came from dozens of throats as the renegades charged.

Smoke and Pearlie knelt at the crest and lifted their rifles. Guns were going off all over the scene in front of them. With that much racket, it was unlikely Black Drum's warriors would hear the shots from up here, at least right away. Smoke searched among the attackers, trying to pick out the war chief.

"I can't tell which of them is Black Drum, if he's even down there," he said. "Just pick your targets and make your shots count."

"Looks like Bagby and his family are givin' 'em a good fight," Pearlie commented as he drew a bead on one of the warriors. "I see half a dozen of the varmints down already."

"Let's add to that," Smoke breathed as he stroked the trigger of his rifle.

Cracking reports rang out steadily from the two men atop the knoll. Each time Smoke or Pearlie fired, one of the Cheyenne jerked, sagged, or threw up his arms and pitched limply from his pony's back. The withering fire they laid down was deadly in its accuracy.

The Indians couldn't fail to notice for very long that they were losing men. With angry whoops, some of them wheeled their ponies. They must have spotted the muzzle flashes from Smoke's and Pearlie's rifles. They charged the knoll—only to be driven from their mounts by slugs that smashed into them. The ones who weren't hit whirled their ponies and fled.

The steady fire from the ranch house and the barn, combined with this new and deadly development, was too much for the renegades. Screeching in fury, they regrouped again and then rode hard to the west, leaning far forward as they galloped out of range. From their vantage point, Smoke and Pearlie were able to send several rounds after them to hurry them on their way. Two more renegades tumbled from their ponies and landed in limp sprawls that signified death.

"Reckon they'll double back?" asked Pearlie as he lowered his still-smoking rifle.

"They don't act like it right now," Smoke replied, "but you never can tell."

"I'll stay up here to keep an eye on the way they went," Pearlie volunteered, "while you go down yonder and check on those folks, Smoke."

"You'll let me know if you see any trouble coming our way?"

Pearlie chuckled. "Oh, you'll know about it, all right. I'll be shootin' to beat the band if I so much as catch a glimpse of a feather or war paint."

Smoke nodded and hurried to his horse. He swung up into the saddle and rode down from the knoll. He set a deliberate pace as he approached the ranch headquarters. He didn't want to rush in, just in case the defenders were still feeling a little trigger-happy and might get spooked.

Instead, a tall, rangy man with a billy-goat beard strode out of the barn and raised the rifle he held in a gesture of greeting. Smoke angled his horse toward the man and nodded.

"Mr. Bagby?" he called. "Amos Bagby?"

"That's right," the man replied.

"I'm Smoke Jensen. I don't think we've met."

Bagby's eyes widened in recognition of the name. "Smoke Jensen!" he said. "No, we ain't met, but I've heard of you, right enough. Was that you up on the knob, shootin' the hell out of those Injuns?"

"Me and a friend of mine, Pearlie Fontaine," Smoke said. He still held his rifle.

"I know Fontaine to nod and say howdy to. Was it just the two of you? You were cuttin' down those red devils like a whole regiment!"

"Just the two of us," Smoke said with a grim smile. "Do you have any injuries?"

"That's what I'm just about to find out." Bagby nodded.

"My boy Richard's sittin' in there with an arrow in his leg, but it ain't bleedin' bad."

The rancher hurried on toward the house. The front door opened before he got there. Another man, who bore a resemblance to Bagby and was probably his other son, stepped out and called, "Pa! Are you all right?"

"Fine," Bagby replied. "How about everybody in there?"

The younger man held up a blood-stained sleeve. "An arrow got through and gave me a gash on the arm, but it's not too bad. Everybody else is all right, I think."

Bagby let out a low whistle of surprise and looked at Smoke. "We were mighty lucky, I'd say. Especially lucky that you and your friend showed up when you did. I don't think it's likely we could've held out against 'em for much longer."

"I'm glad we got here in time," Smoke said.

He hoped that the same sort of luck was smiling down on everyone back at the Sugarloaf.

Chapter 15

While the Bagby womenfolks tended to the two wounded men, Smoke and Amos Bagby checked the bodies of the fallen renegades. The other members of the war party hadn't had a chance to carry off their dead and wounded this time.

Only there weren't any wounded. All the Cheyenne and Arapaho warriors were dead. The ranch's defenders had done some good shooting.

None of the fallen warriors had a small, black-painted drum with him, so Smoke knew the war chief had survived this battle—if he had even been here. Black Drum might have been part of the other group when the renegades split up.

When Smoke and Bagby stepped around one of the house's rear corners, Smoke was surprised to see bodies of three of the raiders sprawled back here, too.

"Looks like they tried to get behind the house, but whoever was posted back here did a good job of driving them off," he said.

"That'd be my grandson, young Marty," Bagby said proudly.

"How young?"

From an open rifle port in the shutter over the window, a boy's voice said, "I'm ten years old, sir." A freckled face topped by red hair looked out at the two men.

"You did fine, son, mighty fine," Bagby said.

"Who taught you to shoot?" asked Smoke.

"My pa and my uncle and my grandpa, sir," young Marty answered. "My sister helped with the loadin', and she done a good job, too."

"I'd say so," Smoke agreed solemnly. He looked at Bagby and added, "You *are* a lucky man."

"And I sure as blazes know it," the rancher said.

Things seemed to be under control here. There was no guarantee the renegades wouldn't return, but Smoke didn't believe that was likely after the losses they had suffered already. He thought there was a better chance the survivors would rendezvous with the rest of the war party.

The question was, where would that reunion take place?

The Sugarloaf was one ominous possibility.

Smoke quickly explained to Bagby how he and Pearlie had found where the war party split up, then said, "I'd like to stay here just to make sure everything will be all right, but—"

"No, if your spread lies in the general direction that other bunch of savages was headed, you got to go check on your own folks," Bagby interrupted. "By grab, if my two boys weren't wounded, I'd come with you, just to give you a hand if you need it. But with both of them not at full fightin' strength . . ."

Smoke nodded and said, "I understand, Mr. Bagby. You need to stay here, just in case those raiders double back. I don't expect them to, but you never know."

Bagby extended his hand. "We're mighty obliged to you, Jensen."

Smoke gripped his hand and said, "Make it Smoke. I'm glad we finally got to meet. Just wish it had been under better circumstances."

"We made it through. This day and age, that's all you can hope for sometimes. Good luck to you and yours, Smoke."

Smoke lifted a hand in farewell and trotted back toward the knoll where he had left Pearlie. Pearlie must have seen him coming, because he appeared at the top of the slope, riding his horse.

A moment later, both men were in the saddle and headed for the Sugarloaf as fast as their horses would take them.

Smoke had told Max Collier and Jed Hightower to stay close to the ranch headquarters while he and Pearlie were gone. Both young cowboys fully intended to follow Smoke's orders, but then Hightower noticed something.

"That damn fool milk cow's busted down the fence in her pen and wandered off again," Hightower reported as he came into the barn where Collier was mending some harness.

"She headed over to that meadow where those wildflowers grow, I'll bet," said Collier. He put the harness aside. "I've never seen a cow go so loco over some wildflowers."

Hightower took off his hat and scratched at his rust-colored hair. "I don't cotton much to the idea of lettin' her wander around like that. Not with Indians maybe somewhere in these parts."

"The fact that there's Indians somewhere in these parts is exactly the reason you shouldn't go chasin' off after her. That's what you were thinkin' about doin', ain't it? Speakin' of damn fools."

"Milkin' her is one of my regular chores," Hightower explained. "I won't deny I've gotten a mite fond of the critter, seein' her every day like that, just the two of us so early in the mornin'-like. As soon as Smoke and Pearlie and Bob rode off, I should've got her and put her here in the barn where she'd be safe." He clapped his hat back on his head and sighed. "I sure hope the Injuns don't get her."

"Oh, hell," Collier said. "If you're that worried, it wouldn't take us but ten minutes or so to ride over to that meadow she likes and see if she's there, and ten more minutes to drive her back here. Less'n half an hour, all told."

Hightower shook his head. "And leave Miss Sally here by herself? No, sir, we can't do that. If we left her alone and somethin' happened to her, Smoke would never forgive us. I don't know about you, but I sure as shootin' don't want a mad Smoke Jensen on my trail."

"Shootin' is right," muttered Collier. "He'd probably fill us full of bullet holes, like he done to all those fellas up in Idaho." He paused. "But if *you* wanted to go look for that darn cow, I don't reckon there's any way I could stop you short of whippin' you and hog-tyin' you."

"Which you couldn't do, anyway."

Collier stood up and said, "I wouldn't be so dadblasted sure about that—"

Hightower lifted a hand to forestall the argument. "We can settle that some other time, maybe, if we want to. Right now, I want to know: Are you sayin' I ought to go after that cow?"

"Well . . . with no milk, Miss Sally couldn't bake as many good things as she does."

"That's right. And you'd still be here to look after things, not to mention I wouldn't be gone very long."

"No, you wouldn't. One thing, though," Collier went on. "If you get to the meadow and she *ain't* there, I don't figure you ought to take any more time lookin' for her. Just turn around and come on back here."

"I reckon I could do that. I'm gonna saddle my horse." Hightower paused. "Thanks, Max."

"Just go on. I don't want that critter to wind up in some red-skin's belly, neither."

A few minutes later, Jed Hightower rode away from the ranch headquarters, heading north. The meadow where they had found the milk cow several times before when it strayed was about a mile from the ranch house.

Despite his determination to do this, worry gnawed at Hightower's guts as he rode. It was a pretty day, birds were singing in the trees, and the whole world seemed peaceful. He knew it might be anything but, though. Indians were stealthy. A lot of times, a fella didn't know they were anywhere around until it was too late. It probably would have been smarter, not to mention safer, for him to just forget about that ol' cow and stay close to home. Smoke could get another milk cow. A man's scalp couldn't be replaced.

This wouldn't take long, he told himself again. And although he hadn't said anything about it to anybody, he had taken to calling the cow Molly when it was just the two of them in the barn. They were friends. And a man didn't just abandon his friends to savage Indians.

He rode through a thick stand of trees and came out at the edge of the meadow, which was a hundred yards wide and twice that long, a big clearing bordered by trees on all four sides.

Smack-dab in the middle of it, munching contentedly on wildflowers, was the big brown cow Hightower had dubbed Molly. She lifted her head and gazed placidly toward him as he rode toward her.

"There you are, dang it," he said. "Come on, you blasted lunkhead. We're not gonna put you in that pen anymore so you can bust out and wander off, not until this whole business with those Injuns is over. You can just stay in the barn." He circled the cow and crowded against her, lifting his right foot from the stirrup to nudge her into motion. "Move along there, Molly. Get on home."

The cow ambled back in the direction Hightower had come from. The young cowboy rode along in her wake.

He wasn't sure what prompted him to glance back over his shoulder. Some instinct, maybe, or it could have been just dumb luck.

Whatever it was, when he looked toward the trees at the far end of the meadow, his heart suddenly slugged so hard in his chest it felt like it was about to bust right out of his body. Four buckskin-clad figures on horseback had drifted out of the trees like ghosts and now sat there watching him. Hightower had good eyesight; he could make out the streaks of black and white and red paint on their faces and the feathers that stuck up from their hair.

"Oh, hell, Molly," he breathed. "Look what you got me into now!"

As if they had been waiting for him to notice them, the four warriors suddenly whooped and sent their ponies lunging forward to race after him. Hightower yanked his hat off his head, whacked it against the cow's rump, and yelled, "Run, damn you, run!"

Then he leaned forward and galloped toward the trees at the near end of the meadow. If he could get there first, he might be able to take cover and fight off the Indians. He had a fully loaded Henry rifle in a saddle sheath. But they were coming after him mighty fast, and it was going to be a close race . . .

Bob Dutton was playing a mournful tune on his harmonica as he rode up to the barn at the Sugarloaf. Max Collier emerged from the big structure and said, "Found that mouth organ, did you?"

"Yeah," Dutton replied, but he didn't sound happy about it.

Collier's face grew more serious as he went on, "What happened at Coleman's spread? Were you and Smoke and Pearlie able to drive off those hostiles?" He frowned. "Where *are* Smoke and Pearlie?"

"The Injuns were already gone when we got there," said Dutton. His voice caught a little as he went on, "I . . . I stayed to bury Mr. Coleman and the other fellas. They'd been wiped out. Smoke and Pearlie trailed the war party. Before they left, Smoke told me to come on back here once I got those men laid to rest, so I did." He looked around. "Where's Jed?"

Worried lines appeared on Collier's face. "He went lookin' for that fool old milk cow. It got out of the pen and wandered off again."

"And you let him do that?" Dutton couldn't hold in the exclamation. Collier and Hightower had been working for Smoke longer than he had, so technically he was low man on the totem pole around the Sugarloaf, but he let out the startled words anyway.

"It wouldn't take him but just a little while to ride up to that meadow where the cow always goes when it gets loose. And I told him that if she wasn't there, just to turn around and get on back here as fast as he can. He ought to be back any time now." Collier waved a hand at their surroundings. "You can see for yourself, it's been quiet around here."

"Doesn't mean it's gonna stay that way. I'll ride out to that meadow and take a look, make sure Jed's all right. Which way is it? I don't really know what you're talkin' about."

"I know where it is, I can go—"

"I'm already in the saddle," Dutton interrupted. "Just tell me how to find it."

Quickly, Collier gave him the directions. Dutton nodded and turned his horse to the north. The horse was getting tired, he could tell, but he called on it for more effort and rode at a fast pace.

When he reached a thick stand of trees, he had to slow down to weave between the trunks. As he did, he suddenly heard a swift rataplan of hoofbeats from somewhere nearby. The next second, several blood-curdling whoops drifted through the air.

The sound of the running horses was enough to make Dutton reach for his rifle. The war whoops prompted him to drag it hurriedly from the saddle boot. He kneed his horse back to urgency.

The sight that greeted Dutton's eyes when he reached the edge of the trees made his pulse race. Jed Hightower rode hard toward him. The milk cow Hightower had been looking for lumbered along well behind him. Closing in on the cow were four painted and feathered warriors. One of them drew back his bowstring, ready to fire an arrow as if he were hunting a buffalo instead of an old milk cow.

Dutton didn't really think about what he was doing. He just brought the rifle to his shoulder in one smooth move and squeezed the trigger. The round that was already chambered exploded from the Henry, whipped past Hightower, and punched into the Indian's chest just before he loosed the arrow. The impact jolted the man back so that the shaft flew harmlessly into the air.

As the echoes of the shot rolled across the meadow, Dutton shouted, "Jed! This way!"

Hightower angled toward him. Dutton's horse was dancing around skittishly, spooked by the shot its rider had fired. Dutton tried to calm the animal, and when the horse settled down a little, he aimed at the three warriors who were still chasing Hightower. The man Dutton had wounded was still mounted but had peeled away from the charge.

Dutton fired again, aiming this time at the pony underneath one of the warriors. It broke stride and went down, and the rider screeched as he was flung over the collapsing pony's head. He sailed through the air for a second, then crashed into the ground, rolled over a couple of times, and lay still.

The other two renegades darted around the fallen man, the slashing hooves of their ponies barely missing him.

Hightower reached the trees and hauled back on the reins, bringing his horse to a stop near Dutton.

"Mighty good to see you, Bob," he called. "Maybe we can fight off those other two."

"The hell with that!" Dutton said. "Look over yonder!"

More Indians were charging out of the trees on the far side of the meadow. Dutton figured there had to be a couple dozen of them—and more were coming out into the open.

Dutton whirled his horse and went on, "Head for the Sugarloaf!"

He wasn't worried about leading the war party back to the ranch. He figured the renegades already knew right where it was and were on their way there anyway.

And once again, their black hearts would be set on murder and destruction.

Hightower wondered if Molly the cow was still alive.

Chapter 16

Sally was finished with the batch of bear sign and looked forward to finding out what the men thought of them. She stirred the beans in the pot on the stove, then set the spoon aside and walked to the ranch house's front door to look out.

She thought about Smoke and tried not to worry. He was better able to take care of himself than anyone she had ever known, but that didn't mean he was invincible. He had been wounded before, and he bled and felt pain like anyone else.

He would never let fear for himself stop him from helping someone who needed it, though. The very idea of that would be completely foreign to his nature.

Sally forced herself to concentrate on what a pretty day it was, warm and with fluffy white clouds floating in the brilliant blue sky. Eventually, the threat from the Indians would be over. The world, this valley, the Sugarloaf . . . they would all go on.

The sound of rapid hoofbeats caught her attention and made her step out in front of the house. She turned to the north and lifted her left hand to shade her eyes from the sun. She spotted two riders heading toward the ranch headquarters. They were still a couple of hundred yards away, but Sally had sharp eyes and recognized Bob Dutton and Jed Hightower.

From the way they were leaning forward in their saddles and galloping their horses, it was like the Devil himself was right behind them, barreling after them.

"Max!" she called toward the barn. "Max, are you in there?"

"What is it, Miss Sally?" he asked as he walked outside. "Is something—Holy cow!"

He had seen Dutton and Hightower, too.

"Get in the house, ma'am. Now!"

Under different circumstances, Sally might have pointed out that he didn't have the right to order her around like that. But not now, not with trouble bearing down rapidly on them. Those two cowboys wouldn't be tearing along hellbent-for-leather if nothing was wrong.

Collier ran toward the barn, where the men had been sleeping while the bunkhouse was under construction.

"I'll fetch some more rifles," he flung over his shoulder to Sally.

That was a good idea, she thought. There were a number of firearms in the house already, but if they were about to be under attack, the more guns, the better.

She stepped inside, picked up the loaded Henry rifle from the table, and carried it back out. Bob Dutton and Jed Hightower were close now. Sally waved a hand over her head and made a sweeping motion with that arm for them to come toward her. They would fort up in the house. Smoke had built it with thick walls, heavy shutters and doors, and rifle loopholes.

As he had phrased it: "Pray there won't ever be any trouble . . . but prepare for a whole heap of it."

The two cowboys galloped up and dropped from the saddles before their horses had stopped completely.

"Better get inside, Miss Sally," Dutton said. "A bunch of redskins aren't far behind us."

"That's what we figured," Sally told him. "Max has gone to fetch more rifles."

At that moment, Collier emerged from the barn, stumbling along under the weight of four rifles.

"I'll give him a hand," Hightower said. He hurried to meet his friend and take a couple of the rifles from him.

"There's plenty of ammunition in the house," Sally went on. "Smoke's been stocking up on it since we heard about that big war party."

Dutton used his hat to swat the two sweating horses on the rumps and send them stampeding away. They could always be recovered later, after the fight.

"I thought for a second we ought to get you and Max and make a run for town," he said. "But I don't reckon we'd get that far before those Injuns caught up to us." He shook his head. "No, we're gonna have to make a stand here, for better or worse."

"We'll hold out until Smoke and Pearlie get back," Sally said with a firm nod. "We have to."

She went back inside, knowing that the three cowboys wouldn't take cover until she did.

They clomped into the house after her. Dutton and Collier started closing the shutters over the windows. Hightower said, "I'm sorry, Miss Sally. That ol' milk cow got loose and wandered off, and I went to look for her. I reckon it was me who led those savages right back here to the ranch."

Dutton looked over his shoulder and said, "You probably didn't have a thing to do with it, Jed. They were already on the rampage and would have gotten here sooner or later." He sighed and shook his head. "They killed Hank Coleman and all the hands at the Triangle EC."

Sally put a hand to her mouth and said, "Oh, no! Those poor men."

"I laid 'em to rest," Dutton went on, "and then headed back here, like Smoke told me to."

"Where are Smoke and Pearlie?" asked Sally.

Dutton explained that they had followed the war party's trail away from the Coleman spread.

"The varmints weren't headed in this direction when they left," he said, "but they must've circled back around to head this way, because they're sure enough out there now."

While they were talking, Sally had taken several boxes of .44 cartridges from a shelf, set them on the table, and opened them. All the rifles were fully loaded at the moment, but they would need more ammunition before long.

Hightower barred the back door and closed the rest of the shutters. The front door wasn't barred yet and, in fact, stood partially open. Dutton stepped out to take a look to the north, muttering, "Those redskins that were chasin' us should have been here by now."

"Come on back in, Bob," Sally said. "You're too tempting a target out there."

"I just don't want them sneakin' up on us—" Dutton began.

An arrow struck his hat from behind and knocked it off his head. He yelped and whirled around, firing his rifle from the hip. He sprayed three swift shots, then dived for the door.

Collier slammed the door behind Dutton, then he and Hightower dropped the bar in its brackets. Dutton had landed sprawling on the plank floor. He rolled over and surged back up to his feet.

"They got around on the other side," he said as he tried to catch his breath. "Reckon they'll come at us from all four ways at once!"

"Each of us will be responsible for one side of the house," said Sally. She tried to sound cool and calm, but inside, her nerves were stretched taut and she wished Smoke was here. "Are you all right, Bob?"

Dutton ran a hand over his close-cropped, sandy hair. "The arrow that ventilated my hat came mighty close to scalpin' me, Miss Sally, but it missed this ol' noggin of mine."

"That's good," she said. "Take the front. I'll cover the south side. Jed, you take the north."

"And I'll have the back," Collier said. "Got it, Miss Sally."

They followed her crisply stated orders and fanned out to the various windows. Sally slipped the muzzle of the Henry she carried through the loophole in the shutters and looked for a target, resting her cheek against the rifle's stock as she did so. She didn't see anything . . .

There! She hesitated just for an instant, long enough to get a good look and make certain that the figure she'd spotted wore buckskins, war paint, and feathers. The Indian had a rifle, too. He fired it toward the house, smoke and flame spouting from its muzzle. The bullet thudded against the thick log wall but didn't penetrate it.

Sally squeezed the trigger. She was expecting the loud crack and the recoil against her shoulder, so she didn't flinch. With a determined expression on her face, she worked the rifle's lever and looked for another target.

Colonel Lamar Talbot pulled back on his horse's reins and brought the animal to a halt. He turned his head to look at the man riding beside him and asked, "Do you hear that, Captain?"

"Yes, sir, I sure do," replied Captain Adam Skinner. "It sounds like gunfire. A lot of shooting going on somewhere up there."

Talbot frowned in thought. "What lies in that direction? Do you know, Captain?"

"I believe that's about where Smoke Jensen's ranch is, Colonel." Skinner paused. He knew quite well that was where the Sugarloaf was located. "Are we going to investigate, or would you prefer to return to our camp for reinforcements?"

Talbot didn't answer immediately. Skinner could tell by the look on the colonel's face that he was weighing the alternatives. They had twenty men with them. Talbot didn't often come along on these patrols, but he liked to get out in the field with the men from time to time, and today was one of those days.

Would twenty men be enough to handle whatever the trouble was? Judging by all the shots he heard, Skinner thought it sounded like a small-scale war had broken out. Of course, with repeating rifles being used, it was difficult to tell how many men might be involved.

Talbot came to a decision. "Let's go take a look, Captain."

"Fine by me, sir," Skinner responded honestly. He never minded action, and when you got right down to it, he didn't want those damned savages to kill Smoke Jensen.

That was a pleasure he hoped to reserve for himself.

He lifted himself in the stirrups, turned to look back at the troopers strung out behind them, and, with a wave of his arm, shouted, "Patrol . . . forward!"

The men surged ahead with Talbot and Skinner leading the way. As they approached Jensen's ranch, the gunfire got louder. Talbot signaled a halt and said, "We're not going to charge in there blindly. Captain, you'll scout ahead and report back on the situation. Take Sergeant Rafferty with you."

"Yes, sir," Skinner said.

Talbot smiled faintly and added, "You know Mr. Jensen's ranch better than any of us, I daresay."

Skinner's rugged face warmed with anger. His failure to secure those horses from Jensen, followed by the brawl with the man, rankled him. No one had ever defeated him in a bare-knuckles scrap before, and he still had a hard time believing that Jensen had been able to.

Talbot hadn't given him much trouble about his lack of success in the mission he'd been assigned. In fact, the colonel hadn't even seemed all that surprised. If anything, that grated on Skinner even more than if Talbot had chewed him out. He had never let the colonel down so far, and he didn't like doing it now.

But that was in the past, and right now it seemed like all hell was breaking loose not far away. Talbot dug his heels into his horse's flanks and sent the animal trotting ahead. Sergeant Rafferty pulled up alongside him. They left the rest of the patrol behind.

"Are we going to engage the hostiles, Captain?" Rafferty asked.

"Only if they don't give us any choice," Skinner said. "You heard the colonel's order. We're just scouting out the situation right now."

"I sure hope we get a little action this time." Rafferty grimaced. "I'm ready to kill some of those savages. We've been here more than a week and haven't spilled any redskin blood!"

Skinner listened to the shots and said, "You're liable to get your wish before this day's over, Sergeant!"

They left the trail and rode into some trees to approach the scene of battle from concealment. After they'd advanced for a few minutes, Skinner dismounted and motioned silently for Rafferty to follow suit. They led their horses forward, using the trees and brush for cover until they reached a spot where Skinner was able to part the growth and peer through the gap at Smoke Jensen's ranch headquarters.

Indians had surrounded the house, using the barn, the corrals and sheds, a parked buckboard, a couple of water troughs, and some trees for shelter as they fired rifles at the house. They weren't using bows and arrows, because those missiles wouldn't be able to penetrate the house's thick walls. Skinner figured those walls were stopping most of the bullets, too. Heavy shutters had been closed over the windows, and he was willing to bet that the doors were barred.

Farther back, out of rifle range, more Indians waited on their ponies. Sergeant Rafferty looked at them and said quietly, "Damn, Captain, there's a whole swarm of the red devils! Must be fifty or sixty, at least."

"And only a handful defending the house," said Skinner.

"But from the looks of the redskins they've put down, they're pretty good shots."

From where he and Rafferty crouched in the brush, several sprawled bodies were visible. Skinner counted them. Nine of the renegades had fallen, and judging by their limp lack of motion, they were either dead or badly wounded. And those were just the ones he could see. There could be others outside his line of sight.

"They've got us outnumbered three to one, Cap'n," Rafferty said. "What are we gonna tell the colonel?"

"We'll tell him what we saw here, nothing more or less," Skinner said. "It'll be up to him to decide what to do."

"You think he'll want to take on those hostiles in a fight?" Rafferty sounded eager and nervous at the same time.

"It wouldn't surprise me a bit, Sergeant." Skinner knew that Colonel Talbot was itching for action, just like the rest of them. "Come on, we'll withdraw now and report back to him."

They hurried back the half mile to where they had left Talbot and the rest of the patrol. With an impatient look on his face, the colonel demanded, "Well? What did you find?"

"It's Black Drum's renegades, all right," said Skinner. "There can't be any other bunch of hostiles that big in these parts. They've got Jensen's ranch house surrounded, but it looked like the folks in the house have held them off so far."

"You don't know how many defenders there are?"

Skinner shook his head. "No way to tell. Not enough to hold those redskins off forever, though, I'd say."

"How many are in the war party?"

"Rafferty and I saw fifty or sixty. Wouldn't you say that was right, Sergeant?"

"Yes, sir," Rafferty responded. "That many of the savages, for sure."

Talbot stroked his chin as he thought about what they had told him. After a moment, he asked, "How many are armed with rifles?"

"Hard to say," Skinner replied. "Half of them . . . maybe."

"So you're saying that we'd be facing twenty-five to thirty riflemen, a force roughly the same size as our own."

Sergeant Rafferty blurted out, "Yeah, but there are just as many hostiles with bows and arrows, Colonel, and they're deadly, too."

"Primitive weapons in the hands of primitive people," Talbot said with a sneer. Then he turned to the troopers, who had dismounted to rest their horses while Skinner and Rafferty scouted the battle. "Mount up, men! We're going to engage the enemy! Be brave, and we will emerge triumphant!"

Skinner and Rafferty glanced at each other. Under his breath, the sergeant asked, "Is this a good idea, Cap'n?"

"It's the colonel's order, Sergeant, so we'll carry it out," Skinner said, but he didn't look or sound completely confident that they were doing the right thing, either.

On the other hand, Skinner didn't want any of those red devils killing Smoke Jensen so long as there was a chance he could do it himself, so he wasn't going to argue with Talbot. Instead, he swung up into his saddle and was at the head of the column as the patrol rode quickly toward the Sugarloaf.

Chapter 17

Sally's shoulder ached from the Henry's recoil, and her eyes watered from the cloud of powder smoke that hung in the room. From time to time, the urge to cough struck her, but she could put up with that as long as it didn't happen while she was trying to aim at one of the renegades.

She wasn't sure, but she thought she had killed a couple of the attackers and wounded at least two or three more. She hoped the men were doing as well or better. When she had to pause to reload, she called out to them to make sure they were still all right. Each time, the three ranch hands answered and assured her they were fine.

If that truly was the case, they had all been lucky. Several times, bullets had struck the loophole she was using and whipped through the room, and she was sure the same thing had happened on the other sides of the ranch house. The constant bombardment of rifle slugs had also chipped away some small openings in the places where the logs were chinked together.

Simply put, the Indians were in the process of shooting the place to pieces . . . and if their ammunition held out long enough, they might just do it!

Finished reloading again, she had just pressed her right

cheek to the Henry's stock and peered out through the loop-hole, when what felt like a breath of hot air brushed across her left cheek and she felt the hair behind her left ear jump. It was such a startling sensation that she almost fell backward.

Then her cheek and her ear began to sting. Sally said, "Oh!" and pulled the rifle from the loophole, then turned and sat down on the floor with her back against the wall. She had the Henry across her lap as she lifted her left hand and gingerly touched that cheek. Her fingertips came away with a very faint smear of red on them. She touched her ear with the same result.

Those were bullet burns, she knew. They were barely bleeding, but they were wounds, nonetheless. One of the shots from outside had kissed her on the cheek, she thought wildly.

She had come that close—*that close!*—to dying just now. She closed her eyes and shuddered at the realization.

The brush with death affected her for her own sake, of course, but even more so, she thought about what it would do to Smoke if anything happened to her. He had already lost one wife, and their child, at the hands of brutal murderers. Even though he didn't talk much about those days, Sally knew the grief had been almost more than he could stand. She didn't want to be responsible for him suffering like that again.

But she couldn't leave this side of the house undefended, either. She drew in a deep, ragged breath, lifted the Henry, stood up and turned once again to the shuttered window.

A few seconds later, the rifle in her hands barked, and one of the renegades spun crazily off his feet as he tried to dart from one bit of cover to another. Sally had drilled him perfectly. She worked the Henry's lever and watched for another target.

Black Drum sat calmly on his pony and watched as his men continued the siege of the ranch house. It was only a matter of time until all the whites were killed, and then Black Drum would burn the buildings to the ground. He would leave death and destruction behind him as a warning to all the other whites that they never should have come to this land.

His scouts had reported seeing a young, attractive woman on this ranch. He hoped that she would survive the battle so he could give her to his men, but if she didn't, it wasn't that important. There would be other women . . . and more death . . . and more devastation . . .

His fingers strayed to the drum's taut-stretched skin and tapped idly on it as he allowed his mind free rein to contemplate all the white man's blood he would spill, all the screams of agony that would rip from their throats. His visions had told him that he could never be defeated, and that rivers of gore would flow whenever he lifted his hand in the signal to kill.

A different sort of drumming, that of rapid hoofbeats, broke into his reverie. He turned his head and saw a large group of mounted warriors trotting quickly in his direction.

At their head rode Wolf Cloud, the warrior he had placed in command of the other group when the war party split up so as to wreak more havoc among the whites in this valley.

Black Drum moved to meet the newcomers. Wolf Cloud came up to him, and both men stopped their ponies.

"You return sooner than I expected," Black Drum said in the Cheyenne tongue. "Were there no more white men for you to kill?"

Wolf Cloud grimaced and then spat. "We found one of their ranches," he reported, "but we were driven away when more white men arrived."

"A large force?"

"I do not know how many there were, but we lost eight warriors, with ten more wounded, and I decided the price we would pay to vanquish them was too high."

For a long moment, Black Drum stared at his lieutenant.

His hand strayed away from the drum hanging by its sling to the tomahawk tucked in a loop of the rawhide cord around his waist. Wolf Cloud saw the movement and stiffened, as if he thought Black Drum might kill him for his failure.

Black Drum considered it.

The messages he had received from the spirits had been very clear: He would always be triumphant over the hated whites. Wolf Cloud's failure was a slap in the faces of those spirits. The defeat might weaken Black Drum's medicine . . .

But then Black Drum suddenly realized what had happened. His medicine had not failed. The spirits had not lied. The fault was his and his alone, because he had been foolish enough to divide his force.

The medicine was embodied in *him* and no one else. Of course Wolf Cloud had failed. He was not Black Drum. Only Black Drum had been chosen by the spirits to triumph over the whites every time he faced them.

His hand moved back to the drum and caressed it. He said, "It is good you did not waste the lives of more warriors in a cause destined to fail. I see this now."

Wolf Cloud appeared to relax a little at this response, but he was still wary.

"I am sorry, Black Drum—"

"No need," the war chief interrupted him. "We are all together again, and in the future we will remain so. What matters now is killing the whites on this ranch and burning their buildings."

"They will all die!" Wolf Cloud declared.

"Yes, in time," said Black Drum, nodding. "In time . . ."

As the patrol galloped toward the ranch headquarters, Skinner gave Colonel Talbot the layout as best he remembered it. Talbot was a sound strategist, and after considering Skinner's report, he said, "We'll sweep in and kill as many of the hostiles as we can in our opening sortie, but ultimately, what we have to do is take the barn, Captain. The part of the horde that's being kept in reserve no doubt will attack when they see us taking a hand. So we'll capture the barn and defend it."

"Yes, sir," Skinner replied. That seemed like a reasonable plan to him. More reasonable than a frontal assault on Black Drum's entire force. The colonel might not think much of bows and arrows, but Skinner knew how deadly they could be in skilled hands.

The Indians had their attention focused on the defenders in the ranch house, but they couldn't fail to hear the thundering hoofbeats as the troopers charged. Skinner drew his pistol as he saw several of the warriors turn to face them.

"Fire!" shouted Colonel Talbot as he brandished the saber he had drawn.

The Indians didn't have time to fight back or even flee before a wave of lead crashed into them. Skinner's horse was practically on top of one of the warriors when the captain fired his gun into the man's face and obliterated it in a crimson smear.

From the corner of his eye, Skinner saw Talbot slashing and chopping at a couple of the warriors with his saber. Both renegades fell with blood spurting from the wounds Talbot's blade had laid open.

Skinner yanked his horse toward the barn, firing at another warrior who lifted a rifle and ran to get in his way. The captain's shot took the man in the chest and spun him halfway around. Skinner blasted another slug into the back of the renegade's head as he charged past.

"Follow me!" he bellowed at several nearby troopers.

The barn doors were partially open. Skinner forced his horse against them and swung them wide. As he entered the barn, his eyes weren't adjusted to the gloom, so he couldn't see very well at first.

He spotted muzzle flashes in the shadows, though, and

aimed at them, ignoring the wind-rip of bullets past his head and pulling the trigger until his pistol's hammer fell on an empty chamber.

When it did, he rammed the gun back in its holster and drew his own saber. A warrior leaped at him, screeching in hate. That cry ended in a grotesque gurgle as Skinner ripped the man's throat open with a slice of the blade.

The troopers poured into the barn behind him and fired right and left, filling the air with an ear-numbing roar. Several renegades who had been up in the hayloft clutched themselves as bullets ripped through their bodies, and then toppled off their perch to land in huddled, bloody heaps in the big aisle that went down the middle of the barn.

Skinner rode down one of the warriors, vaulted from his saddle to run through another man with the saber. The shooting inside the barn trailed away as the last of the Indians who had been in here died.

The gunfire continued outside, though. Skinner turned toward the entrance and saw Colonel Talbot backing into the barn on foot. The pistol in the colonel's hand slammed shots at the enemy.

Skinner looked around and saw that Sergeant Rafferty and most of the other members of the patrol were inside. More than likely, the ones who hadn't made it this far were either dead or badly wounded out there, so Skinner wasn't surprised when Talbot stopped shouting and called, "Close these doors! Assume defensive positions!"

The barn had no windows, but it did have an opening in the hayloft that faced the ranch house. Several troopers scrambled up the ladder to the loft so they could shoot from up there. Two more knelt at the gap between the big front doors and stuck their rifles through the opening. Skinner saw that there were loopholes scattered around the big structure and shouted orders for men to take up posts at those.

Smoke Jensen had built the barn to be defended, thought Skinner. He was sure the house was the same way.

Sergeant Rafferty was one of the men who had gone up into the loft. He came to the edge of the flooring up there and called, "Hey, Cap'n, we can see all those other Injuns from up here! We'll keep an eye on—"

He stopped short, and Skinner could hear other urgent voices up there telling the sergeant something. He asked, "Rafferty, what's going on?"

"Forget what I said about keepin' an eye on those redskins, Cap'n," Rafferty replied. "The rest of 'em are already on their way. Here they come now!"

Chapter 18

Sally was surprised but relieved when she saw the blue-uniformed cavalrymen charge up to the ranch headquarters and attack the Indians. Luck was with her and the three cowhands, she thought. The troopers must have been close enough to hear the shooting.

However, as the battle continued, she realized that the soldiers were pretty evenly matched against the renegades. They weren't going to be able to overwhelm Black Drum's men through sheer force of numbers.

They were making a good fight of it, though, she saw as she watched through the loophole. The Indians had stopped attacking the ranch house and turned all their attention to fighting off the troopers.

Then the newcomers retreated into the barn, and Jed Hightower called from the bedroom on the north side of the house where he had been defending that window, "There was a bunch more redskins sittin' a ways off and watching the battle, Miss Sally, but now they're charging, too!"

"Reinforcements," Sally murmured. "The soldiers really will be outnumbered now." She raised her voice. "Pick off as many of them as you can, Jed."

Hightower's rifle cracked a couple of times before he responded, "Already workin' on it, Miss Sally!"

She wondered if she ought to join him, since the main body of the attack was coming from that direction now. She hated to leave one side of the house undefended, but the shutters were closed securely over the windows. The Indians could hack and batter their way in, using their tomahawks, but that would make enough racket to warn them if they tried it.

She reloaded the Henry, then hurried through the house to the room where Hightower knelt at one of the windows. This was her and Smoke's bedroom, and there were two windows, each shuttered now. Sally knelt at the other one and slid the Henry's muzzle into the small opening.

Hightower's attention was on the charging renegades as he fired twice more, then he glanced over at her and said, "Maybe you'd best find a safer spot, Miss Sally."

The rifle boomed and kicked against her shoulder as she fired.

"And maybe you'd better see about shooting some more of those renegades, Jed," she told him.

She saw the grin that flashed across his face as he worked his rifle's lever and started searching for another target.

Smoke and Pearlie had been pushing their horses as much as they dared as they rode back toward the Sugarloaf. They wouldn't get there any sooner if they wore out their mounts, and both men were savvy enough to know it.

But Smoke's nerves were drawn tight inside him, and if he had given in to the urges he felt, he would be galloping toward home right now.

"There they are again," Pearlie said as he pointed out some tracks. "No doubt about where they're headed."

When they left the Bagby ranch, they had followed the trail left by the retreating war party, but after a while, the direction in which the renegades were headed became obvious, so

Smoke and Pearlie stopped worrying about losing the trail and picked up the pace.

Even if the Indians veered off instead of continuing toward the Sugarloaf, by this time Smoke didn't care. He just wanted to get home and make sure Sally was all right. He couldn't get what had happened to Nicole and little Arthur out of his mind.

He and Sally wouldn't ever be able to have any sort of normal existence if he dedicated himself to staying right by her side and protecting her from now on, he told himself. Life just didn't work that way. Sometimes they would have to be separated. Risks would have to be run.

But Smoke didn't have to like it, and he'd had enough of it for today. He wanted to see her again, hold her in his arms, reassure himself that she was all right.

Once he had done that, he could start thinking again about what to do next.

Suddenly, he reined in, feeling as if somebody had just rammed a foot of cold steel in his guts. Beside him, Pearlie brought his horse to a stop, too, and listened to the same faint sounds Smoke had heard.

"Those are gunshots, all right," Pearlie said after a moment.

"And they sound like they're coming from the Sugarloaf," said Smoke as he calculated distance and direction in his head.

"Maybe, maybe not. It's hard to say—"

"Close enough," Smoke said. He jabbed his heels into his horse's flanks and sent the animal surging forward in a run. He held back a little on the reins, instead of allowing the horse to gallop flat-out. He still couldn't afford to run his mount into the ground.

Pearlie drew alongside him a moment later and matched his horse's speed to Smoke's. "You reckon the bunch we've been followin' teamed up with the rest of the war party?" he asked.

"That's what I'm thinking," Smoke replied. "I don't really care if they did or not."

He didn't have to say what else was in his mind. Sally might be in danger, and that was all that mattered.

Smoke knew this valley like the proverbial back of his hand, so he didn't have to pick his way toward home. He was able to ride at a breakneck pace and still avoid any obstacles. Pearlie kept up with him for the most part, only lagging behind now and then.

As they neared the ranch headquarters, the gunfire grew loud enough for them to hear it easily over the hoofbeats of their mounts. Smoke pulled his rifle from its sheath and worked the lever to throw a cartridge into the chamber. Pearlie did likewise. They topped a brush-dotted slope and half-jumped, half-slid their horses toward the wide trail at the base of it. That trail led to the Sugarloaf.

Once on its hard-packed surface, the horses charged ahead even faster. They were close to home now, so Smoke and Pearlie called on the animals for all the speed they had left. Sharp cracks of rifle fire, interspersed with the heavy booms of handguns going off, filled the air now.

They came in sight of the buildings. Mounted warriors milled around in the open space between the house and the barn, firing rifles and arrows at the structures. More renegades were scattered around the outskirts of the ranch headquarters.

Powder smoke jetted from the loopholes in the shutters over the house's windows, and more fire came from the barn. Some of the Indians were caught in that crossfire. The war party was large and almost surely outnumbered the defenders, but some of the renegades had been reckless and allowed themselves to get in that bad position.

"Looks like those varmints are stuck between a rock and a hard place!" Pearlie called to Smoke.

"Let's make it even hotter for them," Smoke said as he

hauled back on his reins. As soon as his horse skidded to a stop, he brought the Henry rifle to his shoulder and started shooting. The crashing reports came so closely together that they seemed to blend into one long, deadly roar.

Pearlie opened fire as well. Their lead raked the members of the war party between the house and the barn. Several of the renegades pitched from the ponies, fatally wounded by the looks of their limp tumbles.

Smoke searched for an Indian carrying a drum, but the distance was too great, the dust and powder smoke too thick in the air, for him to spot anything like that. He had a hunch that if Black Drum were killed, the war chief's death would take the heart out of the other renegades. They would either surrender or flee.

At the moment, however, all he and Pearlie could do was keep up the pressure on the attackers, raking them with hot lead. It didn't take long for that pressure to have an effect. Yipping and whooping, the ones who were still mounted wheeled their ponies and fled. The warriors scattered around the ranch headquarters broke off their attacks as well and converged on the group heading north.

"They're on the run now!" Pearlie shouted as he lowered his rifle. "Look at 'em go!"

"They're lighting a shuck, all right," agreed Smoke. "Come on. I want to make sure Sally's all right."

He nudged his horse into a lope again and headed for the ranch house. Pearlie called, "I'll keep an eye on the varmints and make sure they don't double back."

As Smoke approached the house, he saw men in blue uniforms emerging from the barn. A few bodies, similarly clad in the outfits of the First Colorado Rifles, sprawled here and there, obviously cut down earlier in the fighting. Smoke was a little surprised that the cavalry was on hand. He had figured that some of his men were defending the barn.

Clearly, that wasn't the case. He spotted Colonel Lamar Talbot striding confidently out of the barn, followed by the burlier figure of Captain Adam Skinner. Smoke ignored both officers for the moment and rode straight to the house.

As he swung down from the saddle, he heard the bar being lifted out of its brackets on the other side of the door, and then the heavy panel swung open so Sally could rush out. No sooner had Smoke's feet hit the ground than she was in his arms, hugging him tightly and pressing her head against his chest.

For a long moment, neither of them spoke, content as they were simply to hold each other. Then Smoke lifted his right hand, stroked her lustrous dark hair, and asked in a voice made husky by emotion, "Are you all right, Sally?"

"I'm fine," she said, "now that you're back." She lifted her head and tilted it back to look up into his face.

"What the—" He moved a finger to touch the red streak on her cheek. "You're hurt!"

"No, just a little scrape from a bullet. That's as close as they came."

Smoke pulled her closer to him again and said fervently, "Well, that's too close!"

Another moment went by before he let go of her and stepped back.

"What about the men?" he asked. "Did Bob Dutton make it back here?"

"He did," Sally said. "He's inside, along with Jed Hightower and Max Collier. None of them are hurt, as far as I know. They all put up a great fight, Smoke. I wouldn't have survived without them."

"They're good hombres," Smoke said, nodding. "Where'd the cavalry come from?"

"I have no idea. But I was certainly happy to see them charge in the way they did. Before that, I was determined that we'd hold out as long as we could, but . . . there were so many Indians . . . and I don't know if we could have lasted . . ."

She broke off as a shudder went through her. Smoke knew how brave she was and knew, as well, that she wouldn't be happy about giving in to her emotions like this, but as far as he was concerned, she didn't have anything to be sorry about. The overwhelming worry he had felt today had left him fairly shaken, too.

"That's not the way the hand played out," he told her, "so let's just forget about it and be thankful."

Her lips curved a little in a slight smile. "Oh, I am," she assured him. "I'm very thankful."

"Hey, Smoke," Pearlie called from behind him. Smoke turned to see his friend approaching with Colonel Talbot and Captain Skinner. Despite his powder-grimed face and a little nick on his cheek that had bled slightly, Talbot looked as urbane as ever. Skinner was his usual more rumpled self. He glared at Smoke and didn't bother trying to hide his dislike.

"Hello, Jensen," Talbot greeted Smoke. "You and your friend certainly came galloping up at just the right time to turn the tide in our favor."

"We were lucky," Smoke said. "Luckier than Hank Coleman and his hands over at the Triangle EC, that's for sure."

Talbot frowned. "What do you mean by that?"

Pearlie said, "I ain't had a chance to tell the colonel what we've been doin', Smoke."

"I gather this attack on your ranch isn't the only atrocity those savages have carried out today?" Talbot went on.

"Not hardly," Smoke said. Quickly, he filled the officers in on the other two raids by Black Drum's war party.

"Them splitting up that way isn't good, Colonel," Skinner commented. "We're already stretched thin as it is."

"Perhaps we killed enough of the rascals that they won't try that again. By the way, Captain, how many men did *we* lose?"

"I don't know, but I'll go check on that right now, sir."

As Skinner walked off to take care of that chore, Talbot turned back to Smoke and Sally and took off his hat.

"I beg your pardon, Mrs. Jensen," he said. "I should have inquired as to your health earlier. I was just caught up in all of . . . this." He gestured toward the bodies, red and white, that littered the ranch yard. "You *are* Mrs. Jensen?"

"That's right, she is," Smoke said.

"I can answer the colonel's question myself, Smoke," Sally said gently. "Colonel Talbot, I've heard a great deal about you, and it's a pleasure to meet you. Believe me, I was very glad to see you and your men when you rode in!"

"I just regret that we didn't get here before the savages launched their attack." Talbot pointed to her cheek. "You're wounded?"

"It's nothing," she said quickly. "A close call, that's all."

Smoke grunted. "Too close for comfort, if you ask me."

"Indeed," Talbot agreed. "You must have been terrified."

"I suppose I would have been," Sally said, "if I hadn't been so busy fighting."

For a second, Talbot looked a little surprised by her answer, but then he chuckled.

"And you gave a good account of yourself, Mrs. Jensen, I'm sure." The colonel put his hat back on and turned as Skinner came up to report to him. "Losses, Captain?"

"Three men killed, Colonel, and six wounded, two of them badly enough that they should head on back to camp."

Sally said, "We can tend to your wounded men here, Colonel, and at least get them in better shape before they have to ride all the way back to your camp."

"I appreciate the offer," said Talbot, "but are you certain about that?"

"Of course. It's the least I can do."

Smoke added, "And Sally has some experience patching up gunshot wounds."

"Very well. On behalf of my men, thank you, Mrs. Jensen." Talbot nodded to Skinner. "See to it, Captain."

"Yes, sir." Skinner asked Sally, "You want us to just bring them into the house?"

"Yes, please," she told him. "I'll get some places ready for them to lie down."

"One more thing, Captain," Talbot said. "Tell the other men to ready their horses. We'll be riding in pursuit of the hostiles as quickly as possible."

"You're going after Black Drum?" Smoke asked with a frown.

Talbot clasped his hands together behind his back. "I still have fifteen men healthy enough to ride, not counting myself and the captain."

"And even with his losses, Black Drum probably has forty."

"He doesn't have that many armed with rifles."

"Some of your men were hit with arrows, Colonel," Smoke pointed out. "You'll still be outnumbered."

Talbot's jaw tightened. He snapped, "I'm not going to let that heathen get away with all the killings he's been responsible for today, to say nothing of all the blood he spilled before he came to this valley."

"Maybe one of the warriors killed here was Black Drum."

"Let's have a look, why don't we?" Talbot suggested.

"I reckon we ought to."

Meanwhile, a couple of men assisted by their fellow troopers hobbled up, and Sally took charge, ushering the wounded men into the house so she could clean and bandage their injuries. Smoke and Talbot walked around the scene of carnage, checking the fallen renegades for one who matched Black Drum's description.

"I don't see him here," Talbot said a few minutes later.

"Neither do I," Smoke admitted. "I've never laid eyes on the varmint, but he's supposed to carry around a black drum with him, and none of these fellas have one." He shrugged.

"Although I suppose one of the other members of the war party could have grabbed it and carried it off. But I don't see why any of them would do that."

"Nor do I," said Talbot. "No, Black Drum made his escape, I'm convinced of that. And I'm going after him." The colonel eyed Smoke. "Will you accompany me and my men, Jensen? You know this valley much better than any of us do, after all."

Smoke looked at Talbot for a couple of seconds, then shook his head and said flatly, "No."

Chapter 19

Talbot looked surprised by Smoke's answer, and so did Pearlie, who had followed along while the two men searched among the fallen warriors for Black Drum.

"I didn't expect you to say that, Jensen," Talbot replied. "After the Indians attacked your ranch, I thought you'd be eager to pursue them."

"A part of me is, Colonel," Smoke admitted. "I don't like what Black Drum has done. He needs to be stopped and brought to justice. But I've fought that bunch once already today, and put my wife in danger doing it. I'm not going to ride off and leave her here again."

He was glad Sally had gone inside. If she had heard him say that, more than likely she would have lit into him like a house afire, insisting that he wasn't going to use her as an excuse for not doing the right thing.

"Very well," Talbot said stiffly. "I suppose if you've made up your mind—"

"I have."

Pearlie spoke up, suggesting, "Why don't I go with the colonel and his men, Smoke? I know my way around these parts pretty darned well, too."

Smoke knew that was the truth. Pearlie hadn't been in the

valley as long as he and Sally had, but there was no chance he would get lost, either. And he could warn Talbot if the troopers were approaching a good spot for Black Drum's renegades to lay an ambush.

"If you're sure you want to do that, it's fine with me," Smoke said.

Bob Dutton had walked up in time to hear the conversation. He said, "I'm comin' along, too. I've got a score to settle with those redskins. Those fellas they killed over at the Triangle EC were friends of mine."

Talbot looked at the young cowboy, sizing him up, and said, "We can't allow personal grudges to interfere with doing our duty, son."

Dutton shook his head. "It won't, Colonel. I'll follow orders, just like I was one of your troops. I just want another shot at those renegades."

"And you'll have it, as far as I'm concerned." Talbot glanced at Smoke. "As long as your employer agrees."

"I don't have any say over things like that," replied Smoke. "You go ahead if you want, Bob, and you'll have our best wishes going with you."

"Thanks, Mr. Jensen."

"We've talked about that. It's Smoke."

Dutton grinned. "Thanks, Smoke. Would it, uh, be all right if I got a fresh horse from the string? Mine's been ridden to hell and gone today."

"Mine, too," added Pearlie.

Smoke nodded and told them, "Both of you go ahead. Take any of the horses you want, except Drifter."

Pearlie chuckled. "It ain't like I'd ever try to ride that rapscallion anyway. Drifter's a one-man horse."

He and Dutton headed off to the barn to throw their saddles on fresh mounts. Talbot turned back to Smoke and eyed him with keen interest.

"I believe you and Captain Skinner already had a discussion about providing remounts for my men . . ."

"This is an entirely different situation," Smoke said. "Tell them to go ahead and get fresh horses, too. That'll give you an advantage over the war party. Their ponies have been ridden long and hard today."

"I appreciate that, Jensen."

"Sure," Smoke said easily. "I'll be obliged to you for that . . . and even more so if you bring my two men back safely."

"Well," Talbot responded, "I expect Black Drum will have something to say about that."

Black Drum felt his pony faltering under him and drew back on the reins. As he came to a stop, so did the other members of the war party.

He didn't count them, but he knew that somewhere between forty and fifty remained. They had fought three battles today and lost men in each clash. And only one of the battles could be considered a clear victory. In the other two, his men had been forced to flee. His thoughts were mired in a gloomy swirl.

What had happened? Until today, his campaign of blood against the hated whites had gone so well. What had changed to ruin his medicine?

No matter how hard he tried, he couldn't come up with a reason for this latest failure, as he had earlier about Wolf Cloud's attack on the other ranch.

As if he knew that Black Drum was thinking about him, Wolf Cloud edged his pony forward. His left hand was pressed to his side, over a dark bloodstain on his buckskin shirt. A white man's bullet had ripped through him, and his coppery face was haggard from pain.

"Our ponies tire," Wolf Cloud said, "and so do the men. Five are hurt badly enough that they must rest soon."

"Six," Black Drum said. "You will not be able to go on much longer, my friend."

Wolf Cloud sat up straighter on his pony's back as a stubborn expression came over his face.

"This wound is nothing," he declared with a sharp, horizontal slash of his hand. "The bite of an insect."

Black Drum knew that wasn't true. Wolf Cloud had lost a considerable amount of blood. If he continued pushing himself, he might pass out and topple off his mount. It would be better if he rested, and that was true of the other badly wounded men, too.

Black Drum looked around. His gaze settled on a shallow ridge topped with rocks and thick brush, fifty yards away. He nodded toward it and told Wolf Cloud, "Take the other wounded men and go up there to rest. Go on foot. Leave your ponies with us."

Wolf Cloud stared at him, eyes widening slightly. After a couple of seconds, he said, "The white soldiers may be following us."

"They may," Black Drum said serenely.

"If they are, they will ride along here. Men hidden on that ridge could ambush them and slow them down. Perhaps even cause them to turn back . . . although that is unlikely."

"Even such a delay would be helpful for the rest of the war party," Black Drum said. He was glad that Wolf Cloud had grasped what he was saying so readily.

Wolf Cloud drew in a deep enough breath that it made him wince from the pain of his injury. He nodded slowly and said, "As always, your words are wise, Black Drum. Your plan is the best for everyone and will give the others a better chance to get away, so they can fight again and kill more whites on another day."

"I am glad you agree, my old friend." Black Drum extended his hand, and the two of them clasped wrists. "I will play a song for you."

"A death song to usher me into the spirit world."

"A song to honor a friend."

Wolf Cloud jerked his head in a nod. He turned his pony and called out to the men. The five warriors who had suffered the worst wounds walked their ponies forward. Quickly, Wolf Cloud explained the plan to them. They frowned as understanding of what they were being asked to do dawned on them. But none argued.

They were Cheyenne warriors. They would do what their war chief thought best. One by one, they swung down from their ponies. A couple could hardly stand because of their injuries, but the other men helped them.

"Leave your rifles," Black Drum told them.

The men handed their weapons to friends. Some who didn't have bows and arrows were given those in return. Once that was done, Wolf Cloud led them toward the ridge on foot. One of the men broke a branch off a bush and used it to brush out their footprints behind them, so that any pursuers would be less likely to notice that half a dozen men had departed from the rest of the war party.

Wolf Cloud glanced back once. Black Drum had already waved the others on, but he still sat upright on his pony, watching the warriors who would ambush the white men. He began tapping out a steady rhythm on the drum at his waist. Wolf Cloud sang with it, chanting the words of his death song as he turned and led the other men who limped and hobbled toward the ridge. They began to chant, as well.

Pearlie rode alongside Colonel Talbot as the soldiers followed the tracks left by the war party. Captain Skinner was behind the colonel, and Bob Dutton rode next to the captain.

Pearlie didn't much cotton to having Skinner behind him like that. The troopers had rubbed Pearlie the wrong way right from the start, but Skinner more so than any of the others. He had seen in Skinner's eyes that the captain held a grudge against Smoke. Skinner didn't strike him as the sort of man who would forgive and forget, either.

However, they all had other concerns at the moment, like tracking down those renegades. The Indians still outnumbered them, Pearlie knew, but today's clashes had dealt some serious blows to Black Drum's forces.

"Tell me, Mr. Fontaine," Talbot said, breaking into Pearlie's thoughts as if he knew what the other man was musing about, "do you think we can defeat the hostiles once and for all if we catch up to them today?"

"I reckon you want me to be honest, Colonel?"

"Of course. I wouldn't have asked you otherwise."

"Then, considerin' the numbers, I don't figure that us wipin' 'em out is very likely. *But*, if we can make 'em go to ground and hole up somewhere, we might be able to keep 'em pinned down long enough for you to send back to Big Rock for the rest of your bunch. That might be enough to finish the job."

"That seems like a sound strategy. Is there enough light left in the day for us to accomplish that goal?"

Pearlie squinted at the sky. "Well, see, there's your problem. I ain't sure we got enough hours of daylight left. And to be honest, Colonel, I don't much want to be roustin' around out here after dark with a bunch of renegades lookin' to lift my scalp."

"Indians are superstitious children in many ways," scoffed Talbot. "They won't even fight after dark, will they?"

"I sure wouldn't want to bet my hair on that," Pearlie said. "And that's what we'll be doin' if we don't catch up to them before nightfall."

From behind them, Skinner asked, "What do you suggest we do, then, if we don't catch them? Just let them go and allow them to remain unpunished for their atrocities?"

"Didn't say that." Pearlie kept a tight rein on his temper. "But we might have to wait and fight 'em again some other day."

Bob Dutton said, "I hope it doesn't come to that. I've got scores to settle with those varmints."

"We all do, young man, on behalf of the innocent settlers Black Drum and his men have killed," Talbot said. "He has the blood of hundreds of men, women, and children on his hands, and I intend to see to it that they're avenged."

Pearlie heard the anger and passion in the colonel's voice. Despite what Talbot had said to Dutton, the colonel seemed to be taking his job a little personally, too.

The Indians hadn't been trying to cover their trail when they rode away from the Sugarloaf. All they'd cared about was putting distance between themselves and their enemies. Because of that, it wasn't difficult to track them at first, but as the afternoon went on, Pearlie could tell that their quarry had slowed and started being more careful. He was a good tracker—not Smoke's equal, or anywhere close to Preacher's level—but even though the trail became more difficult to discern, he didn't lose it.

There were still a couple hours of daylight left when Pearlie suddenly felt the skin on the back of his neck prickle. That was instinct trying to tell him that something was wrong, he realized. He looked around quickly and didn't see anything threatening, but he slowed his horse, anyway.

Colonel Talbot reined in, too, and asked, "What is it, Fontaine? Did you spot something?"

"No, not really," Pearlie replied, "but my gut's sure tryin' to tell me that somethin' ain't right—"

His gaze was still roaming over their surroundings as he spoke, and it abruptly came to rest on a small ridge about fifty yards to their left. There were rocks and brush up there, but he didn't think the cover was thick enough to conceal any horses.

It could hide men, though, and as his words stopped short with that realization, a flight of arrows arched out of the brush and whipped down among the troopers. One man let out a gurgling scream as he clutched at the shaft that seemed to have sprouted like magic from the side of his neck. Another man howled in pain from an arrow embedded in his thigh.

Without being ordered, several of the soldiers jerked their rifles to their shoulders and opened fire on the rise. The slugs tore through brush and whined off rocks, but another volley of arrows sailed out and rained down on the men. One of the troopers was hit in the chest this time, and a horse screamed as an arrow lodged in its neck.

"Get back!" Colonel Talbot shouted, his voice cutting through the commotion. "Back out of range!"

The men wheeled their horses, except for the one who had been wounded in the neck. He succeeded in pulling the arrow loose, but a flood of crimson came with it. As his mount danced around skittishly, spooked by the gunfire, the wounded trooper swayed in the saddle and then toppled to the ground. The horse bolted, dragging him.

For a second, Bob Dutton looked like he was going to chase after the runaway, but Pearlie called to him, "Forget it, kid! That fella's a goner."

Nobody could lose that much blood and live, Pearlie knew.

Dutton grimaced but abandoned the idea and rode after Pearlie, Talbot, and Skinner. The rest of the patrol retreated as well, scattering a little as they pulled back out of range of the hidden bowmen.

No shots had been fired yet from the ridge. That told Pearlie the renegades hidden up there didn't have rifles. He had been in a lot of fights in his life, and that experience gave him a pretty good idea of what was going on here: Black Drum had left some men on the ridge to ambush them and delay the pursuit.

More than likely, those warriors were wounded. Pearlie hadn't seen any hoofprints leading in that direction, so he knew the renegades had walked to the ridge.

Black Drum, that son of a gun, had abandoned those men. Sacrificed them so he and the others would stand a better chance of getting away. It made sense, Pearlie supposed . . . but he didn't see how an hombre could do that to men who were supposed to be his friends and fellow warriors.

When the troopers had pulled back another hundred yards, they were out of range of the arrows. A few more shafts flew from the brush atop the ridge, but they fell short.

The man with the arrow in his chest was still alive. A couple of the troopers helped him down from his horse and got him stretched out on the ground. As bad as the wound looked, he might live if the arrowhead had missed his heart or anything else vital.

Sergeant Rafferty brought his horse up next to the officers and asked, "Do you want us to keep shooting at the ridge, Captain?"

"Yes, make it hot for those red devils—" Skinner began.

"You'll just be wastin' ammunition if you do," Pearlie said.

Skinner glared at him. "You're not giving the orders around here, Fontaine."

"No, but I figure you might want to listen to some good advice," Pearlie said coolly. "Those renegades will be hunkered down well enough behind those rocks that you won't hit them. It'd be pure dumb luck if you did."

"I don't have to listen to you—"

"Perhaps you should, Captain," Talbot interrupted. "Go ahead, Fontaine."

Pearlie thought the colonel actually looked interested in what he had to say, so he went on, "More than likely, those fellas don't have horses up there, and there's a good chance they're wounded, too." He explained his theory about why Black Drum had left the ambushers behind. "They can't get away from us, and if we circle around and stay out of range, they can't stop us, so it seems to me the best thing to do is just go around 'em and keep chasin' the rest of the war party."

Talbot stroked his chin and frowned in thought. "I don't like the idea of leaving enemies alive behind us," he said. "That doesn't seem to be strategically sound."

"I don't think there's more than six or seven of them. They're a-foot, and they're hurt. They really ain't that much of a threat, Colonel."

"Assuming, of course, that your theory is correct."

Pearlie shrugged and said, "Well, yeah, I reckon so."

Talbot shook his head. "No, it's late in the day already, and as you yourself pointed out earlier, it might be unwise to continue our pursuit of Black Drum after night falls. Not only that, those savages just killed another of my men and badly wounded two more. I'm in no mood to let them get away with that."

Skinner nodded curtly and said, "I agree with you, Colonel."

"So, we're going to engage these hostiles. Captain, I want five men to ride around and attack them from the rear to flush them out of hiding. The rest of us will maintain our position here in front of the ridge and be ready to intercept the hostiles when they attempt to flee."

Pearlie said, "They probably won't try to get away. They're liable to put up a fight right where they are."

"In which case, they'll be dealt with there," Talbot replied. "Captain?"

Skinner said, "Yes, sir," then turned in his saddle and called, "Rafferty! Take four men and go around behind that ridge. You'll engage the hostiles first."

"Yes, sir," said Rafferty. "Are we trying to capture them, or . . . ?"

Talbot said, "Give them a chance to surrender, Sergeant."

"They won't take it," Pearlie muttered to Dutton.

"And if they refuse," Talbot continued, "use all necessary force to subdue them."

"Yes, sir!" Rafferty wheeled his horse and started calling names. The troopers he summoned rode forward.

Pearlie said, "Colonel, I'm goin' with the sergeant and those other fellas. That'll make the odds more even."

"And I'll go, too," Dutton chimed in.

Talbot smiled. "You men are civilians and not under my command, even though it could be argued that by accompanying us, you've placed yourself so. However . . . by all means, go ahead, if that's what you want to do."

Pearlie nodded and turned his horse. Dutton fell in alongside him as they joined Rafferty and the other four troopers. The group backtracked to swing around the ridge and come up behind the renegades hidden there.

"At least this way I'll have a chance to get some of those murderers in my gun sights," Dutton said.

"Just don't let them plant any arrows in you," Pearlie warned.

Chapter 20

The terrain on the far side of the ridge fell away gradually, so Pearlie, Dutton, and the troopers would have to advance up a slight slope. There wasn't much cover, either, so if they just charged in, the renegades were bound to see them and would greet them with flying arrows.

Rafferty called a halt when they were still well out of bowshot and considered the situation.

"That brush won't stop bullets," he said after a moment. "It seems to me that if we just rake the crest with rifle fire, we should be able to pick them all off fairly quickly."

"The colonel said to give them a chance to surrender," Pearlie reminded him.

Rafferty spat. "He also said to use all necessary force. Looks to me like it's necessary—"

"Hold on, Sergeant," Pearlie said. He pointed toward a gully that meandered toward the ridge. "A couple of fellas could slip up that gully and get right on top of those renegades, if they was careful enough. Then they'd have the drop on 'em and could force them to call it quits."

"Don't you think they already know we're back here?" Rafferty asked with a scowl. "They must have seen us split off from the rest of the patrol, and if they've got any sense, they'll know we did that in order to flank them."

Pearlie considered that, then said, "Yeah, but if you and the other fellas dismount back here and sort of mill around with the horses, they'll think we're all still tryin' to figure out what to do next. They won't see me and Bob sneakin' up on 'em."

Rafferty rubbed his heavy jaw for a moment, then finally nodded.

"That sounds like it might work, all right, but it won't be you and the kid, Fontaine. I'm coming with you."

"Suit yourself, Sergeant."

"Wait a minute," Dutton objected. "I want a crack at those varmints."

"You'll get it if they spot us, or if they decide to fight instead of surrenderin'," said Pearlie.

"That's right," Rafferty added. He looked at the troopers. "If there's any shooting up there, the rest of you charge and shoot anybody who's not me or Fontaine. Got it?"

The men nodded in understanding of the orders.

Rafferty drew his revolver and nodded to Pearlie. "All right, let's go."

Pearlie hung his hat on his saddle horn and told Dutton, "You stay here with the soldiers, Bob. But if them renegades start the ball, I expect you to come ready to dance."

"I will, Pearlie," the young cowboy said. "You can count on that."

"Move those horses around," Rafferty ordered. "Stir up some dust."

Once the troopers had done that, Pearlie and Rafferty crouched low and went over to the gully. They slipped down the bank into it. The gully was about five feet deep and perhaps that wide. The men would have to crouch in order to avoid being seen as they worked their way toward the top of the ridge.

Pearlie took the lead. Rafferty didn't object. Brush clogged the gully in places, and the two men had to struggle their way through it. Pearlie was lucky; the range clothes he wore included leather chaps and a cowhide vest, so the branches didn't claw at him as badly as they did at Rafferty. He heard the sergeant cursing under his breath behind him.

Black Drum's ploy was working, Pearlie thought. Leaving a small group of warriors behind to ambush the troopers *had* slowed down the pursuit. It would have been a gamble whether or not the patrol would have caught up to the war party before nightfall anyway, but by dangling the bait of those wounded warriors in front of Talbot, Black Drum had insured that the rest of the war party would get away.

Pearlie could almost admire the man as a leader, while still believing he was pure evil for the atrocities he and his followers had committed.

From time to time, Pearlie risked a glance over the top of the gully to see how close they were to the top. Finally, he turned and whispered, "All right, Sergeant, they ain't more'n twenty or thirty feet from us, there in the brush that'll be right in front of us when we climb outta this gully. Won't take us but a second or two to get there. You ready?"

"I damn sure am," breathed Rafferty. "Let's go."

Pearlie nodded. With his Colt in his right hand, he used his left to help him climb up the bank and emerge from the gully. As soon as he was out, he broke into a run and heard Rafferty scrambling after him. From this angle, he could see the renegades kneeling behind rocks as they sporadically fired arrows toward the distant patrol.

"Drop them bows!" shouted Pearlie as he thrust the revolver out in front of him. "Get your hands up!"

Rafferty pounded along to his right and just behind him. "Surrender!" he bellowed at the Indians. "Give it up now!"

As Pearlie suspected, all the warriors were already wounded, with scattered bloodstains showing on their buckskin garb. They tried to whirl around and meet this new threat, but their injuries slowed them down too much. Pearlie and Rafferty had them covered before they could bring their bows to bear. A couple of the men didn't even have arrows nocked, so they had no chance to fight back. All they could do was slump against the rocks in attitudes of defeat.

The others weren't going to give up without a fight, though. Grimacing, one man aimed his bow at Pearlie and pulled back the arrow.

"Don't do it!" Pearlie yelled at him.

Pearlie couldn't afford to give the man more than a split-second to change his mind. When that didn't happen, Pearlie pulled the trigger an instant before the warrior released the arrow.

That was enough. Pearlie's bullet slammed into the man's chest and knocked him backward against the little boulder he had been using for cover. He loosed the arrow, but it sailed at least a dozen feet above Pearlie's head. The warrior dropped his bow as he bounced off the rock. He pitched forward on his face.

At the same time, one of the warriors got off an arrow aimed at Rafferty, but the shot was rushed. The shaft flew past the sergeant's left shoulder, missing by a foot or so. Rafferty fired, and the Indian doubled over as the slug tore into his belly. He stumbled forward and collapsed.

Two more Indians had arrows nocked, but they let the tension off on the strings and lowered the bows. Pearlie motioned with his Colt and ordered, "Throw 'em on the ground." He didn't know if any of the Cheyenne understood English, but he thought they could figure out what he wanted them to do.

After a second of hesitation, the two men tossed their bows and arrows to the ground. Pearlie motioned with his gun again and said, "Get your hands up."

Reluctantly, three of the warriors did so. The fourth man started to lift his arms, then grimaced and clutched his side where a large bloodstain was visible on his shirt. Still making a face, he slowly twisted to the ground and didn't move again. He had either passed out or died from his injury.

By now, the shots had drawn the rest of the patrol. They thundered up the slope on horseback, along with Bob Dutton, but reined in sharply when they saw Pearlie and Rafferty covering the three captives.

Rafferty said to one of the troopers, "Slauson, ride back down to the colonel and let him know we have prisoners."

"Yes, sir!"

"Cover them, men," Rafferty went on. To the renegades, he said, "Toss down any knives and tomahawks you have, then move over there, away from your weapons."

They complied with the order and then shuffled and limped to one side.

Pearlie bent over the warriors who had fallen and checked them for signs of life. When he straightened from that task, he shook his head and told Rafferty, "They're all done for."

The sergeant grunted. "No great loss, and it's certainly no more than they deserve."

Knowing how much blood Black Drum's war party had spilled, Pearlie couldn't really argue with that sentiment.

Dutton dismounted and walked to him. "Are you all right, Pearlie?" the young cowboy asked.

"Yeah, it wasn't much of a ruckus. I knew if we could get up here without them spottin' us, they wouldn't be able to put up a real fight."

Dutton nodded toward the three prisoners and asked, "What's gonna happen to them?"

Pearlie scratched his beard-stubbled jaw and said, "I don't rightly know. I reckon that'll be up to Colonel Talbot."

The colonel was riding up to the ridge now, along with Skinner and the rest of the patrol.

"There's a part of me that wants to just gun the varmints

down," Dutton said as he glared at the three renegades. "After what they did at the Triangle EC—"

"I know, son. And I ain't sayin' you're wrong to feel that way. But it ain't up to us."

Colonel Talbot and Captain Skinner dismounted and talked to Rafferty, getting the sergeant's report on the engagement. When they were satisfied with that, Talbot strode over to face the prisoners.

"Do any of you men speak English?" he demanded.

At first, none of the renegades responded. Then, with a surly look on his face, one of the warriors said, "I speak the tongue of the filthy white men."

Rafferty took a step toward the man and growled, "Why, you redskinned—"

Talbot held up a hand to stop him and said, "That's all right, Sergeant. The prisoner has a right to his opinion."

"He doesn't have a right to anything except a bullet in the head, to my way of thinking," said Rafferty. "With all due respect, Colonel."

Talbot motioned him back and addressed the captive who had spoken. "What's your name?"

"I am called Walks Like Bear."

"And who are these men?" Talbot asked as he nodded toward the other two prisoners.

With obvious reluctance, Walks Like Bear said, "Blue Feather and Falling Horse."

Talbot pointed at the three bodies. "And those men?"

"Wolf Cloud, Paints His Pony, and Runs at Night."

"None of you are Black Drum?"

Walks Like Bear sneered at Talbot and said, "I have told you our names."

"Did Black Drum survive the battle at Smoke Jensen's ranch?"

Captain Skinner said quietly, "He probably doesn't know

who you're talking about, sir. They're too ignorant to know the names of the people they attack."

Talbot looked annoyed at the interruption, but after a glance at Skinner, he said to Walks Like Bear, "Was Black Drum still alive the last time you saw him?"

"Black Drum will kill every white man in this valley," the warrior said, answering the question but only indirectly. "The white women and young ones will die, too. The spirits have willed it. All whites are bad."

Talbot ignored that and asked, "Where is Black Drum hiding?"

That question drew a harsh bark of laughter from Walks Like Bear. "Black Drum does not hide! You think he is like a prairie dog, burrowing into the ground?"

"More like a worm," Skinner snapped.

"You will see worms," Walks Like Bear said as his lips drew back from his teeth in a hate-filled grimace. "You will feel worms as they rise from the earth to devour your stinking carcass, white man! *That* is the fate that awaits you for trying to steal the real people's land!"

"So you can't tell me where to find Black Drum?" asked Talbot.

"I cannot. I would not, if I could."

Talbot nodded and said, "Very well."

Without Pearlie noticing, the colonel had unfastened the flap on his holster. He drew his gun and raised it in a smooth motion, cocking the hammer as he did so. Walks Like Bear didn't have time to do anything except widen his eyes slightly as he realized what was about to happen.

Talbot pulled the trigger. The gun boomed, and Walks Like Bear's head jerked back as the bullet struck him in the forehead, bored through his brain, and exploded out the back of his skull in a grisly pink mist. The warrior's knees buckled. He thudded to the ground.

Pearlie couldn't find his tongue for a second. When he did,

he blurted out, "Dadgum it, Colonel, you just killed that man in cold blood!"

Talbot holstered his revolver and snapped the holster flap.

"I executed an enemy prisoner, Fontaine," he said. "There's a big difference." The colonel smiled thinly. "Besides, I believe *you* killed one of the savages a few minutes ago, according to Sergeant Rafferty's report."

"He was tryin' to kill me," Pearlie snapped. "There's your big difference."

Skinner said, "Keep a civil tongue in your head, Fontaine. That's an officer you're talking to."

"Not an officer I answer to."

Despite that defiant declaration, Pearlie was keenly aware that he and Dutton were very much outnumbered by the troopers. Talbot could do anything he wanted, and the two civilians couldn't stop him.

The sudden shot had taken the two surviving warriors by surprise, and even though they stiffened and leaned forward as if they wanted to attack Talbot, they didn't move otherwise. Their faces were full of hate as they stared at the colonel, though.

Skinner nodded toward the two renegades and asked, "What are we going to do with these prisoners, Colonel?"

Talbot faced them and said, "Neither of you speak English?"

They both stared blankly at him.

"If you can tell me where to find Black Drum, I might be persuaded to spare your lives," Talbot went on.

That didn't get any response, either.

"They don't understand you," said Pearlie. "And I don't reckon they'd help you, even if they did."

"I suspect you're right." Talbot shrugged. "Very well. I find them both guilty of murder and sentence them to be hanged by the neck until dead. Carry out that sentence, Captain."

Skinner nodded curtly, turned to Rafferty, and said, "You

heard the colonel, Sergeant. Find a suitable tree and string up these filthy redskins."

"Yes, sir!"

None of the troopers seemed to be surprised by this grim turn of events. Pearlie stared at Talbot, who looked as slick and unruffled as ever, as though he hadn't just sentenced two men to death. Then Pearlie looked over at Dutton and said, "We can't let 'em do this, Bob."

"Why the hell not?" Dutton said. "Those Indians *are* murderers. They've helped massacre who knows how many innocent people, includin' women and kids."

"Yeah, but it ain't hardly legal, doin' it this way."

Talbot heard Pearlie's words and said, "I disagree with you, Fontaine. I'm a military commander, and these men are the enemy. In the field like this, I have every right to pass judgment on them and see that the sentence is carried out."

"Yeah, but . . ." Pearlie's voice trailed off as he frowned. He wasn't a soldier. He truly didn't know what was allowed and what wasn't.

"Besides, I know a few things about your background," Talbot went on coolly. "I'm told that until fairly recently, you made your living selling your skill with a gun. Surely you didn't worry about legal niceties every time you fought in a range war or helped some railroad tycoon crush his business rivals."

"Sounds like a hypocrite to me," jeered Skinner.

Pearlie couldn't muster much of an argument for that. He and Dutton stood by while Rafferty had some of the troopers grab the two renegades by the arms and wrestle them down from the ridge. They dragged the men across the trail to a cluster of trees. The Indians figured out what was going on when two men tossed ropes over sturdy branches.

Pearlie and Dutton remained on the ridge with their horses while the preparations went on. The rest of the patrol, including Talbot and Skinner, went down the slope to watch. The warriors struggled, but with several men holding each of them, they couldn't prevent Rafferty from slipping nooses over their necks.

Dutton looked over at Pearlie and said, "You're not really that upset about this, are you? Those men are killers. They've got it comin'."

"Yeah," Pearlie admitted. "I suppose they do. If Talbot took 'em back and had a trial, the way it played out in the end likely wouldn't be any different."

"You've seen hangings before, haven't you?"

"I've seen more hangin's than years you've been alive, kid," Pearlie said. "And I don't doubt that every hombre I've seen get his neck stretched deserved it, too. But still, seein' fellas get strung up that way puts sort of a hollow feelin' in my guts."

"Well, come to mention it, I reckon I know what you mean." Dutton shook his head. "It doesn't help the way those troopers are carryin' on that way."

The soldiers had formed a ring around the two men who stood under the trees with ropes around their necks. The circle was big enough that Pearlie and Dutton could see the prisoners clearly from where they were. The blue-uniformed troopers were jeering and catcalling at the renegades, whooping with laughter and slapping each other on the back, having themselves a grand old time.

Pearlie thought he saw the warriors' lips moving. They were chanting their death songs, he figured.

Talbot and Skinner stood off to one side, watching calmly. Talbot allowed the troopers to carry on their celebration for a few minutes, then looked at Skinner and nodded. Skinner called out commands.

On the ridge, Dutton made a face and said, "This doesn't really seem like the way the cavalry usually handles things, does it?"

"No," Pearlie said. "It don't."

Troopers took hold of the other ends of the ropes that had been tossed over the branches. They began hauling on them. Cheers erupted from the other men as the prisoners were lifted off the ground. Their hands and feet were free, so they were able to kick madly and claw at the nooses. One of the warriors reached up and got hold of the rope above the noose and pulled on it to relieve the strain on his neck.

But both men had been wounded in the previous battle and had lost blood. Their strength gave out quickly. Their arms dropped to their sides. For a short time, they continued kicking hard enough to make themselves sway back and forth at the ends of the ropes.

Then it was over, and that swaying slowly stopped, leaving them hanging limp and lifeless.

Pearlie blew out a disgusted breath, turned to their horses, and said to Dutton, "Come on, kid. Let's go home."

Chapter 21

"He had them hanged?" Smoke said. "Just like that?"
"Just like that," replied Pearlie.

They stood in front of the ranch house at the Sugarloaf. It was early evening, past dusk, and while a faint glow remained in the western sky, shadows cloaked most of the landscape around the ranch. Smoke and Pearlie were both keen-eyed enough to see each other in the gloom. Lights burned in the house and the barn but little of the illumination from them spilled out of the buildings.

Pearlie and Bob Dutton had ridden in a short time earlier. Smoke, alert for the sound of hoofbeats—or anything else that might prove important—had gone out to see who was coming. He'd carried a Henry rifle with him, and the rifle was now canted back, the barrel resting on his shoulder.

Pearlie and Dutton had dismounted, and Pearlie had handed his mount's reins to the young cowboy. "Take 'em on into the barn and see to 'em," he'd said. "When you're done, you can check at the house. I 'spect Miss Sally's keepin' some food from supper warm for us."

That was true. Sally wouldn't let any man go hungry if it was in her power to feed him.

Earlier, the wounded troopers had been taken into Big

Rock. The local undertaker had returned with his wagon to collect the bodies of the slain soldiers but had balked at tending to the dead renegades.

"I'm afraid I don't know how to conduct, ah, heathen burial arrangements," the man had told Smoke.

"Well, for one thing, they're not buried," Smoke said. "The Cheyenne put their dead in trees, and if there aren't any trees available, they'll build platforms to put them on. We'll take care of that. My hands and I have already wrapped the bodies in blankets, and we'll take them up into the hills tomorrow and find good places for them."

"Seems like a lot of trouble to go to for savages and killers," the undertaker had commented.

"They're not either of those things anymore," Smoke had told him. "They're just dead."

"Hmmph. If it was up to me, I'd dig a big hole and just dump them all in it."

"Punishing a man once he's gone from this world doesn't make any sense. It's just a waste of time."

"Have it your way, Mr. Jensen. I'll leave it to Colonel Talbot to decide what he wants to do with the remains of his men."

Now, as Smoke stood in the gloom with Pearlie, he thought about that conversation. Once Pearlie had made sure that Sally wasn't in earshot, he had told Smoke what had happened when the patrol caught up to the wounded renegades Black Drum had left behind.

"Do you know what Talbot did with the bodies?" Smoke asked.

"Left 'em for the scavengers, I reckon. I know he left those last two danglin'. I looked back from a high spot and saw them still hangin' from that tree, and the troopers were already mounted up and movin' out, headed back to Big Rock, I reckon." Pearlie paused. "I reckon maybe he figured leavin' 'em like that would serve as a message to Black Drum."

"It'll send a message, all right," muttered Smoke, "but disrespecting the dead won't make Black Drum any fonder of white folks."

"No, I don't imagine it will," Pearlie allowed. "On the other hand, it don't seem likely that varmint could get any more kill-crazy than he has been so far. He's already next thing to a hydrophobia skunk."

Smoke laughed, but there was no humor in the grim sound. "No doubt about that," he said. "I'm just glad you and Bob got back all right." He explained his plans for the dead renegades. "Tomorrow you and I will take those bodies up into the hills and put them in the trees . . . but not until I've gotten back from taking Sally into Big Rock. She's going to stay a while with friends, until things get a little safer in these parts."

Pearlie hesitated, then said, "Uh, Smoke . . . does Miss Sally *know* you're takin' her to town so she'll be safe?"

Smoke chuckled again, this time with genuine amusement. "Why do you ask? You think she'd give me an argument if she knew?"

"Well . . . you're a heap better acquainted with her than I am, but I've known her long enough I figure there's a good chance of that happenin'."

"You're probably right," Smoke admitted. "I need to go ahead and tell her tonight, though, so she'll have time to get ready. She'll really be upset if I spring it on her as a surprise."

"You think Black Drum's liable to come back and attack the ranch again?"

"It wouldn't surprise me a bit. He tried three raids today, and two of them failed. You and I played a big part in beating him both times. He'll want to even the score for that."

"Yeah, I expect he will. But he lost men in every one of those scraps, Smoke. That war party ain't as big as it was."

"Maybe not," said Smoke, "but there are still plenty of those renegades to cause trouble."

"You don't reckon Black Drum might give up and head back to the reservation?"

Smoke shook his head. "He knows better than that. There wouldn't be anything waiting for him but a hang rope. No, once he started slaughtering innocent settlers and burning down ranches and towns, there was only one way this was going to end."

Pearlie didn't have to ask what Smoke meant. Both of them already knew the answer to that.

The only way to stop Black Drum was to kill him.

As Pearlie predicted, Sally didn't like the idea of going to town for the duration of the Indian trouble. Hiding out, she called it.

"And I've never been one to hide from trouble," she insisted. "I didn't run away when we first met up in Idaho, did I?"

Smoke frowned slightly. "I'm not quite sure what you mean by that."

"I mean that getting involved with Buck West . . . and then falling in love with Smoke Jensen, once I found out who you really are . . . wasn't exactly the safest thing I could do, now was it? Especially since there were so many people around there who wanted you dead."

"Well, I suppose that's true," he admitted. "But to tell you the truth, there were times I wondered if I ever should have gotten mixed up with you."

"Smoke!"

"For your sake, I mean," he went on hastily. "Lord knows, deciding to pull in double harness with you is just about the smartest thing I've ever done."

"Well," she said, perhaps mollified by his words but not quite ready to admit it just yet, "I suppose that helps. But I still don't like the idea of hiding out in Big Rock."

"It's just until Colonel Talbot and his men finish dealing with Black Drum."

"Do you think the soldiers will be able to run them to ground?"

"I hope so."

Smoke didn't mention that he intended to offer his services to the colonel, if that would help end the threat sooner. He had come to that decision earlier this evening. Pearlie and the other hands could keep things running on the Sugarloaf and protect the ranch.

With Sally's grudging acceptance of the trip to Big Rock, Smoke was able to relax enough to get a good night's sleep. He needed it after the long day of riding and fighting. The iron constitution that nature and his rugged life had given him meant that he woke rested and refreshed the next morning.

After breakfast, Sally finished her packing. Then Smoke loaded her bags in the buckboard and helped her onto the seat before stepping up beside her.

"Keep your eyes open," Smoke told Pearlie and Bob Dutton, who stood nearby. "Black Drum's probably going to want to lick his wounds for a few days before he tries anything else, but we don't have promises of that."

"Don't worry," Pearlie said as he lifted a hand in a gesture of farewell. "We'll take care of the place."

"I'll be back later." Smoke flapped the reins against the backs of the team and got the two draft horses moving.

Smoke was every bit as wary as he'd advised Pearlie and Dutton to be, but they didn't run into any trouble on the way into the settlement.

Sally was friends with a number of ladies in Big Rock, but she had insisted that she would be staying at the Dunn Hotel while she was in town. She didn't want to inconvenience anyone by barging in on them, as she put it. Smoke didn't figure any of the ladies would have minded if Sally stayed with them, but he wasn't going to argue over something as minor as that. If she wanted to stay at the hotel, that was fine with him.

He stopped the buckboard in front of the big, two-story building, set the brake, and wrapped the reins around the lever. He had just jumped to the ground and started around the vehicle to help Sally down when he noticed Captain Adam Skinner walking along the street toward them, headed in the direction of the camp.

Skinner saw Smoke at the same time and stopped short, but he paused only for a second. Then he came on stubbornly. Smoke considered letting Skinner walk on past before he assisted Sally from the buckboard, but then he decided he wasn't going to allow the captain's presence to affect what he wanted to do.

He reached up, slipped his hands under her arms, and swung her to the ground with an ease that looked effortless. No sooner had her shoes touched the dirt of the street than Skinner stopped again, this time only a few feet away. He took his hat off, put a smile on his face, and said, "Good morning, Mrs. Jensen. It's a pleasure to see you again . . . especially since it's under better circumstances."

Sally turned to him and returned the smile. "Good morning to you, too, Captain. Those men who were wounded yesterday, how are they doing today?"

"Our surgeon believes they'll be all right, ma'am. Thank you for asking, and for helping to take care of them. The surgeon said you did a fine job." Skinner glanced at Smoke, gave him a brief nod, and said, "Jensen."

"Hello, Captain." Skinner seemed to be making an effort to act civil, so Smoke was willing to do the same. But he could tell by the look in Skinner's eyes that the man hadn't forgotten that brawl they'd had . . . or the fact that Smoke had won that fight. Smoke wasn't likely to forget it himself.

Skinner looked at the bags in the back of the buckboard

and asked, "Have you come to town to stay for a while, Mrs. Jensen?"

"Yes, Smoke thinks it's a good idea if I do until the Indian threat is over. I can't say that I completely agree with him, but I don't want to worry him, either."

"Well, I hope it's not long before we have all those hostiles rounded up and taken care of, ma'am."

After the grim story Pearlie had told him the night before, Smoke had a pretty good idea what Skinner meant by "taken care of."

Skinner put his hat on and bid Sally a good day, giving Smoke another curt nod as he walked off. Sally watched the captain go, then said quietly, "That man doesn't like you, Smoke."

"You noticed that, eh? Well, the feeling's mutual."

Smoke carried the bags into the hotel and up to the room they rented on the second floor. He would have stayed long enough to have lunch with her, but he still wanted to pay a visit to the military camp and he had that grisly chore to take care of out on the Sugarloaf, too.

He took her in his arms and kissed her goodbye instead, and after clinging to him for a moment, she looked up at him and said, "As soon as you think it's all right, I want to come home."

"And I want you home," he told her. "Don't ever doubt that."

He kissed her again, then left the hotel, climbed into the buckboard, and drove toward the open area on the edge of town where the First Colorado Rifles were camped.

"Jensen's in town today," Skinner reported to Colonel Talbot.

"Is that so?" Talbot was sitting at the folding table in his tent. He turned in the chair so that he could stretch his legs out in front of him and cross them at the ankles. He picked up a cup of coffee that Skinner knew was liberally laced with brandy and sipped from it before he went on. "What business is that of ours, Captain?"

"None, really, sir, but I know you planned to visit some of the other merchants and leading citizens today to see if they wanted to, ah, contribute to the defense and well-being of their settlement. I wasn't sure if you'd want to do that while Jensen is around."

Talbot's casual attitude disappeared in a heartbeat. He pulled his legs in and sat up straight to glare across the table at Skinner, who was still standing.

"Are you insinuating that I have some reason to be *afraid* of Smoke Jensen, Captain?" he asked coldly.

"No, sir, but . . . Hell, we've been riding together long enough I think I can be honest with you . . . Lamar." Skinner's use of Talbot's first name made it plain that the conversation had ventured into different areas than the talks they usually had as colonel and captain. "Mostly what we've done since we came here is fight Indians and lose men. We've gotten some supplies from these townies but hardly any money."

"The reason we formed the First Colorado Rifles was to kill savages," Talbot said. His mouth was a thin, hard line as he spoke.

"Yeah, but it takes money to supply a bunch of fighting men . . . and to keep them happy. They're not going to keep on burying their friends and risking their necks if there's not a payoff pretty soon."

Talbot stared at Skinner for several long seconds, then grunted in acknowledgment of what the captain had said.

"You're right, of course. Black Drum will lie low for a time, in all likelihood. We need to increase the pressure on the townspeople and persuade them to part with more of their cash."

"We could forget about Black Drum and just *take* what we want—"

As soon as the words were out of his mouth, Skinner knew he had made a mistake. Talbot shot to his feet and crashed a fist down on the table.

"Damn it, that would make us outlaws! We are *not* outlaws! We are a military unit, duly constituted and sworn—"

Talbot was already mad, so maybe it was time for the showdown that Skinner had always known was coming, sooner or later.

"Duly constituted and sworn in by *us*, Lamar," he broke in. "You know good and well we don't have any official authority, and so do the men. They go along with playing soldier so nobody suspects us, but it's always been about the loot we can collect."

"No!" thundered Talbot. "It's about killing savages and making the frontier safe—"

Skinner held up a hand to forestall the rest of the rant.

"Sure, it's about killing redskins," he said heavily. "I like seeing the filthy savages die just as much as you do. But like I said, that takes money."

Talbot trembled from the depth of the anger he was feeling. He said, "You forget yourself, Captain."

Skinner met his stare squarely, took a stub of a cigar from his shirt pocket, and stuck it in his mouth. Around the stogie, he drawled, "No, you do, *Colonel*."

That finally seemed to penetrate Talbot's rage and remind him of the reality of their situation. He drew in a deep breath that made his nostrils flare and then slumped back into the chair to gaze gloomily at the table in front of him.

"Look, you're the boss of this outfit, Lamar. Always have been and always will be." Skinner figured it would be a good idea to smooth Talbot's ruffled feathers now that some things had been gotten out into the open. "And I know you count on me not to let you lose sight of the real objective."

Talbot nodded slowly and said, "That's true. I *do* need to be more diligent about letting the citizens of Big Rock know that they're going to have to pay to keep themselves and their town safe."

"Sure," Skinner said with a casual wave of his hand. "They always come around. And Black Drum's giving us a helping hand whether he intends to or not." A grin appeared on the captain's rugged face. "You should hear the talk around town this morning. Those raids yesterday have got just about everybody scared out of their skin. If you talk to them, they'll fall all over themselves giving you money, I'll bet. I just thought it might be a good idea to wait to do it until Jensen's not around."

"You think Jensen might stick his nose in our business?"

"From everything I've heard about him," said Skinner, "he's just the sort to do that."

"What about Sheriff Carson?"

"Carson doesn't really worry me. You or me either one, we can take Carson. Same goes for Fontaine. But Jensen?" Skinner shook his head. "I'd just as soon not have to draw down on Smoke Jensen if I don't have to."

Talbot nodded in agreement.

Skinner chewed his cigar for a second, then went on, "There's one more thing about Jensen. He brought his wife into town this morning. She's going to stay in Big Rock as long as Black Drum's on the loose."

"What does that have to do with us?"

Skinner's grin was more of a leer. "You've seen her, Lamar. Most men never get within shouting distance of something that fine."

"Mrs. Jensen *is* very attractive," Talbot allowed.

"Damn right. When we finally pull out of here, I wouldn't mind taking her with me."

Talbot stared at him for several seconds, then laughed abruptly.

"What?" Skinner snapped. "You don't think I could handle a woman like that?"

"You were just warning me about Smoke Jensen and saying you didn't want to have to draw on him. Now you say you want to take his wife away from him. How do you intend to do that, Adam, without killing him?"

Skinner didn't respond immediately. When he did, his voice had a flinty edge to it.

"I never said Jensen wouldn't have to die. But there's more than one way of accomplishing that."

Before either of them could say anything else, a private stuck his head in the tent's entrance flap and said, "Beggin' your pardon, Colonel, but you've got a visitor headin' this way. A civilian."

"Who might that be, Private Hemphill?" Talbot asked as he came to his feet again.

"That fella called Jensen, Colonel. Smoke Jensen."

Chapter 22

Smoke brought the buckboard to a halt at the edge of the camp. As he climbed down from the vehicle, he was struck once again by how slovenly the troopers were in their appearance, with beard stubble and dirty, wrinkled uniforms. Clearly, Talbot and Skinner weren't very strict when it came to discipline and regulations in the ranks.

On the other hand, Smoke had seen some of these men in action and knew that they were good fighters. A fella didn't have to be all that neat about his uniform if he was good at his job, Smoke supposed. But most military officers he had been around didn't think that way.

Sergeant Rafferty walked up to him and asked, "What are you doing here, Jensen?"

"I came to see the colonel," Smoke replied coolly. "Is that all right with you, Sergeant?"

"It's not up to me—"

Colonel Talbot interrupted him by walking up and saying, "Hello, Jensen. What brings you here?"

Smoke ignored Rafferty and turned toward Talbot. From the corner of his eye, he saw the sergeant's beefy face flush even darker with anger. Obviously, Rafferty didn't like Smoke's dismissive attitude, but he didn't say anything else. Instead he stalked off.

Talbot wasn't wearing his hat, but other than that he was in full uniform and, unlike the troopers under his command, it was crisp and clean, as usual. Somehow, he seemed able to avoid dust and sweat no matter what the conditions.

"I'd like to talk to you for a few minutes, Colonel," Smoke said.

"There hasn't been any more trouble at your ranch from the renegades, has there?"

"No, we haven't seen any sign of them since yesterday. But that war party is what I want to talk to you about."

"Of course. Come with me. We'll go to my tent."

Talbot led the way to the large command tent and ushered Smoke inside. The colonel waved toward a chair in front of a folding table and asked, "Can I get you a cup of coffee?"

"No, I'm fine, but thanks, anyway," said Smoke. He sat down while Talbot went behind the table and took a seat there. "Where's Captain Skinner?"

"Oh, he's around somewhere, I'm sure. I don't keep up with his whereabouts every moment. Would you like for me to send for him?"

"No, that's not necessary. I just want to volunteer my services, Colonel, and I figure you're the one who'll make the decision on that."

Talbot cocked an eyebrow and looked surprised. "Volunteer," he repeated. "You don't mean you want to join the First Colorado Rifles, do you?"

"No, I'm not enlisting," Smoke said with a smile. "I have a lot of respect for the army, but I don't reckon I'm cut out to be a military man. I was thinking I could work *with* you, though, as a civilian scout."

Talbot leaned back in his chair and regarded Smoke intently.

"Now that's an intriguing idea," he said. "The army makes regular use of civilian scouts, especially out here on the frontier."

"I know. An old friend of mine called Preacher has helped out the military a number of times."

Preacher's name didn't appear to mean anything to Talbot. The colonel said, "Do you believe you could help us track Black Drum to his lair?"

"I think there's a good chance of it. I know you asked me to come with you on Black Drum's trail yesterday and I refused. That's been kind of gnawing at me. I don't reckon it would have made any difference if I had ridden with you—Pearlie's told me all about what happened—but I still feel like I ought to do my part."

"And I appreciate you saying that. I understand your concern over your wife's safety, though."

"She's in town now," said Smoke, "and she'll be staying until the threat from that war party is over."

Talbot inclined his head. "You understand that it will almost certainly be necessary to kill Black Drum in order to end that threat?"

"I do." Smoke's voice hardened. "He's the one who came here to the valley and started murdering innocent folks, and he killed plenty on the way, too. He's responsible for that, nobody else. Whatever happens to him . . . he's got it coming."

"I'm glad that we're in agreement on that. Very well, Jensen, I accept your offer." Talbot stroked his chin and frowned in thought. "Captain Skinner will be taking a patrol out tomorrow. Are you willing to ride with them? I know that you and the captain have had some, ah, disagreements . . ."

"That's fine, Colonel," Smoke answered without hesitation. "I'm perfectly willing to work with Captain Skinner as long as he's willing to work with me."

"Oh, he will be, don't worry about that. Adam is a fine officer and won't allow any personal feelings to interfere in the performance of his duties." Talbot came to his feet and extended his hand over the table. "Welcome . . . unofficially . . . to the First Colorado Rifles."

Smoke stood up and shook with the colonel. "What time is the patrol leaving?"

"First thing in the morning, right after breakfast."

"I'll be here," Smoke promised.

Skinner came back into the tent a few minutes later, after Smoke Jensen was gone, and asked, "What the hell did he want?"

Talbot leaned back in his chair and chuckled. "You're not going to believe this, Adam . . . or perhaps you will. Jensen volunteered to serve as a civilian scout for us and help us track down Black Drum."

Skinner's eyebrows rose. "What did you tell him?"

"I accepted his generous offer, of course."

That shocked Skinner even more. He stared at Talbot and said, "Why in blazes would you do that?"

"Come on, Adam, you're smarter than that. You said just a short time ago that Jensen might interfere with our plans for the town *and* you mentioned that you have plans of your own for the man's wife. We'll all be better off in the long run if Smoke Jensen isn't around anymore. Isn't that what you strongly implied?"

"Yeah, but . . ." Skinner's objection trailed away. "Are you suggesting this gives us a good chance to get him out of the way, so he can't ruin everything for us?"

Instead of answering the question directly, Talbot said, "I told him that you're leading a patrol through the valley tomorrow and asked if he would be willing to accompany it. He agreed without any hesitation."

"So if something were to happen to Jensen while we're out on that patrol . . ."

Talbot spread his hands and said, "It seems like a good outcome all around, doesn't it?"

"Well, not for Jensen, and probably not for his wife, but for you and me . . ." Skinner grinned. "Yeah, I'd say that might work out just fine, Colonel."

"All you have to do is send some men on ahead of the patrol with orders to locate a good ambush site. Then when Jensen is killed, it'll be easy enough to blame it on the renegades. Just make it look good. That will be one less obstacle the two of us will have to contend with."

Skinner was nodding as he considered the plan. "I like it," he said.

"Be careful that nothing goes wrong, though," Talbot cautioned. "As you pointed out, Jensen would be a bad man to have for an enemy."

"Nothing will go wrong," declared Skinner. "By the time that patrol gets back here tomorrow, Smoke Jensen will be a dead man, just one more victim of that crazy redskin Black Drum."

Smoke had to drive the buckboard back through Big Rock to get to the trail leading to the Sugarloaf, and as he did so, Sheriff Monte Carson stepped out from the front door of his office and raised a hand to stop Smoke.

"Hello, Monte," Smoke greeted his friend. "How are you today?"

"All right, I suppose," Monte replied, "but I'm worried about something. Wouldn't mind having a word with you about it, if you don't mind."

"Of course I don't mind," Smoke said, even though he knew he needed to get back to the ranch so he could help Pearlie with those dead renegades.

"Why don't we go down to Louis's place and get a cup of coffee? He can help me tell you about it."

Intrigued now, Smoke nodded and got the buckboard moving again, heading toward Louis Longmont's saloon.

The place wasn't busy this early in the day. A few men

stood at the bar nursing beers, and one friendly, low-stakes poker game was going on. Two men playing dominoes at another table seemed more animated than the card-players.

Louis Longmont was at his usual table with several sheets of paper, a pen, and an inkwell in front of him. As Smoke and Monte walked up, Smoke smiled and asked, "Writing a book, Louis?"

"Letters to old friends," Louis replied. "Although I *could* write a book if I wanted to. Perhaps I should write one about you, Smoke."

Smoke laughed and said, "Only if you wanted to be sure nobody would ever read it. I don't figure anybody would ever be that interested in my life."

"Reckon we could get some coffee and talk for a spell, Louis?" Monte asked.

"Of course." Louis signaled to the bartender to bring the coffee. As the other two men sat down, he went on, "Now, what's this about?"

"I'm as puzzled as you are," Smoke said. "Monte's being mysterious."

"Nope, I just figured we might as well be in pleasant surroundings since we're gonna be talking about something *un*-pleasant." Monte sighed. "I mean what Colonel Talbot and Captain Skinner have been up to."

Smoke frowned. "Fighting Indians?"

"That was yesterday. Before that, they were trying to extort money from the businessmen and citizens here in Big Rock."

Smoke leaned back in his chair and didn't try to keep the surprise off his face.

"They tried to get some horses from me, and I heard about the trouble folks have had with the soldiers expecting to get supplies for free," he said.

"And free drinks, too," Louis said. "Now I see why you included me in this discussion, Monte."

The sheriff said, "Yeah, free supplies, drinks, and anything else they want. Some of those troopers have been mighty bold with their talk around the ladies, too. But the past few days, Talbot and Skinner have been going around town and talking to folks, dropping hints that they need to contribute to a fund to be used for the town's defense. Some people have done it, too. But I figure all the money those two have collected has actually gone right into their own pockets."

"You don't know that for sure, though," Smoke said.

Monte shrugged. "I don't suppose I do. But have you ever heard of something called a protection racket, Smoke?"

"Can't say as I have."

The conversation was interrupted then by the bartender's arrival carrying a tray with three cups of coffee on it. He set them on the table, and when he was gone, Monte resumed, "I've heard fellas from back East talk about such things. A gang of criminals tries to get folks to pay them for protection from trouble that might wreck their businesses . . . but it's the same crooks who'll do the wrecking if they don't get paid."

Smoke shook his head and pointed out, "What's going on here isn't the same thing. The threat from Black Drum and his followers is real. I've seen the results with my own eyes, and swapped lead with them, too."

"Oh, sure, it's not exactly the same thing," Monte agreed. "The army and the renegades aren't working together, and I don't mean to suggest that. But that's no reason Talbot and his bunch can't make money off the deal, is it?"

"Can't argue with you there. I'm surprised the army would allow such a thing, though."

"The army can't do anything about it if they don't *know* about it, can they?"

Louis said, "It sounds to me like someone should inform them of the situation."

Monte looked back and forth between Smoke and Louis

and said, "That's exactly what I'm thinking about doing. I'm going to send a telegram to the War Department in Washington and ask them if they know about Talbot and Skinner."

The telegraph had come to Big Rock with the railroad a few months earlier, connecting the settlement with the rest of the world.

Smoke nodded and said, "That's a good idea. In the meantime, Skinner's going to be busy tomorrow. He's leading another patrol through the valley. I know because I'm going with them."

It was Monte's turn to look surprised. Louis raised an eyebrow, as well, and said, "I was under the impression you two don't get along."

"I don't reckon the captain will ever be one of my favorite people," Smoke said dryly, "and I'm pretty sure he feels the same way about me. But if it'll end the threat from that war party any sooner, I'm more than willing to help."

"And end those officers trying to bamboozle money out of folks, too," Monte added. He lifted his coffee cup. "I'll drink to that."

The three men clinked their cups together.

When Smoke got back to the Sugarloaf, Max Collier and Jed Hightower loaded several blanket-wrapped bodies into the back of the buckboard. The corpses of the other dead renegades had to be draped over saddles and lashed into place. The smell of death made the horses carrying those grim burdens skittish. Pearlie tied them all together in a string and knotted the lead rope around his saddle horn. Smoke would drive the buckboard.

"Are you sure you don't want us to come with you, Smoke?" Bob Dutton asked as he, Collier, and Hightower watched the procession get ready to leave.

"No, you boys stay here and keep an eye on the place,"

Smoke told him. "I'm not expecting trouble, but you never know. I have a place in mind to lay these bodies to rest, and it's in earshot of the ranch if there's any shooting. If we hear anything, we'll light a shuck back here in a hurry."

Dutton muttered, "I still think you're doin' more for those savages than they'd have any right to expect. More than they'd ever do for any white men they killed, that's for sure."

"No reason we can't be better than them, is there?"

Dutton sighed and said, "No, I reckon not."

As they rode away from the ranch headquarters, Pearlie asked quietly, "Why *are* you doin' this, Smoke? It ain't like you to worry too much about what happens to varmints who try to kill you."

"I'm not worried about them," Smoke said. "I don't care if their spirits spend eternity wandering the wasteland between this world and the next. Figured hoisting their carcasses up in some trees was easier than digging a hole big enough for all of them, though."

"Well, speakin' purely on a practical basis, you may be right," Pearlie conceded.

They traveled several miles into the foothills of the mountains. Smoke stopped the buckboard when they reached a stand of trees with a number of thick branches protruding from the trunks. For the next couple of hours, he and Pearlie worked at placing the bodies in the trees, arranging the blanket-shrouded shapes so that they rested securely on branches and tying them in place. The elements would take care of things after that.

On the way back to the ranch headquarters, Smoke told his friend about the conversation he'd had with Monte Carson and Louis Longmont, and also about the offer he had made to Colonel Talbot.

"You're throwin' in with that bunch, Smoke?" Pearlie asked, clearly astounded. "But from what Monte told you, they ain't nothin' but owlhoots."

"Next thing to it, maybe," Smoke agreed, "but the threat from Black Drum is real, and even if Talbot and Skinner are trying to pull some sort of extortion scheme in addition to their army duties, they're the best chance we have of ending the threat. Once those renegades are dealt with, they won't have any reason to stay in these parts and cause more trouble for folks."

"After what I saw of 'em while I was ridin' with 'em, I ain't surprised to hear they're up to no good. That Colonel Talbot's a cold-blooded hombre. The way he shot that Injun and then had the other two strung up . . . Well, I don't figure there's much I'd put past him, Smoke."

"I feel the same way," Smoke said, nodding. "That's a good reason to get them gone from these parts, just as quickly as we can."

Chapter 23

Smoke had an early breakfast with the crew on the Sugar-loaf, then headed into town after discussing the day's work with Pearlie. Instead of splitting up to take care of different chores as they normally might, the four ranch hands would stay together and remain close to headquarters. The rene-gades would love to find the place undefended so they could burn the ranch house and the other buildings without any risk to themselves.

The sun was barely up when Smoke, riding Drifter, reached the army camp on the outskirts of Big Rock. Cooking fires still leaped and crackled as the troopers prepared their breakfast. Smoke headed for Colonel Talbot's tent. Before he got there, Captain Skinner stepped out of the tent, saw Smoke, and raised a hand in greeting.

"Jensen," he said. "You got here on time."

"I said I would," Smoke responded, his voice as cool and crisp as the morning air around them. "How many men will be in this patrol you're leading?"

"Twenty, not counting Sergeant Rafferty and myself. So you'll make twenty-three, I guess, total. How do you think that stacks up against Black Drum and the rest of those sav-ages?"

"If we run into them, we'll still be outnumbered, I'd say," allowed Smoke. "I think he still has at least forty warriors. But that's considerably fewer than he had before. And we'll be better armed. He didn't just lose men in those fracases the day before yesterday. He lost rifles, too."

Skinner nodded. "That's the way the colonel and I see it. Even outnumbered, we'll be more than a match for those filthy heathens."

Smoke hoped the captain's optimism proved to be well-founded.

"If we can pin them down somewhere, I'll send a fast rider back for the colonel and the rest of the men," Skinner continued. "Then we can wipe them out, once and for all."

Smoke nodded. "If luck's with us, maybe it'll play out that way."

"How do you plan on doing that scouting you talked about?" asked Skinner. "You'll just ride out ahead of us and search for signs of the redskins?"

"That's right. I'll probably range half a mile or so in front of the rest of the patrol. I ought to take one of your men with me so I can get word back to you in a hurry if I find anything."

"One of the troopers, eh?" Skinner nodded. "All right. That sounds fine to me. I'll pick a good rider, so he can move fast if he needs to."

"That'll be fine."

"We'll be ready to ride in about ten minutes."

Smoke nodded his agreement and watched Skinner stride off to gather the men who would be going on the patrol.

He thought Talbot might emerge from the tent, but he didn't see any sign of the colonel before Skinner returned, leading a group of men on horseback. The captain said, "We'll pick up the trail north of your place, Jensen, where we had to turn back yesterday."

"All right," Smoke said, thinking about what had happened at the spot Skinner mentioned. That was where Talbot had shot down one of the Cheyenne prisoners in cold blood, Pearlie had said, and then had the other two captives hanged. Those bodies might still be dangling from the hang ropes . . . unless Black Drum and his men had returned to retrieve them.

If that turned out to be the case, then Black Drum and his followers would be more rage-filled and thirsty for white man's blood than ever before, Smoke knew. He wasn't sure if Talbot's ruthless actions made the situation any worse than it already was, but it sure as blazes couldn't have helped matters.

Those gloomy thoughts were going through Smoke's head as he and Skinner rode out, side by side at the head of the patrol.

This would only end in death. Black Drum had known that from the time he left the reservation. It was true that the spirits had promised him victory. His visions had told him that he would slay many, many whites and spill their blood on the land they had stolen. But even so, deep in the recesses of his mind, he had been aware that there were too many of the hated whites. He could not kill or drive them all away.

His medicine could do only so much.

He could not have said what his followers believed, nor did he care. They helped him achieve as much of his vision as possible, and that was the only thing that mattered. In the end, they would all die, and so would he.

But what songs those to come would sing about his sacred war against the white invaders. Glory and honor would follow his name forever.

Despite all that, he felt a pang of regret as he looked up at the limp, hanging bodies of Blue Feather and Falling Horse. Their faces were blue and swollen, as were the grotesque

tongues that protruded from their mouths. They had died ig-
noble deaths.

As had Walks Like Bear, whose body lay nearby. As far as
Black Drum could tell, one of the white men had shot down
Walks Like Bear as if he were a mad dog. At least Wolf Cloud,
Paints His Pony, and Runs at Night, whose corpses also lay
nearby, appeared to have died in battle.

The war chief's fingers tapped on the taut skin head of the
drum at his waist. He nodded toward the hanged men and ordered, "Take them down. Gather these fallen warriors. We
must send them to the next world in proper fashion, so that
the spirits of our ancestors will be pleased and welcome
them." Black Drum paused. "And then . . ."

"And then what?" asked one of the other warriors when
Black Drum's voice trailed off.

"And then we will go to the town the whites call Big Rock,"
Black Drum declared. "We will kill them all and burn the
town to the ground, as we did the other white settlement to
the east."

He was aware of the men casting wary glances at each other
but chose to ignore that. None of the warriors moved or spoke
for a long moment. Finally, one of them said, "There are many
whites in that town."

"Women and old men," scoffed Black Drum. "And men
with no hearts to match those of the Cheyenne and the Arapaho."

"That is true, but they probably have many rifles."

"And no true sight to aim them," Black Drum insisted. He
tapped harder on the drum. "Our medicine is strong! The
spirits favor us. We cannot be defeated!"

He knew not all of them believed him. But enough did, and
the others would not allow themselves to be disgraced by
abandoning their quest now. Too many had died already. Giving up would mean their deaths were for nothing.

One of the warriors suddenly thrust the lance he carried into the air and let out a shrill, piercing whoop. Another followed suit, brandishing his bow and yipping. More and more shouts and cries rose from their throats until the sounds filled the air and echoed back from the foothills.

"We ride for Big Rock," Black Drum declared when the tumult died away. "But not until we have taken care of our fallen friends. Then we will ride in a circle and attack the town from the east, where they will not expect us. We must be among the white soldiers, killing them, before they know we are there."

Several of the older warriors nodded in approval of the plan, while the younger ones began shouting and yipping again, carried away by their enthusiasm.

That was good, thought Black Drum. They would need that fervor before the day was over. He wanted to kill as many of the whites as possible and to see their ugly buildings ablaze before the inevitable end came.

If his medicine would allow him to do that, then this would, indeed, be a good day to die.

Smoke, Captain Skinner, and the rest of the patrol reached the spot at midday. Smoke recognized it from what Pearlie had told him about the events two days earlier.

Skinner reined in and gazed at the empty branches of a tree not far from the trail.

"Looks like the savages came back for their friends," he commented. "Buzzards wouldn't have been able to cut down those carcasses." A look that was half grin, half grimace appeared on his rugged face. "I hope the carrion birds feasted some on those bodies before the rest of the savages came along to get them, though. That'd give 'em a good idea about the fate that's waiting for all of them."

None of the other bodies were still there, either, so Smoke knew Black Drum had taken them for a proper ceremony and laying to rest. Would the war chief go back to the Sugarloaf to retrieve the bodies that had been left there? Smoke had warned Pearlie about that very possibility.

On the way up here, he had considered detouring to the ranch to see how things were going. It wouldn't have been very far out of the way. But he had stuck to the duty he'd volunteered to do and led the patrol to this spot instead.

"Can you backtrack them from here, Jensen?" Skinner asked. "It looks to me like they picked up the bodies and then went back the way they came from."

"Yeah, it's hard for that many riders to move without leaving a trail," Smoke said. "I'll start scouting on ahead now. I wouldn't put it past Black Drum to try something tricky, like laying an ambush for us."

"Neither would I," Skinner agreed. He turned his head and called, "Private Hemphill!"

The tall, rawboned private rode up to join them. Smoke recalled that Hemphill, along with Sergeant Rafferty, had caused trouble in both Louis Longmont's saloon and Don Baker's mercantile. In fact, Hemphill had threatened Bob Dutton with a gun. That was what had led to Hank Coleman firing the young cowboy.

Skinner said, "Hemphill's a good rider, and that's a fast horse he's on. That's what you asked for, isn't it, Jensen?"

"It is," Smoke said. He didn't cotton much to the idea of Hemphill coming with him, but as long as the trooper did his job well, Smoke supposed it didn't matter whether he liked the man. He looked at Hemphill and went on, "If we find any sign of those renegades, Private, you'll ride back to let Captain Skinner know about it. That sound all right to you?"

"Whatever the cap'n wants me to do," Hemphill replied in a flat, surly tone.

"Those are your orders," Skinner snapped. "You know what to do, Hemphill."

"Yes, sir, I sure do."

Smoke told Skinner, "If you need us, fire three shots in the air. We'll turn around and light a shuck back to wherever you are."

"Just find those redskins," Skinner said.

Smoke nodded and heeled Drifter into motion. Hemphill came with him, riding alongside in silence.

The trail curved between two hills. It wasn't long before the rest of the patrol was out of sight behind them. Smoke didn't expect much conversation from Hemphill, and he wasn't disappointed. The trooper didn't say anything other than a few grunted words when Smoke pointed out things about the tracks they were following.

The trail led higher into the foothills. Rocky outcroppings were common, and when the war party's tracks led through a narrow gap between two of them up ahead, Smoke reined in and studied the scene carefully.

"What's the matter?" Hemphill asked. "We're supposed to be followin' those tracks, aren't we? Why'd we stop?" That was the most he'd said to Smoke since they left the rest of the patrol.

"Because that little gap up there is a good spot for an ambush," Smoke said. "Black Drum could have warriors on those piles of rock on both sides of the trail, just waiting to bushwhack us."

"Ah, you're crazy. Nobody but a mountain goat could climb up there."

"No, it wouldn't be as difficult as it looks at first glance. And we don't even know how rugged it is around on the other sides. Might be an easy climb back there."

"So what are we gonna do?"

Smoke considered and said, "I think we'd better try to circle around and pick up the trail somewhere farther on."

"The hell with that. Waste of time."

Hemphill jabbed his boot heels in his horse's flanks and sent the startled animal loping ahead, straight toward the gap.

Smoke was so surprised that a couple of heartbeats went by before he called, "Hey, wait, you blasted fool."

Hemphill ignored him and continued riding.

If Smoke had been the type to curse, he would have been turning the air blue right about now.

Instead, he muttered, "Loco varmint," and started after Hemphill. The private was already too close to the gap for Smoke to catch him before he got there. Smoke had only two choices: abandon Hemphill to whatever his fate might be, or forge right on through the gap with him.

Smoke didn't abandon his companions, even when they were acting like damned fools.

He reached for his rifle and pulled the Henry out of its saddle sheath. It was entirely possible that there weren't any renegades lurking in the gap and that he and Hemphill would ride right on through, unharmed. But he was going to be ready if any trouble broke out . . .

The noise was a small one, especially with hoofbeats echoing against the rock outcroppings. But Smoke's keen ears heard it anyway: the clatter of a small chunk of stone bouncing down on his right. Rocks didn't fall by themselves very often.

It was more likely that something—or some*body*—up there had knocked it loose.

Even as that thought flashed through his mind, Smoke twisted in the saddle and raised the Henry to his shoulder. As he did, a rifle cracked somewhere above him. Dirt kicked up to his left, and he knew the shot had missed him and Drifter by only a narrow margin. He saw the spurt of powder smoke from the hidden bushwhacker and loosed two rounds in that direction, working the Henry's lever swiftly between the shots.

Drifter was used to gunfire, so he didn't budge as the booming reports filled the air. Not even he could keep from jumping a little, though, as a slug from the left side nicked his shoulder.

Smoke expected that crossfire and pivoted to meet it, throwing two more shots in the direction of the second ambusher.

What happened next surprised him, though. Private Hemphill whirled his horse around, yanked his pistol from its holster, and charged toward Smoke, flame spouting from the gun's muzzle as he fired.

For a split-second, Smoke wondered if Hemphill was trying to get a shot at one of the bushwhackers and just doing a really bad job of it. But then he felt as much as heard the wind-rip of a bullet going past his ear and knew that Hemphill was trying to kill *him*.

There was only one explanation for that: Hemphill expected this ambush and was part of it.

Smoke could puzzle out the rest of it later. He whipped the Henry around again and fired as another of Hemphill's slugs kicked up dirt and rock a few feet in front of Drifter. The trooper was rushing his shots. Smoke didn't rush, but his actions were still blindingly fast as he drew a bead and squeezed the rifle's trigger.

At the Henry's sharp crack, Hemphill blew backward out of the saddle, crimson flying in the air from his bullet-shattered right shoulder.

Then Smoke hauled on the reins and jumped Drifter to the left. Both bushwhackers hidden above him continued firing. Smoke heard the bullets whine as they passed close to him, but none of them found their target.

In little more than the blink of an eye, he was too close to the base of the outcropping on the left for the man up there to have an angle on him. That rifle fell silent. The man on the other side of the gap continued firing, though. His shots were coming too close for Smoke's comfort. When Smoke looked up there, he caught a glimpse of dark blue fabric among the rocks.

That was enough. Smoke's rifle cracked again, and the man on the right side of the gap abruptly stood up, dropping his rifle and clutching at his body where the .44 round from the Henry had ripped through him. The rifle clattered down the slope. The wounded man groaned and pitched forward. He tumbled several feet and then sailed clear of the outcropping to plummet through empty air and strike the ground with a meaty thud.

That hombre was out of the fight, and Private Hemphill appeared to be, too. But more rocks rattled above Smoke, and when he craned his neck to look, he spotted the second bushwhacker—another of the troopers—trying to shift his position so he'd have a clear shot again at Smoke.

For a second, their gazes locked, and Smoke saw the fear that twisted the man's face. He tried to bring his rifle to bear, but he didn't have time. Smoke fired again.

The bullet caught the man under the chin and blasted upward through his head at an angle. He dropped his rifle and toppled forward, turning over completely once in the air before crashing to the ground not far from Drifter's hooves. The big stallion snorted disdainfully at the bloody corpse.

Smoke didn't like killing men he had fought alongside, especially soldiers, but they had called the tune. And it was looking more and more like maybe they weren't actually soldiers—

The sound of a gun hammer being cocked brought his attention back to Private Hemphill. The trooper had struggled to his feet and was trying to line up a shot on Smoke with the revolver that he now clutched in his left hand. Hemphill's right arm hung limp and blood welled from his wounded shoulder. The gun in his other hand wavered around.

Smoke pointed the Henry at him and called, "Better drop it, Hemphill. Otherwise you won't give me any choice but to shoot you again, and it'll be for keeps this time."

Hate burned in Hemphill's eyes, but he saw reason. His hand opened and the gun thudded to the ground at his feet. But then he grinned as he swayed back and forth, and he said, "Hear that?"

Smoke heard it, all right. Horses pounding closer, moving fast.

"That'll be the cap'n and the rest of the bunch," Hemphill jeered. "And when they get here, Jensen, you're a dead man!"

Chapter 24

When the Good Lord made Smoke Jensen, He hadn't included any backup in Smoke's nature. Running from trouble was something he just didn't do.

However, he had learned the value of a strategic retreat, and now seemed to be an appropriate time for just such a tactic. He dug his boot heels into Drifter's flanks and sent the stallion leaping ahead in a gallop.

Behind him, Hemphill yelled in surprise. Smoke cast a glance over his shoulder and saw the private scrambling after the revolver he'd thrown down. Hemphill scooped up the gun and fired wildly after Smoke, but Drifter's speed had already carried man and horse to the outer fringes of effective handgun range. Smoke didn't know where Hemphill's bullets went, but he didn't think any of them came close to him or Drifter.

Smoke had faced overwhelming odds before, but usually on ground of his own choosing. He didn't know for sure that every member of the patrol would try to kill him if Skinner ordered them to, but he figured there was a pretty good chance of it.

This ambush, along with what he had learned about the shady activities of Talbot and Skinner back in Big Rock, convinced him that the so-called First Colorado Rifles weren't real soldiers at all. He realized that suspicion had been lurking in the back of his head all along, based on various things about the way the troopers looked and conducted themselves that just hadn't seemed right.

And yet they had battled Black Drum and the other renegades, just as an actual cavalry unit would, and had done so effectively, too. It was a complicated situation, Smoke decided, and the details could be hashed out later.

For now, the best thing for him to do was to avoid a confrontation with Skinner and the rest of the patrol.

As he galloped out of the gap between the massive rock piles, he spotted two horses tied in some nearby trees. Those would be the bushwhackers' mounts. This whole attempt on his life had been planned from the start, he thought. Smoke had no doubt that Skinner was behind the attempt and had given them their orders.

But was Talbot involved, too? Smoke suspected that was the case, but he didn't know for sure.

He kept riding hard, heading for a nearby ridge topped by a thick growth of pine trees. Drifter started up the slope, his powerful muscles making it seem easy.

Before Smoke reached the top, he heard the sharp cracks of rifle fire behind him. A slug whistled past him, not too far away. Smoke angled the stallion to the right for a couple of strides, then back the other way. More bullets struck the ground and threw up gouts of dirt. Others tore through the clumps of brush that he passed. But none of them came perilously close.

With a final lunge, Drifter reached the crest and darted between two of the pines. Smoke reined in and turned the horse so he could look back down the slope and see if the phony cavalrymen were pursuing him.

Instead, they had stopped in the gap between those outcroppings and weren't shooting anymore since he had reached the cover of the trees. He saw them milling around down there and spotted Skinner. The captain was waving his arms and yelling orders, although Smoke was too far away to make out any of the words.

Smoke lifted the Henry to his shoulder and fired four swift rounds, aiming high enough that the bullets all struck the rocks and ricocheted off with loud, menacing whines. He saw several of the troopers duck instinctively in their saddles. He hoped that would spook them enough to make them give up on the idea of coming after him.

However, Skinner clearly wasn't going to do that. He bellowed more orders and continued waving his arms, and the troopers started up the slope toward Smoke in a ragged line. Most of them looked nervous, as if they expected bullets to be coming their way at any second.

In fact, Smoke could have picked off several of them with no trouble, but until he knew exactly what was going on here, he didn't want to kill anyone that he didn't have to. He knew this valley much better than any of those men did. He wouldn't have any trouble giving them the slip.

He faded back deeper into the trees, then turned and rode Drifter at a fast lope down the far side of the ridge, across a broad, open meadow, and into more trees. His pursuers were being cautious, but several of them topped the ridge in time to spot him disappearing into the shadows under the pines a quarter of a mile away. Faintly, Smoke heard their shouts.

He knew they would be coming after him. He also knew that up ahead was a rocky stretch where it would take a good tracker to follow his trail. The men might have a tracker that skilled among them, but there was a good chance they didn't. Anyway, that wasn't the only ploy Smoke could use to get away from them.

He allowed Drifter to pick his own path over the rough

ground and stuck with the rocks for half a mile. Then he rode down into a wash and followed it for another half mile before leaving it and riding for several hundred yards in a shallow creek he had known was there.

By then, his route had curved back around toward the site of the ambush. He thought Skinner might still be there, and Smoke wanted to have a word with the captain . . . or whatever he really was.

A short time later, he came across the same tracks he and Hemphill had been following as they scouted ahead of the patrol. With a faint smile on his face, Smoke turned the stallion to the left to follow the hoofprints once again. He could have turned right and lit a shuck for the Sugarloaf, and none of his pursuers would have known where he'd gone until it was too late to stop him.

Instead he was riding right back toward men who, a short time earlier, had been doing their best to kill him.

He had his limits, though, and he wasn't going to run again. He wanted to have this out with Skinner. With luck, he might catch the captain without a dozen or more troopers to back him up.

Smoke came in sight of the gap where the unsuccessful ambush had taken place. He angled to the right, into some trees, so he could approach without being seen. It took him about ten minutes to work his way around to a spot where he could ride out and confront Skinner without much, if any, warning.

Skinner was pacing restlessly back and forth in front of the gap, puffing furiously on a cigar. Clouds of gray smoke wreathed his head.

A couple of the troopers stood nearby with their horses and Skinner's mount. It had been a fifty-fifty chance whether Skinner had accompanied the rest of the patrol in pursuit of Smoke, or had waited here for them to bring him back. Smoke's gamble that Skinner stayed behind had paid off, at least for now.

He swung down from the saddle, left Drifter concealed in the trees, and slipped forward through some brush until he was able to step into the open no more than twenty feet from Skinner. Smoke hooked his thumbs in his gun belt and stood there facing the man squarely. Skinner, who had just swung around to pace back toward Smoke, stopped short and stared at him in amazement.

"Jensen!" he blurted out a second later. "How—"

"It's not easy tracking a fella through his own stomping grounds," drawled Smoke. "I left those other hombres a long way behind and circled back around to you, Skinner." Without taking his eyes off the man he was convinced was a phony captain, he added sharply to the two troopers, "You boys had better keep your hands away from those guns. If I see you reaching, I won't take it kindly."

Skinner spat out the cigar butt and said, "Don't let him buffalo you, damn it! Shoot him!"

One of the troopers swallowed nervously. "Smoke Jensen's got himself a big reputation as bein' fast on the draw, Cap'n. We ain't gunfighters—"

"Shut up, you coward!" Skinner roared. Smoke could tell that he was itching to reach for his own gun, but he didn't want to risk such a showdown, either. Even if Smoke hadn't been who he was, getting a pistol out of a cavalry holster with its flap closed was a cumbersome operation.

After a moment, Skinner got his anger under control with a visible effort and went on, "What do you want, Jensen?"

"For starters, I'd like to know why you tried to have me killed."

Skinner shook his head. "I don't know what you're talking about."

Smoke nodded toward the bodies of the troopers he had killed, which had been picked up and laid on their backs nearby, with blankets draped over them. Their legs stuck out in plain sight, though, in high-topped boots and uniform trousers.

"Those are two of your men I was forced to ventilate, to keep them from killing me," he said.

"Whatever they did, I had nothing to do with it," Skinner insisted. He smirked. "I guess there's just something about you that makes men want to shoot you, Jensen."

"Are you sure it doesn't have anything to do with you and Talbot wanting to get me out of the way, since I've figured out that you're all just a bunch of outlaws and not real soldiers at all?"

Smoke could tell by the surprise in Skinner's eyes that his speculation had found its target. The two troopers caught their breath, too.

Skinner recovered quickly. "I still don't know what you're talking about. We're the First Colorado Rifles—"

"You can call yourselves whatever you want," Smoke broke in. "That doesn't mean the army actually sent you here. In fact, I'd bet a hat the army doesn't even know you fellas exist. But we'll find out soon, because by now Monte Carson's wired the War Department to find out what's really going on." Smoke shook his head slowly. "You and Talbot overplayed your hand by trying to extort money from the settlers in Big Rock. That's not something the real army would have done . . . but no-good owlhoots would have."

"You're just spinning some crazy yarn," Skinner said, but his heart didn't seem to be in his denials anymore. "We're not outlaws, and I didn't try to have you killed."

"That's not what Private Hemphill said. Where *is* Hemphill, anyway?"

Smoke had just realized that the wounded man should have been here, too. He had figured Hemphill was too badly hurt to join the others in chasing him.

A slight crackle of brush behind him was the only warning

he had, and that might not have been enough if Hemphill hadn't been compelled to yell gloatingly, "I'm right here, Jensen!"

Smoke dived to his left as a gun roared.

He landed on his shoulder and rolled, came up on one knee with the Colt in his hand. He saw Hemphill rushing toward him. The wounded private had a crude bandage wrapped around his right shoulder, and once again he was using his left to shoot at Smoke. Hemphill must have been in the brush, probably answering the call of nature, when he got here, thought Smoke. Then Hemphill had laid low until he decided the time was right to strike.

Hemphill's second shot sizzled through the air only a few inches from Smoke's right ear. Smoke triggered the Colt and Hemphill doubled over as the slug punched into his guts. His furious charge turned into an awkward stumble. He got off another shot, but it went into the ground as his feet just before he collapsed.

Smoke twisted toward the other troopers. Instead of opening fire, they had rushed him, and they were close enough that when one of them left his feet in a diving tackle, Smoke didn't have time to get out of the way.

The man's shoulder crashed into Smoke's chest and drove him over backward. Smoke hit the ground hard enough, with the trooper's weight bearing down on him, that the impact made the Colt slip out of his fingers. It skidded away, out of reach as the trooper pinned him to the dirt and started hammering punches at him.

The second man hurried up and aimed a kick at Smoke's ribs. Smoke couldn't avoid it. The boot toe slammed into his side and sent pain shooting through him.

He slipped a short, upward punch through the arms of the man on top of him and caught the hombre under the chin. Even though the blow had traveled only a foot or so, it packed enough power to rock the man's head back sharply and make his jaws click together. Smoke bucked him off and tried to roll away from the other man's frantic kicks.

Unfortunately, that brought him within reach of Skinner, who had grabbed a rifle from a scabbard on one of the horses and was waiting to strike. He thrust the rifle butt at Smoke's head and landed a glancing blow with the brass plate on the end of it.

That was enough to make Smoke's senses spin madly. He couldn't get out of the way as the second trooper kicked him again. Pain filled his body and mind.

Strong hands cruelly gripped his arms and hauled him to his feet. Before he could even try to struggle free, Skinner stepped in and hit him with the rifle butt again, this time driving it into Smoke's stomach. Smoke would have doubled over, but he couldn't with the two troopers hanging on to him so tightly.

Skinner tossed the rifle aside and said, "Hold him, you two." He clenched his fists. "I'm going to teach him a lesson." An evil leer stretched across the captain's rugged face. "Of course, he won't have a very long time to appreciate that lesson before he dies."

Those words penetrated to Smoke's groggy mind and warned him that he had only moments to act. If he allowed Skinner to wallop him several more times, even with bare fists, he would be too senseless to put up a fight. He knew Skinner and the troopers would beat him to death.

That meant it was now or never.

With every ounce of his willpower, Smoke ignored the pain and forced his muscles to work. As Skinner closed in on him, fists cocked to batter him more, Smoke jerked both knees up. That threw all his weight on the men holding him and caused them to stagger. He straightened his legs with a snap and drove both boot heels against the man's broad chest.

Skinner flew backward, and the reaction from the devastating kick made the troopers stumble again. One of them lost his footing and his legs buckled underneath him. He fell to the ground and took Smoke and the other soldier with him.

Smoke's right arm came free. He lifted the elbow in a sharp blow to the chin that levered the other trooper's head back. In a swift continuation of the same move, Smoke slashed the hard edge of his open right hand across the man's exposed throat. The man writhed on the ground, twitching and moaning as he tried to breathe. He pawed feebly at his throat.

The second trooper swung a wild punch at Smoke. The blow mostly missed, just grazing the side of Smoke's head above his left ear. Smoke twisted, grabbed the man by the shoulders, and rammed his knee into the man's groin. He screamed and curled up around the agony below his waist.

Smoke got a hand on the ground and pushed himself up. His head was actually starting to clear a little now. Exertion and the satisfaction of fighting back were responsible for that.

Skinner had rolled several yards when he landed after that vicious kick from Smoke. He had come to a stop now and was trying to struggle back to his feet at the same time Smoke was doing likewise. They came upright together and lunged at each other, slugging fiercely.

For a long moment, they stood toe to toe, battling like a couple of wild animals. Smoke was able to block most of Skinner's punches, but some of them got through and slammed into his face and body with devastating force.

Smoke gave better than he got, though. Skinner was slightly taller and maybe twenty pounds heavier, but Smoke was faster, his punches were just as powerful, and he landed more of them. Skinner began to give ground. His arms sagged, allowing even more of Smoke's punches to thunder home.

Smoke whipped a hard left to Skinner's solar plexus. Skinner gasped for air, and his arms dropped even more. Smoke threw a roundhouse right that landed squarely on Skinner's jaw and slewed his head sideways. Skinner's eyes rolled up in their sockets. He crumpled to the ground and landed on his side, groaning. He wasn't out cold, but he wasn't going to be getting up anytime soon, either.

Smoke stepped back, breathing hard. His hands throbbed from the punishment he had just given them by battering them against Skinner's head and body. He grimaced as he flexed his fingers, but he could tell that he hadn't broken any bones. His hands might hurt, but he could still use them.

His ribs hurt, too, where he'd been kicked several times. He drew in a deep breath. Again, pain made itself felt, but he was convinced none of the ribs were cracked.

He looked around, spotted his Colt lying on the ground, and quickly stepped over to it to scoop it up. He checked the barrel, the cylinder, and the action. Dirt hadn't fouled the weapon. He moved back so he could cover all three men.

Both troopers still lay on the ground, moaning. The one Smoke had hit in the throat appeared to have recovered enough that he was able to breathe again, but he was pale and shaken. The man Smoke had kneed in the groin was still curled up in a ball, but he wasn't howling in pain anymore. The sounds he made were more like whimpers.

Neither man looked like he would be a threat anytime soon.

Nor did Skinner. He was only half-conscious as he lay there breathing heavily, the air rasping in his throat.

That left Hemphill. Smoke had a pretty strong hunch that the hombre was dead, and that proved to be the case. All the life had bled out of the crumpled heap the private formed on the ground.

Smoke moved from man to man, disarming them with his left hand as he carefully kept them covered with his right. He threw the pistols well out into a thicket of thorny brush, then did the same with the rifles he took from saddle boots on the horses. The weapons could be retrieved later, but not without a heap of scratching and clawing from those thorns.

When the three men recovered enough to ride, he planned to force them onto their horses and then take them back to Big Rock as his prisoners. With his testimony that they had tried to kill him, Monte Carson would be willing to lock them up. That might prompt a showdown with Talbot and the rest of the so-called soldiers, but Smoke figured he would deal with that problem when the time came.

He wondered if Monte had gotten any response from his telegram to Washington yet. There might not have been enough time for that.

Smoke scanned the country to the north. He didn't see any signs of the rest of the patrol. They were probably still out hunting him. He needed to move quickly . . .

The swift drumming of hoofbeats made him frown and turn his head. The sound came from the direction of town. He looked around and spotted a lone, blue-clad figure riding hell-bent-for-leather toward him. What was a single cavalryman doing out here, and in such a hurry, to boot?

A cold feeling stirred inside Smoke as his instincts warned him that something was wrong—bad wrong.

A minute later, the trooper drew rein and gaped in amazement at the sprawled bodies of Skinner, Hemphill, and the other two men, as well as the blanket-covered shapes of the two dead bushwhackers.

Smoke had him covered. He said, "Take it easy, mister. I've already shot three men today, and I'm not really in the mood to make it four."

"Jensen!" the man said with a gulp. "What the hell . . . Is Cap'n Skinner . . . dead?"

"No, but he's my prisoner now, and so are you. Shuck that revolver and throw it over in the brush. Same with the rifle."

"But—"

"Just do it," Smoke said in a flat, dangerous voice. The trooper swallowed hard again and did as Smoke ordered. Then Smoke went on, "What are you doing out here by yourself?"

"The colonel sent me," the man replied. "He ordered me to find Cap'n Skinner and the rest of the patrol and bring them back to Big Rock as fast as I could."

"Why would he do that?" Smoke wanted to know.

Eyes wide with excitement, the trooper said, "Because that loco Injun Black Drum and all his warriors are attackin' the settlement! If we don't get some help, he's liable to burn the whole damn town to the ground!"

Chapter 25

Two hours earlier, Sally Jensen left the Dunn Hotel after having lunch in the hotel dining room. She had spent the morning in her room, reading one of the books she had brought with her from the ranch house. She and Smoke were both readers and since there was no place in Big Rock to buy books, they had volumes shipped in regularly on the train from back East.

But Sally enjoyed being active, too, so after eating, she decided to walk around town and visit with some of the people she knew. She dropped in first at the sheriff's office and said hello to Monte Carson.

"Afternoon, Sally," he greeted her with a smile as he stood up and came around the desk. He held a chair for her and went on, "What brings you here? Not trouble, I hope."

"No, not at all," she replied with a smile of her own as she sat down. "You know that Smoke wanted me to stay here in town until the threat from Black Drum and his war party is over?"

"Yeah, Smoke mentioned it. It's a good idea, if you ask me, the way those Indians have been rampaging around the valley."

"Well, I didn't want to add to his worries, so I agreed. But

I'm already tired of sitting in a hotel room, so I thought I'd circulate around town a little. You think that's all right, don't you?"

Monte had settled back down in his chair. He pushed aside the paperwork he'd been dealing with and shrugged.

"I don't see why not," he said. "We can't rule out the possibility of Black Drum attacking the town, of course, but I don't think it's very likely. Surely he's got more sense than that."

"There haven't been any more reports of attacks?"

"Not that I'm aware of."

"Smoke has gone with a cavalry patrol today to see if he can help them track down the war party. I don't like it when he rides off into possible danger like that, but . . ."

"I suppose you must be getting used to it by now," Monte supplied when Sally's voice trailed off.

"Not really, but there's nothing I can do about it, either."

Monte chuckled. "Yeah, I reckon Smoke Jensen's sort of like one of those forces of nature you hear about. When he thinks something is the right thing to do, there's no holding him back. It'd be like arguing with a tornado." The lawman's face grew more solemn as he continued, "What you said about the cavalry, though . . . Has Smoke mentioned anything about them to you?"

A frown creased Sally's forehead. "No, not really. I know he and that Captain Skinner don't get along, and I get the impression that he's uneasy about the rest of them."

"He may have good reason to be. I've been doing some checking . . ." Monte stopped and shook his head. "No, never mind."

Sally said, "You can't just start saying something like that and then not go on."

"Right now, anything I could say about those troopers would be sheer speculation. Nothing but gossip, really. But I'm expecting a telegram anytime now that I hope will tell me a lot more."

Sally laughed. "You know that's maddening, don't you?"

"Didn't mean it that way. Just spoke without thinking." In an apparent effort to change the subject, Monte went on, "How about a cup of coffee?"

"Well . . . I suppose that would be all right," Sally said with a somewhat dubious glance at the battered old coffeepot sitting on the potbellied stove in the corner.

Monte grinned and shook his head.

"I wasn't talking about that mud," he told her. "I wouldn't ask a lady to drink any of that devil's brew. What I had in mind was that we'd stroll down to Louis's and have some of that coffee he likes."

"That's an excellent idea," Sally agreed. "Smoke and I have gone into Longmont's many times."

"Well, it's a saloon," Monte said as he got to his feet again. "So I reckon it's not really proper for an unaccompanied lady to go in there, especially a married lady. But there won't be any problem since you'll be with me."

"There shouldn't be any problem anyway," Sally responded with a trace of tartness in her voice. "A lady should be able to go anywhere she pleases without having to worry so much about propriety. But I suppose that's the way of the world, at least right now. Things may change someday."

"Yeah, Louis says he plans to hire a cook and make the place as much a restaurant as it is a watering hole. When he's done that, anybody will be welcome in there."

"Even married ladies," Sally said dryly.

Monte just chuckled again as he offered her his arm and they left the sheriff's office.

Quite a few men spoke to Monte and tipped their hats to Sally as they walked along the street toward Louis Longmont's saloon. Most folks in Big Rock knew that Sally was married to Smoke Jensen, but they also knew that Sheriff Carson was one of Smoke's best friends, so they didn't see anything wrong with Sally and Monte strolling arm in arm along the street.

When they reached Longmont's, Louis greeted them and escorted them to his private table.

"We came for some of that coffee of yours," Monte said as he held Sally's chair for her.

"Of course." Louis signaled to the bartender. "I'm glad to see you, Sally. I hope you'll feel free to come in here anytime."

"That's just what I was telling Monte," she replied.

"And I told her you planned to make this into a fancy restaurant, as well as a fancy saloon," Monte added as he thumbed his hat to the back of his head.

"Well, it's a far cry from fancy, as yet," said Louis, "but in time, in time . . . I heard a rumor that Smoke has joined forces with the cavalry for the time being."

"He rode out with the patrol that left earlier today," Sally said. "Do *you* know anything about this mystery involving the cavalry, Louis? Monte dropped some hints about it but won't give me the details."

"Well . . ." Louis said, clearly as reluctant as the sheriff to discuss the matter. "I'm aware that Smoke harbors certain suspicions . . ."

"Which didn't stop him from volunteering to do some scouting for them," Monte pointed out. "I figure Smoke thinks it's more important to deal with the problem of Black Drum—"

Before he could go on, a man slapped aside the batwing doors at the saloon's entrance and rushed into the room.

"There's a bunch of shootin' out at the cavalry camp!" he announced at the top of his voice. "Somebody said the Injuns are attackin'!"

Louis and Monte leaped to their feet. Sally started to get up, too, but Monte put a hand on her shoulder.

"Better stay right here," he told her. "If it is an Indian attack, you'll be safer here than if you try to get back to the hotel, because Louis will look after you. Won't you, Louis?"

"Of course," the gambler said. A pistol had appeared already in his hand as if by magic, drawn from the shoulder holster under his coat.

"And I'll go see what this ruckus is all about," Monte went on. He had drawn his gun, too. They could all hear the shots coming from somewhere outside. Most of the saloon's customers charged out of the place, eager to find out what was happening and to reach their families, if they had any, or to find a good place to fight if they had to.

"You said the Indians weren't likely to attack the town," Sally said to Monte.

"Yeah, but you can't ever be sure what they'll do. Stick close to Louis. I'll be back if I can!"

With that, the sheriff ran out of the saloon. Sally hated to see him go. Her heart hammered inside her chest.

"You'll be all right," Louis assured her. "I'll see to that."

"I know that," said Sally, "but you won't be offended if I say that I wish Smoke was here, will you?"

"Not at all. I wish he was, too!"

"Maybe you have a spare gun I can use if I need to?" Sally suggested.

Louis hesitated, then nodded.

"Smoke has told me that you're an excellent shot," he said. "I think that would be a very good idea."

The screaming echoed in Lamar Talbot's head, but the pounding of his heart grew louder and louder until it drowned out the terrified shrieks. Each pulse was like an explosion going off in his brain, detonating faster and faster until it seemed as if his skull would come flying apart . . .

Summoning up his determination, he shoved the memories

out of his head. They had come crowding in when one of the men in the camp had looked down at the arrow suddenly protruding from his guts and started screaming.

Talbot had been nearby, walking past the rope corral where the horses were kept, when the man cried out. The sound of the man's screams, as well as the sight of that arrow, instantly had transported Talbot back twenty-five years and hundreds of miles to the Texas plains, to the little homestead on the Brazos river, to the early evening when Lamar Talbot's life had changed forever.

The sun had gone down a short time earlier, but young Lamar and his pa hadn't headed home for supper yet. Some of the cows had strayed, and they were out about half a mile from the cabin, searching for the fool critters. It was early spring, warm but not oppressive, and a big round moon had risen in the east while a reddish-gold arch of light from the sunset remained in the western sky. Lamar's pa had stopped for a moment to gaze at that moon, and a worried frown appeared on his weathered face.

"What's wrong, Pa?" Lamar had asked.

"That moon. I think it's what folks around here call a Comanche moon. The filthy savages like to come raiding by its light." The elder Talbot sighed. "We'd better forget about those missin' cows for now, son. We can look for them again tomorrow and hope the coyotes don't get any of 'em in the meantime."

Lamar's heart had started to slug harder in his chest. "You think the Indians might come around tonight, Pa?"

"No, not really. But just in case, I want to get back to your ma and sisters, get the shutters fastened and the door barred before it's full night. It's not dark enough yet to be real worried—"

That was when the distant boom of a shotgun had rolled over the landscape, followed by the sharper cracks of rifle fire.

Lamar's pa had said as bad a word as Lamar had ever heard come from his lips. He broke into a run toward home and flung over his shoulder, "You go around to where the tunnel comes out! Your ma's liable to send the girls that way! You find 'em and protect 'em!"

Lamar and his father had spent weeks digging and reinforcing the escape tunnel that ran a hundred yards from under the cabin's floor to the face of a bluff that overlooked the broad, slow-moving Brazos. Other settlers in the area had advised Lamar's pa that it was a good idea to have such a tunnel, in case the Comanches came raiding.

A quarter of a mile upstream along that bluff from where the tunnel came out was a small cave with a lot of rocks and brush in front of the entrance. Lamar's sisters, twelve and fourteen years of age, had had it drummed into their heads that if they had to flee from the savages, they were to crawl through the tunnel and then head for that cave, where they would hide until Lamar or one of their parents would come to get them.

As the shooting continued, Lamar ran after his father and called, "Pa! What're you gonna do?"

"Run off those damn savages!" replied the elder Talbot, never slowing. "That is, if your mama ain't killed 'em all first!" He waved his arm. "Now circle around and get to that tunnel, like I told you!"

Lamar wanted to go with him, but at the same time, he was scared to defy his father's order. He veered to his right and dashed through the brush, ignoring the way it ripped at his clothes and sometimes at his skin.

He heard only one rifle firing now. The girls had practiced some with the weapons, and he was convinced that they had been shooting, too, at first. But now, with only one person still putting up a fight, that had to mean his ma had sent the girls through the tunnel. They were his responsibility. His duty was to keep them safe.

He reached the river sooner than he expected, so soon that it took him by surprise and he had to skid to a fast halt before he toppled off the bluff. He looked around, disoriented for a moment in the fading light. He wasn't sure exactly where he had come out and didn't know which way the tunnel exit was.

Then he got his bearings, slid down the bluff to the narrow strip of land between the slope and the river, and started running north along the bank. He saw a bend up ahead and knew the tunnel was just beyond it.

Then shapes moved through the gathering shadows in front of him, and guttural voices called out quietly to each other.

Lamar threw himself to the ground behind a bush and clutched the rifle as he peered through a gap in the branches.

Four Indians, bare-chested and wearing hide leggings, feathers sticking up from their heads and with their black hair in braids, slid down the bluff and started north. They must have suspected that the white settlers had an escape tunnel and were looking for the other end of it. If they found it, that meant they would find Lamar's sisters . . .

He drew a bead on the back of one of the Indians. He could press the trigger and kill the savage before the man knew what was going on.

But Lamar had only a single-shot rifle, and he knew that if he gunned down one of the raiders, the other three would turn around and come after him. Even if he didn't fumble at all and reloaded perfectly, he would only have enough time to fire one more shot. At best, that would still leave two of the Indians to kill him.

Besides, he had never pulled the trigger on anything except rabbits for the stew pot and an occasional coyote. He had never killed a man. And despite what some people said about the Comanche not being human, those were men over there, nearing the bend in the river.

The blood rushed and boomed inside Lamar's head. His sisters were smart. They would look around as best they could before they ventured out of the tunnel. They would spot the Indians and stay where they were, not coming out until the savages were gone. He told himself that, and then he told himself that he couldn't be any use to the girls if he went and got himself killed by shooting just one of those red-skinned heathens . . .

Then the Indians went out of sight around the bend, and a moment later, his sisters began to scream.

Forcing himself to remain calm, Colonel Lamar Talbot pulled the revolver from its holster and turned to see half a dozen warriors rushing out of the trees. Two of them fired the rifles they carried, while the others used their bows to launch arrows at the troopers scattered around the camp.

More shots from all around told Talbot that this was just one small part of the attacking force. Black Drum's war party seemed to be on three sides of the camp, with only the side toward Big Rock open. Coolly, Talbot fired two shots at the Indians he could see and was rewarded by the sight of a savage stumbling. Without waiting to see if the warrior collapsed, Talbot ran through the camp and shouted, "Retreat! Retreat to the town! Establish a defensive line there! Retreat!"

He and his men could fort up in the buildings in Big Rock. Their tents offered them no real protection here in camp.

As one of the troopers dashed past him, Talbot lunged and grabbed the man's arm, jerking him to a stop. The man turned a panic-stricken face toward him. Talbot holstered his gun and slapped the man to settle him down and get his attention.

"Listen to me," Talbot said in a low, urgent voice. "Get a horse and ride north to the spot where we fought the Indians before. Find Captain Skinner and the rest of the patrol. Tell them that the Indians are attacking and we're going to retreat and defend the town. Do you hear me, Private? Find them and bring them back here!"

"Y-yes, sir," the man stammered. "You mean now?"

"Of course now, you infernal idiot!" bellowed Talbot. He gave the man a shove. "Go! And if you fail, I'll hunt you down and kill you myself!"

Terror flared in the trooper's eyes. He was more afraid of the colonel than he was of the Indians. Talbot knew that, and it was exactly the way he wanted things.

Of course, if the man failed in his mission, there was a very good chance Talbot wouldn't still be alive to hunt him down . . . but the trooper's thought processes didn't get that far. He turned and sprinted toward the horses, determined to carry out the orders.

Talbot pulled his gun again, shot another Indian, and continued making his way toward Big Rock, shouting, "Fall back! Fall back!" to his men as he passed them.

* * *

Fear clenched a cold fist on Smoke's guts as he looked at the wild-eyed trooper on horseback who had brought the news.

Not fear for himself. He had felt that emotion only rarely in his adventurous life. But he could know fear for those he loved, and that sensation filled him now, body and soul.

Sally was in Big Rock.

"You're sure about that attack?" he asked sharply.

"Damn right I'm sure. The redskins hit our camp first. We didn't even know they were anywhere around."

Smoke nodded. That was often the way it happened when a war party launched an assault.

"We put up a fight," the trooper went on, "but there were too many of 'em and they had surprise on their side. Colonel Talbot ordered everybody to fall back into town. He grabbed me, told me to get on a horse, and ride for reinforcements."

"So he and the rest of the soldiers forted up in the settlement?"

"That's what they were gonna do," the man said, "but I don't know if they made it. I lit a shuck outta there, just like the colonel ordered."

"What about the people in town? They knew what was going on and were ready to defend the place?"

The trooper shook his head. "Mister, I just don't know. Like I said, I fogged it outta there as fast as I could."

Smoke already regretted the two or three minutes he had spent questioning the man, and yet he had needed to know what the situation was. All thoughts of taking Skinner and the others back to Big Rock as his prisoners fled his brain now. All that mattered was getting to Sally as quickly as he could.

But there was one more thing that needed to be said. "When you start back to town, go by the Sugarloaf ranch. You know where it is?"

The trooper nodded. "Yeah, I know."

"Tell the men you'll find there to head for town as fast as they can, and to bring plenty of ammunition with them."

The addition of top-notch fighting men such as Pearlie Fontaine, Bob Dutton, Max Collier, and Jed Hightower might make a difference in the battle against Black Drum and his warriors.

Smoke was swinging up in the saddle already as he gave the trooper that order. He pulled Drifter around and heeled the stallion into a run. He flashed past the man, who called, "Hey, wait—"

Smoke didn't hear what else the trooper said, if anything. He didn't have any more time to waste.

Sally's life was in danger, and nothing would stop him from reaching her side.

Chapter 26

When Monte Carson ran out of Louis Longmont's saloon, he turned toward the sound of gunfire. As he looked toward the eastern end of town, his keen-eyed gaze spotted several soldiers running from the direction of their camp. A couple of them stopped and turned back, lifting the rifles they carried to fire at something Monte couldn't see.

He saw one of the troopers reel, though, and then turn around to reveal the arrow embedded in his chest. The man dropped his rifle and pawed at the shaft, then collapsed.

The soldier who'd been beside him turned to run again, but too late to escape his fate. He cried out, arched his back, and stumbled on for a few steps before pitching forward on his face. An arrow stood straight up from where it was lodged between his shoulder blades.

Monte knew he couldn't do anything to help either of those men, but before he could decide on his next move, the decision was made for him. A rifle cracked somewhere close, and he felt the wind-rip of the bullet as it fanned his cheek.

Whirling instinctively toward the attacker, he saw an Indian standing atop a nearby building, behind the structure's false front. The warrior was trying to reload the single-shot rifle he held. Monte's Colt came up and roared, and the Indian's head jerked as the slug blew away a fist-sized chunk of his skull. He went over backward, tumbling out of sight down the roof's far slope.

The savages weren't just chasing the troopers out of their camp, Monte realized. They were already in the town! Screams and shouted curses filled the air, along with the crackle of rifle fire interspersed with the heavier booms of pistols going off. Somewhere a shotgun thundered.

Monte saw citizens running along the street in wild panic. He shouted at them and waved his left arm, saying, "Head for Longmont's! Get inside the saloon!"

It was a sturdy building, as good as any in Big Rock to defend. The problem was that the town's inhabitants were scattered among the homes and businesses. Those caught on the street by the attack could seek shelter in Longmont's, but the others would have to hunker down wherever they were and hope that the Indians wouldn't come for them.

Not that it would matter if Black Drum had his way, Monte thought grimly. He had a hunch the war chief would try to burn the town and use flames to kill everybody he couldn't murder with arrows or bullets.

An arrow flew past Monte's head. Another grazed his upper left arm, ripping his shirt sleeve but narrowly missing the flesh underneath it. He spun toward an alley mouth where several warriors had appeared. His gun blasted again and again.

The Indians scattered, ducking back out of sight. He didn't know if he had hit any of them or just caused them to withdraw for the moment. He kept his gun ready as he backed swiftly toward the batwinged entrance of Longmont's.

People were streaming in there, seeking shelter. Louis appeared on the porch, revolvers in both hands. He fired the guns, back and forth, snap shots that didn't even seem to be aimed. But Monte saw a couple of Indians running along the other side of the street tumble down as the gambler's bullets found them.

Then Monte reached the door and stood to the left of it

while Louis was on the right. They continued firing, covering the townspeople who were trying to reach cover. After a few minutes, Monte didn't see any other citizens of Big Rock headed this way, so over the din of gunfire, he called to Louis, "We'd better get inside while we can!"

"Yes," Louis agreed after firing a final shot. Then he exclaimed, "No, wait!"

Colonel Lamar Talbot had just come into view, running toward them. The colonel was hatless and had his pistol in his right hand, the saber from his scabbard in the left. His left sleeve was bloody, but he didn't appear to be incapacitated by the wound. In fact, as a warrior leaped from an alley mouth at him with an uplifted tomahawk, Talbot struck first, ramming the saber completely through the Indian's body so that several inches of bloody steel stuck out the man's back.

When the warrior fell in his death throes, Talbot struggled to pull the saber free. Monte shouted, "Forget it, Colonel! Get in here while you can!"

Talbot looked up, seemed to realize what was going on, and abandoned the saber. A couple of bounding leaps brought him to the saloon's porch.

"Have you seen any of my men?" he asked breathlessly. "I can't find them!"

"They're probably scattered around town, taking cover wherever they can," Monte told him. "The only ones I've seen are a couple who were killed by the renegades."

"Black Drum is attacking the town with everything he has left," said Talbot. "We have to hold him off. I've sent for reinforcements!"

"Get on inside. We'll fight from in there."

Talbot nodded. He stumbled a little as he pushed through the batwings. Maybe the loss of blood from his wound was affecting him, or maybe he was just shaken by the battle, Monte thought.

The colonel had a crazed look in his eyes, that was for sure.

Monte hurried into the saloon next, followed by Louis. As Louis ducked through the batwings, an arrow struck the swinging door on the right and embedded there. Louis slammed the inner doors behind him.

"Break the glass out of the windows!" he called. "Every man with a gun, get ready to fight!"

The racket of shattering glass filled the air. The saloon's big front windows had been freighted out from Denver and had been pretty expensive, Monte knew. Louis could replace them, though, once all this was over.

Assuming, of course, that the saloon—and the rest of the town—was still standing by then . . .

Smoke rode hard toward Big Rock, but he had to rein in and walk Drifter for a while every now and then. The big black stallion possessed plenty of strength and stamina, but even he had his limits. And it wouldn't do Smoke any good or get him to Sally's side any faster to run the horse into the ground.

During one of those stretches, he paused at a high spot and hipped around in the saddle to look behind him. A thin column of dust rose in the distance. Smoke kept watching, and after a moment he spotted the group of riders kicking up that dust. From the number of them, he was pretty sure he was looking at Skinner and the rest of the patrol.

None of those men were to be trusted anymore, but right now Smoke was glad to see they were following him. Their guns might be needed when they got back to Big Rock. Smoke hoped that Black Drum's war party hadn't overrun the town and that the slaughter wasn't going on already.

With a sigh, Smoke kneed Drifter back into a run. The urgency he felt inside him wouldn't let him delay any longer.

The hour it took him to ride back to Big Rock was one of the longest in his life. When he got close enough, he began to hear gunfire. That was oddly reassuring, because it meant the battle was still going on. He didn't see any smoke billowing into the air, so he knew the town wasn't on fire.

Despite the eagerness he felt, it wouldn't be a good idea to charge in without knowing what was going on. He circled the settlement and approached from the side where the cavalry camp was located. Leaving Drifter ground-hitched, he took his rifle and started ahead on foot, making use of trees and brush to keep his advance hidden.

Smoke's first look at the camp made his mouth tighten into a grim line. The rope corral was in a shambles, and the horses were gone. Whether they had been stampeded or stolen by the Indians didn't matter. The tents were wrecked and flattened, too, more evidence of the attack.

The real proof of what had happened here, though, was in the bloody form of a dozen soldiers, all lying motionless in death, some skewered with arrows, the others drilled with rifle bullets. Smoke saw one man whose head was such a gruesome ruin that he had to have been hacked to death with a tomahawk.

Smoke had no way of knowing for sure how many warriors Black Drum had left. Estimates based on the losses from previous battles indicated that the war party numbered forty to fifty men. Possibly a few more, but it couldn't have been much larger than that.

The so-called First Colorado Rifles, with the Skinner-led patrol gone, had had around thirty-five men to oppose the renegades. Now, with the men who had been killed here in the first wave of the attack, there couldn't be more than twenty-five soldiers left in town. Smoke saw two warriors lying dead on the ground among the flattened tents and figured that Black Drum had lost more men than that, but even so, the troopers who had retreated into Big Rock had to be outnumbered.

There were other fighting men in the settlement, though—

Monte Carson and Louis Longmont, among others. They would pitch in and help the troopers try to hold off the war party. Judging by the sounds of the shots he was hearing, Smoke believed the battle had settled down to one main confrontation. The defenders had holed up somewhere, and the renegades were trying to root them out.

All those thoughts flashed through Smoke's mind in a matter of heartbeats. Sooner or later—sooner, more than likely—Black Drum would resort to setting the buildings on fire. So Smoke didn't have any time to waste. With the Henry rifle held at a slant across his chest, he trotted through the devastated camp toward the settlement.

Sally knelt behind one of the saloon tables and thumbed fresh cartridges through the loading gate of the Henry rifle she held. Several tables had been overturned and shoved up to the busted-out front windows to provide extra cover for the defenders.

During the first part of the battle, Monte and Louis had insisted that she stay down on the floor behind the bar with the girls who worked in the saloon. That was the safest place for them.

But Sally had never been one to cower in fear, and after three men had been wounded in the fighting, one of them badly, she had slipped out from behind the bar, picked up a fallen Henry, and taken one of the places at the windows. Monte, over at the other front window, had seen what she was doing, and she could tell he started to say something to her. Then he thought better of it, gave a fatalistic shrug, and went back to shooting at the renegades who had gathered in the building across the street to pour lead at the saloon. The building housed a dress shop, and it had never seen customers like the renegades who packed into it now.

There was no way of knowing how many rounds had flown

back and forth across the street in the past hour. Hundreds, certainly. Maybe a thousand or more. Miraculously, no one inside the saloon had been killed yet. The defenders had no idea if any of the Indians had been wounded fatally.

Colonel Talbot was behind another table at the same window as Sally. From time to time, he rose up enough to fire several shots from his pistol, then sank down again to mutter to himself. During one of the occasional lulls in the gun-thunder, Sally heard him saying, "Should have been with them, should have been with them."

She supposed he was talking about the soldiers under his command.

Over at the other window, Louis Longmont crouched next to Monte and said, "I'm surprised they haven't attempted an all-out frontal assault yet."

"Black Drum probably doesn't have enough men left for that," replied Monte. "And they're scattered through the town, too, trying to wipe out the other pockets of resistance. You can tell that by the sound of the shooting."

Louis nodded. "Yes, it appears he's committed enough warriors over there across the street to keep us pinned down while the rest hunt for other survivors." A humorless smile curved the gambler's lips. "He's saving us for last, I think."

Monte grunted and said, "The best for last, I reckon." He looked around the room. "Where do you figure the rest of those soldiers are?"

"They must have scattered, too. They never struck me as a well-organized fighting force."

"That's because they're really outlaws and not soldiers at all," Monte said bitterly. "I'm more convinced of that than ever."

"I think you're right, old friend. Still, they'll fight for their lives, and they're keeping some of Black Drum's forces occupied. We should be grateful for that small favor, anyway."

"Yeah . . . but is it just postponing the inevitable?"

"Time will tell," mused Louis. "And with any luck, help may be on the way."

Normally, Smoke would follow the sound of shooting toward trouble, but with guns blasting all over Big Rock, that wasn't going to work today.

Instead, he worked his way behind some houses a couple of blocks from the center of town. As he crouched behind a shed, he spotted a couple of renegades sneaking toward the back door of one of the dwellings.

He didn't know if anybody was inside the house, but he was absolutely certain those two war-painted Cheyenne warriors didn't belong here, so he stepped out from behind the shed, brought the rifle to his shoulder, and called, "Hey!"

The two Indians jumped a little in surprise and whirled toward him. Smoke's rifle cracked twice, as fast as he could work the Henry's lever, and both renegades collapsed with blood and brains leaking from their bullet-bored skulls.

With all the other shooting going on in Big Rock this afternoon, it wasn't very likely anybody else had noticed those two reports. Smoke lowered the rifle and trotted on, circling the house.

As he did so, he suddenly came face-to-face with another renegade. The warrior had good instincts and reflexes. He reacted instantly, thrusting the lance he held at Smoke's midsection.

Smoke's reflexes were quicker, though. He used the Henry's barrel to knock the lance aside. The renegade had put a lot of power behind the thrust, so when it missed, he stumbled forward, off-balance.

That put him within reach of Smoke, who slammed the rifle butt into the middle of the warrior's face. The blow crushed the man's nose and shattered the bone behind it. He fell clumsily and lay there twitching with crimson leaking not only from his nose but from his ears, as well.

The injury would be fatal, Smoke was convinced of that, but he drew the knife on his left hip, bent, and cut the renegade's throat, just to be sure. Then he wiped the blade on the man's buckskin leggings and sheathed it again.

That was three of Black Drum's men accounted for, he thought as he cat-footed toward the front of the house.

But he knew there were plenty more where those came from.

As if to prove that, no sooner had he stepped into the open than an arrow came out of nowhere and knocked his hat cleanly from his head. Guided by his instincts, Smoke pivoted sharply and spotted the man who had launched the shaft at him. The warrior already had a second arrow nocked and was pulling back the bowstring.

Smoke figured he was going to get his shot off first, and so he would have if an arrow hadn't flown in from a different direction with no warning and struck the Henry's breech. The unexpected impact knocked the rifle aside just as Smoke squeezed the trigger, so his shot went wild. The other Indian fired his second arrow.

Smoke twisted just enough that the flint head missed him, going between his left arm and his body. The wooden shaft slapped against his ribs and bounced off. He triggered the Henry from the hip and saw the renegade fly backward as the .44 slug punched into his chest.

Twice, he had come within inches of killing Smoke Jensen.

He wouldn't get a third chance.

But that left the other renegade drawing a bead on Smoke, who, as he spun around, went for his Colt instead of trying to lever another round into the Henry's chamber. That was even faster. The revolver exploded, and the renegade who had been trying to fit another arrow to his bowstring stumbled and dropped both bow and arrow. His right hand went to his throat, but he couldn't stem the blood that welled out from bullet-ripped arteries. He stumbled and fell facedown, didn't move again.

Five, thought Smoke as he pouched the iron. He knew better than to believe that he could wipe out the entire war party this way, one or two renegades at a time, but the more of them he killed, the fewer the town's defenders would have to deal with.

Not seeing any more Indians at the moment, he ran toward an alley that he knew would take him to Center Street. His goal was the Dunn Hotel, because he figured that was where Sally was most likely to be.

And finding her, ultimately, was what he wanted to do more than anything else.

So it was pretty simple. He would kill any of Black Drum's warriors who got in his way.

Chapter 27

Smoke reached the alley mouth and looked out at Center Street. Bleak lines appeared in his cheeks as his mouth tightened. Half a dozen bodies lay in the street—four men and two women—skewered by arrows or bloody from gunshot wounds. He could see the faces of two of the men, twisted in agony by the pain of the deaths they had suffered. They looked familiar to him. He had seen them in town before, but he wasn't personally acquainted with either of them.

That didn't matter. They were innocent people who had been going peacefully about their business, only to be cut down brutally and unexpectedly. Nothing could bring them back, but every one of the renegades Smoke killed was that much more weight on the other side of the scale.

He didn't see any soldiers or members of the war party, only the slaughtered settlers. The Dunn Hotel was on the other side of the street, about fifty yards away to his right, diagonally. He glanced to his left, toward Louis Longmont's saloon, wondering if his old friend was all right. He would check on Louis later, he decided, and Monte Carson, too, but right now he wanted to find Sally, and since he had left her at the hotel . . .

Smoke sprang onto the boardwalk in front of the buildings on this side of the street and trotted along it. He would be out in the open when he crossed the street, so he wanted to make that time as short as possible. He wouldn't venture out until he was directly across the street from the hotel.

He hadn't gone very far along the boardwalk when two warriors emerged from an alley in front of him. They spotted him instantly and tried to swing the rifles they carried toward him. Again he chose to use his Colt instead of the Henry. In a blur of motion, he drew the gun and slammed out three shots.

The first bullet took the renegade on Smoke's right in the belly and doubled him over. Bending forward like that caused Smoke's second shot to strike him in the top of the head, shattering his skull. The third shot, fired so close on the heels of the first two that the reports sounded like one long peal of thunder, cored through the other renegade's heart and made him corkscrew to the ground.

Neither man had had time to fire a return shot.

Smoke stayed where he was on the boardwalk long enough to slide fresh cartridges into the Colt's cylinder, replacing the ones he'd fired. He filled all six chambers, rather than leaving one empty so the hammer could rest on it as he normally did. At times like this, a man needed a full wheel.

He had just slipped the revolver back into the holster when swift footsteps slapped the planks behind him. As he whirled, from the corner of his eye he saw a man hurtling through the air toward him. The renegade had left his feet in a diving tackle.

Smoke didn't have time to get out of the way. The warrior crashed into him, wrapping his arms around Smoke's waist as he drove him over backward. Smoke landed hard enough on his back that all the air was forced from his lungs, leaving him gasping and stunned for a second.

That was long enough for the renegade to jerk a knife from its sheath at his waist and raise it in his right hand while his left clamped around Smoke's throat to pin him to the boardwalk. The knife flashed down at Smoke's chest.

With the same near-supernatural reflexes that made him

perhaps the fastest man on the draw on the whole frontier, his left hand shot up and caught the Indian's right wrist, stopping the knife with its tip a mere three inches from the breast pocket of Smoke's shirt. The muscles in Smoke's forearm quivered as he strained to hold the blade back.

At the same time, his right fist came up and hammered the warrior's jaw. The blow knocked the man to the side but didn't loosen his grip on Smoke's throat. Smoke writhed in his grasp and forced the renegade's right arm down. He slammed the back of the man's right hand against the planks. That made the knife's bone handle slip out of his fingers.

Smoke hit him again, and this time the punch knocked the Indian away from him. The man rolled against the building's front wall. Smoke had just started to reach for his gun when a desperate, flailing kick landed the warrior's foot in his stomach. Smoke hadn't caught his breath completely yet, and that just made the situation worse.

But no situation was bad enough that it couldn't get even worse, as was proven a heartbeat later as a second warrior leaped onto the boardwalk and pointed a rifle at Smoke.

Gasping for air or not, Smoke knew he had to move. He rolled toward the street as the renegade's rifle cracked. The bullet chewed splinters from the boardwalk less than a foot from his head. As he came over his back, Smoke palmed out the Colt again and tipped it up. Flame gouted from the muzzle. The slug pulped the renegade's lips, shattered his teeth into a million pieces, and blew the lower part of his brain out the back of his head.

The first man, lying on the other side of the boardwalk, scooped up his knife from where it had slid and flung it at Smoke in the same motion. The edge sliced across Smoke's forearm, cutting through his shirt sleeve and leaving a shallow gash in the flesh underneath. The wound stung, but not bad enough to make him drop the gun.

He snapped a shot at the warrior, but the man was already moving and the slug narrowly missed him, thudding into the wall behind him instead. He lunged for the rifle dropped by the man Smoke had just shot. It was a Henry repeater, not one of the single-shot weapons many of the renegades carried. He worked the lever as he came up on his knees to take a shot at Smoke.

Before the warrior could tighten his finger on the Henry's trigger, Smoke's Colt boomed again and a red-rimmed black hole appeared in the warrior's forehead, centered between his eyes and just about an inch above them. His head went back, and the rifle slipped out of his suddenly nerveless fingers. He flopped forward. A dark red pool spread on the planks under his head.

Smoke scrambled to his feet and picked up his own rifle. Leaving the two renegades he had just slain behind him, he loped along the boardwalk until he was across the street from the hotel. He crouched next to a parked wagon for a moment and looked around.

A lot of shooting was going on, further along the street toward Longmont's Saloon, but he didn't see any more of Black Drum's renegades down here in this area. He started to sprint across the street toward the hotel.

He had gone only a couple of steps when more shots blasted and bullets kicked up dust around his feet. He zigzagged and glanced up. An Indian with another Henry was firing at him from one of the hotel's second-floor windows.

Smoke's heart plummeted when he saw that. Sally's room was on the second floor. If the renegades had taken over the hotel already, what did that mean as far as her fate?

He couldn't answer that question if he was dead, so he poured on the speed and continued darting back and forth to make himself harder to hit.

When he was close enough, he left his feet in a huge bound

that carried him onto the hotel's front porch. The second-floor balcony formed the roof of that porch. Smoke heard heavy footsteps thud on the balcony and knew the Indian who had been shooting at him had climbed out of the window. He pointed the Henry up and cranked off three rounds, aiming at the hurrying footsteps. Splinters rained down around him as the slugs punched through the boards.

A loud grunt came from the balcony, followed by a crash. That was the railing along the front of the balcony breaking as the warrior's bullet-riddled body reeled into it. Along with the broken pieces of whitewashed wood, the renegade fell into the street. He writhed once and then sagged into the immobility of death.

Smoke hit one of the hotel's front doors with his shoulder and knocked it open. He burst into the lobby and almost slipped on a throw rug. As he caught his balance, furious, high-pitched yips came from the stairs on the other side of the lobby. A couple of renegades with war paint on their faces started down them, leaping several stairs at a time, which actually worked against them because they kept almost losing their balance.

From the corner of his eye, Smoke caught sight of a more immediate threat. Another warrior stood on the second-floor balcony and had an arrow nocked and pulled back. The Henry in Smoke's hands cracked a shaved fraction of a second before the warrior loosed the arrow.

That was enough to throw off the renegade's aim. The arrow flashed past Smoke and thudded into the trunk of a potted palm beside the entrance. The tree's fronds trembled from the impact.

Up on the balcony, the Indian who had fired the arrow came up on his toes and dropped the bow as Smoke's bullet ripped through his torso at an angle. He fell forward. Instead of breaking through the balcony railing, as had happened outside, this time the dying man flipped over it and turned a somersault in the air before landing with a crash on his back, atop the now-deserted registration desk. His left arm and leg hung limply on the front side of the counter and twitched a couple of times as the man died.

Smoke turned toward the other two renegades, who had reached the bottom of the staircase by now and charged him, brandishing tomahawks. The Henry belched fire and smoke again, and one of the men flew backward, howling in pain.

The other warrior threw the tomahawk he held. It struck Smoke on the right shoulder. Luckily, as it turned over in the air, it was half a revolution off and the heavy wooden handle hit Smoke, rather than the sharp flint head.

The tomahawk might not have inflicted a serious wound, but it struck hard enough to make Smoke's right arm go numb. He couldn't work the rifle's lever, so he dropped it and used his left hand to jerk his knife from its sheath.

The warrior had yanked out his own knife after throwing the tomahawk. Somewhat awkwardly because he had to use his left hand, Smoke parried the slash that the renegade aimed at his throat. Sparks flew as steel rang against steel. Having turned away the warrior's attack momentarily, Smoke thrust his blade at the man's chest, but the renegade twisted out of the way and tried again to cut Smoke, who jumped back and barely avoided the swipe.

Smoke could draw and fire a gun with his left hand almost as well as he could with his right. The difference wasn't enough to matter. But he hadn't done all that much knife-fighting with his left hand, so within moments he was sweating and breathing hard as he struggled to keep the warrior from lodging eight inches of cold steel in his body. The blades flashed back and forth almost too fast for the eye to follow. Only Smoke's superb reflexes saved him.

After that first thrust, he was forced to fight purely defensively. It was all he could do to parry the renegade's attacks. He gave ground slowly. The renegade pressed him, closer and closer to slipping his knife through Smoke's desperate parries.

But all the while, feeling was seeping back into Smoke's right arm. He let it swing a little behind him, where his enemy couldn't see it as well, and flexed his fingers. When he felt like they were working well enough, he took a quick step back to put a little distance between them and let the hand holding the knife sag even more. His chest rose and fell raggedly. Air rasped in his throat.

As Smoke thought might happen, the renegade paused to leer at him in gloating triumph before finishing him off. That gave Smoke plenty of time to draw the Colt, raise it, and blow the man's brains out. The warrior had just enough time to look startled before he died.

Smoke left the Henry where he had dropped it and, with the Colt in his fist, bounded up the stairs, taking them three at a time. When he reached the second floor, he shouted, "Sally! Sally, are you here?"

"Help! Help us!"

The response came from behind the closed door of one of the rooms, but it was a man's voice, not Sally's familiar tones. Smoke grabbed the knob with his left hand anyway and twisted it. He threw the door open and looked into the room to see two men and five women huddled there. One of the men was wounded, clutching a blood-dripping left arm with his right hand, but he was the only one who appeared to be injured. They were all pale and shaking in terror, though.

The other man was the desk clerk from downstairs. He exclaimed, "Mr. Jensen! Oh, thank heavens. We heard the shooting below and prayed that someone had come to rescue us."

"What happened?" Smoke asked.

The clerk nodded at the others and said, "These are the only guests who are still alive, as far as I know. When the savages attacked, I retreated up here and gathered everyone I could find. I . . . I have a gun . . ."

He held up a small pocket pistol which wouldn't have done much good against the war party, but at least he'd been willing to try to fight back.

"I heard screams from elsewhere in the hotel," the man went on, "and I suppose that was because the savages were killing the other guests." He nodded toward the wounded man. "Mr. Hennessy here barely escaped from them with his life."

"One of them shot me!" said the wounded man.

Everything the clerk had said so far had made Smoke's spirits plummet even more. In a thick voice, he forced himself to ask, "My wife . . . ?"

"She's not here!" the clerk said. "She left before the Indians attacked."

Smoke felt as if he'd been given a sudden, unexpected reprieve from a death sentence. He asked, "Did she say where she was going?"

"I . . . I believe she said something about saying hello to the sheriff and then paying a visit to Mr. Longmont's establishment."

Smoke bit back a groan. Earlier, he had thought for a second about heading to Louis's himself, but he had come here to the hotel instead. Now the knowledge that Sally might be down there gnawed at his guts.

On the other hand, by coming here first he had undoubtedly saved the lives of these folks, and he also knew that if anybody in Big Rock could keep Sally safe, Louis Longmont was the man. Well, Louis and Monte Carson. If, by some chance, the two of them were together, and Sally was with them . . .

He knew what he had to do. He said, "Ladies, one of you tear some strips off a sheet and use them to bind up this man's wound. If anybody's got a flask of whiskey, it would be a good idea to pour some of it on the bullet holes before you bandage them."

"I . . . I might have some spirits," said one of the women. "Purely for medicinal purposes, of course."

"Get that done while all of you hunker down here," Smoke went on. "I didn't see any more renegades in the hotel, and I reckon they would have shown up before now if they were here. You ought to be as safe here as anywhere else in town right now." He looked at the desk clerk. "But keep that gun of yours handy, anyway."

"I will, I assure you," the man said. "What are you going to do, Mr. Jensen?"

"Find my wife," Smoke replied grimly.

Chapter 28

Smoke left the hotel through the back door and hurried along the alley between the two rows of buildings. His gaze darted from side to side constantly, searching for any signs of danger.

Even so, he was taken a little by surprise when the rear door of a building slammed open and a shape hurtled out of it at him. The warrior must have spotted him through a window and then lain in wait for him until Smoke came even with the door.

The renegade clutched a lance that he thrust at Smoke. The wooden point, sharpened and hardened in fire, caught the right side of his shirt and ripped it, scraping his skin but not really penetrating it. Smoke clamped his arm down on the lance to trap it and grabbed it with both hands. He heaved, which flung the renegade to the side. The man let go of the lance as he tripped and sprawled in the dirt of the alley.

Since Smoke already had hold of the lance, he flipped it around, raised it, and thrust down as he leaped toward the fallen warrior. The man rolled onto his back just in time for Smoke to bury the lance in his chest, driving it deep into the heart. The warrior grunted in pain as he grimaced and clutched the lance, but after a second his fingers slipped away from it and his arms fell loosely to the sides. The eyes staring up at Smoke went glassy in death.

Smoke left the lance where it was and hurried on. He had to cross a street to get to the block where Longmont's Saloon was located, but nobody shot at him as he ran through the open space, so that was an improvement.

Gunfire from up ahead drew his attention to a shed at the rear of a property on the next street over. Two warriors made a dash from the shed toward the rear door of what Smoke recognized as his friend's establishment. Shots from a window in the saloon building dropped one of the renegades. The other whirled back and sought the shed's cover again.

Smoke's Colt roared and knocked the warrior into a rolling sprawl. When he tried to push himself up, Smoke drilled him with a second slug. This time the renegade stayed down.

Smoke wasn't surprised that the defenders inside the saloon were covering the back. He would expect that sort of caution from an experienced fighting man like Louis.

But from inside the building, the defenders couldn't see everything. The roof, for example. Movement there made Smoke glance up. One of the renegades was on the roof and had a blazing torch in his hand. He had his back to Smoke as he was about to set fire to the building's false front.

The Colt angled up and blasted. The torch-wielder arched his back as the bullet struck him from behind. He came up on his toes and tottered forward, then dropped the torch and slid down out of sight.

Smoke bit back a curse. The torch was still burning up there. He holstered the Colt, looked around, and spotted several empty crates stacked against the rear wall of the saloon. They had held bottles of liquor originally, but now they would serve another purpose.

Quickly, he rearranged the crates so that he could climb on top of them, and that brought him in reach of the rain gutter that ran along the back edge of the roof. He stretched his arms up, caught hold of the gutter, and with a grunt of effort hauled himself up far enough to kick a leg high and catch a toe in the gutter as well. From there it wasn't hard to pull himself up and roll onto the peaked roof.

The exertion made the arm that had been cut by the thrown knife ache. A thread of blood trickled down his side where the lance had scraped him, too. He ignored both of those minor annoyances. He saw the renegade he had shot lying slumped near the building's false front, as well as the burning torch, which was the most important thing right now. Smoke scrambled to his feet and hurried along the roof's slope, his superb balance helping with that challenge.

The wooden shingles on the roof were starting to catch fire, as were the boards of the false front. Smoke reached for the torch so he could fling it into the street and then put out the flames, but before he could grasp it, a couple of bullets exploded up through the roof and narrowly missed him.

Blast it! The defenders inside the saloon had heard his rapid footsteps and mistaken him for one of the renegades.

He couldn't blame them for their reaction. He probably would have done the same thing in their place.

But he didn't want to get shot, either, especially when he might be getting close to being reunited with Sally. So he threw himself backward as more shots came through the roof in the same area as the others. Then, circling that spot, he cat-footed toward the torch, moving quietly enough that he hoped those down below wouldn't hear him this time.

He reached the burning brand, grabbed it, and threw it well over the top of the false front so it would clear the awning over the boardwalk and drop into the street, where it could burn out harmlessly. Then he whipped off his shirt, which was already torn and bloody in several places and used it to beat out the flames. That left the roof and the false front charred here and there but not really damaged seriously.

The threat of Longmont's turning into a blazing inferno was thwarted, but only for a moment. Before Smoke could do anything else, a flaming arrow arched down out of the sky, missed him by several feet, and lodged at an upright angle in the roof.

Smoke lunged, caught hold of the shaft, and tugged it free before the flames could catch. He tossed the burning arrow into the alley at the side of the building, hoping it would go out harmlessly down there.

He had barely done that when another fire arrow thudded onto the roof behind him and to his right. As he turned toward it, the defenders inside the building started shooting through the roof again. Grimacing, Smoke snatched up the second arrow and threw it off the building as well, while at the same instant, a slug punched upward through the roof about an inch from his right foot and sizzled past him on its journey into the sky. If it hadn't been traveling at a slight angle, it would have struck him in the arm. A slight angle the other way, and the bullet would have ripped through his leg.

This was getting too blasted dangerous, even for him. He sprang to the window that was built into the false front and peered through the opening. He spotted one of the renegades on the roof of the building opposite Longmont's. The warrior had another arrow nocked and aflame, and he was leaning back as he prepared to launch it on its arching flight across the street.

The range was a little long for a handgun, but in his hurry to reach Sally, Smoke had left the Henry rifle back at the hotel. He drew the Colt, knelt to steady himself, and lined up the shot in less than the blink of an eye. The revolver roared and bucked against his palm.

The Indian on the other roof fell back as Smoke's bullet

struck him in the head and killed him instantly. Nerveless fingers released the bowstring. The blazing arrow flew almost straight up in the air, slowing until it finally stopped, twisted, and plummeted back down as gravity took over. It landed on the roof of the same building from which it had been fired.

Smoke didn't wait to see if that building was going to catch on fire. He started to turn, only to be tackled by the warrior he had shot earlier, the one who had climbed up here with a torch to start with. Smoke had figured the renegade was dead, but he hadn't had time to check.

The man appeared to be badly hurt, judging by the grimace on his face, but he had regained enough strength that he wasn't out of the fight. His tackle drove Smoke backward against the false front. Nails groaned as the combined weight of the two men threatened to pull the structure loose and send it crashing down on the awning below.

The boards and nails held, and Smoke got his feet planted and shoved the warrior away from him with a left hand to the chest. The man was badly wounded and appeared to be unarmed, but his eyes burned with the light of fanaticism.

That hate kept him on his feet as he lunged at Smoke again, this time with his hands outstretched toward his enemy's neck. Clearly, he wanted to lock those hands around Smoke's throat and choke him to death.

Instead, Smoke's right fist exploded on his jaw and knocked him off his feet. The renegade rolled down the roof and went over the edge with a strangled yell that ended abruptly when he landed with a thud in the alley.

Carefully, Smoke made his way over to the edge and peered down at the warrior. The grotesque angle at which the man's head sat on his shoulders told Smoke that he'd broken his neck when he landed. He wouldn't get up and keep fighting this time.

Smoke lowered himself over the edge, feet first, and hung

by his hands for a second before dropping the rest of the way into the side alley. A few steps brought him to the front corner.

He couldn't get to the saloon's entrance. He would have had to venture into a crossfire to do that, and lead was still storming back and forth across the street in a deadly barrage.

He might be able to get in the back, though, especially if he called out to let the defenders know who he was. He didn't want to be mistaken for a renegade and get shot by one of his friends.

He had just turned to attempt that when he heard a low rumble that grew rapidly in volume.

Horses, he realized. A lot of them.

Black Drum and the rest of his renegades could be trying a last-ditch mounted attack, but Smoke wasn't sure there were that many of them left. He had lost track of how many he had killed since he reached Big Rock, but he knew he had whittled down the war party considerably.

He sprang to the alley mouth and looked to the west, where the hoofbeats thundered. A group of blue-uniformed troops galloped along Center Street, with Captain Adam Skinner at their head.

Skinner was being rash. He was about to lead his men right into that crossfire. The defenders inside the saloon would hold their fire when they saw the soldiers, but by that time, some of the men might have been cut down already.

Smoke didn't like or trust any of those so-called troopers, didn't believe they were the real thing and was convinced they were outlaws. But that didn't mean he was going to stand aside and watch while they were slaughtered. Even Skinner . . .

Despite the danger in which he was putting himself, Smoke dashed into the street and waved his arms to get Skinner's attention.

Skinner saw him, all right. The captain's features twisted into a hate-filled scowl. He yanked his revolver from its holster and galloped straight at Smoke, flame spurting from the muzzle of his gun as he fired.

For a split-second, Smoke thought Skinner must have taken him for one of the war party. After all, he was bare to the waist, and he supposed that in the dust and confusion, somebody might mistake his skin, bronzed from working shirtless in the sun, for the coppery hue of a Cheyenne warrior and not notice the pale hair on his head.

But then Skinner bellowed, "Jensen!" and kept coming as Smoke dived aside, away from the bullets that whipped through the air where he had just been.

Skinner wasn't going to pass up this chance to kill him. Smoke knew that now. The captain might try to pass it off as an accident and claim that he thought Smoke was an Indian. Or he might be so full of hate that he just didn't care anymore.

Either way, Smoke had no choice. He hit the dirt, rolled, and came up on one knee with the Colt in his hand. It belched fire and lead twice in the space of a single heartbeat, and Skinner went backward off his horse as the bullets plowed into him.

That shocked the troopers with him into yanking back on their reins, which saved their lives because they were about to be caught in the crossfire. At that moment, howling in fury, a dozen renegades burst out of the building where they had taken cover. It was on fire now from the flaming arrow that had gone straight up and then back down to land on the roof. Black smoke curled from the shot-out windows.

The Indians opened fire on the troopers, who reacted instinctively despite their shock at seeing Skinner shot off his horse. They returned the fire, and the defenders in Longmont's Saloon blasted away at the renegades, too. The Indians no longer had any hope of winning. Smoke knew they just wanted to die in battle.

All but one, who darted in a different direction. As he did

so, the small drum hanging from a sling around his shoulder swung out so that Smoke could see it.

Black Drum . . . and he was trying to get away. Abandoning the warriors he had led on the long, bloody-handed trail of slaughter.

Smoke charged after him.

Black Drum ducked into an alley. The renegades might have stashed their ponies somewhere nearby, and the war chief could be trying to reach them.

If Black Drum escaped, he could recruit more warriors and continue his campaign of death. He could claim that his medicine had protected him and allowed him to get away so he could keep on killing whites.

Smoke couldn't let that happen.

"Black Drum!" he shouted as he entered the alley. "Turn and face me!"

Black Drum stopped short and turned. His hand strayed to the drum at his waist, and his fingers tapped a ragged rhythm on its skin head.

His other hand jerked a pistol from behind the sash at his waist.

Smoke felt the wind-rip of the bullet past his left ear as he triggered the Colt. The hammer clicked harmlessly on an empty chamber. Black Drum pulled the trigger on his gun again, but rage and frustration appeared on his face as it failed to fire, too. It was as empty as Smoke's gun.

Screeching furiously, Black Drum threw the revolver aside and charged at Smoke.

Smoke shoved his Colt back in its holster and met the war chief's attack. They came together like two titans, grappling and heaving and slugging. The sweat and dust that covered their torsos made it difficult for either man to get and maintain a grip as they staggered back and forth in the alley.

Then Black Drum stuck his foot between Smoke's calves

and tangled their legs together. Smoke fell heavily, but on his way down he grabbed the rawhide sling by which the drum hung at the war chief's waist and dragged Black Drum down with him.

They rolled through the dirt. Black Drum jabbed a knee into Smoke's belly, making him gag. Smoke landed his left fist in the renegade's face and felt hot blood spurt across his knuckles from Black Drum's nose. The two men panted hard from the exertion of their battle. This was a fight to the death, and both of them knew it.

With dust filling his mouth and nose and sweat dripping into his eyes and stinging them so he could hardly see, Smoke hooked his left arm around Black Drum's shoulders and heaved so the war chief wound up lying on top of him. Smoke still held the rawhide sling in his right hand. He looped the slack around Black Drum's neck and started revolving his wrist, twisting and tightening the cord. Black Drum tried to writhe away from him, but Smoke's other arm clamped around him like a band of iron and kept him from escaping.

The drum banged against Smoke's arm as he took up all the slack in the sling. Even when it was tight around Black Drum's throat, Smoke continued twisting it.

Black Drum kicked his legs and tried to hit Smoke, but he was in an awkward position and couldn't get any power behind the blows. Smoke wrapped his own legs around the renegade's lower limbs and clung tighter to him as he increased the pressure. Black Drum's struggles became more frantic. He made tiny bleating noises as he fought to get air into his lungs, but the rawhide sling cut deeply into the flesh of his throat and closed it off. He bucked and heaved. Smoke held on like he was sticking to the saddle of a wild bronc that didn't want to be ridden.

Black Drum waved his arms in the air, but the movements became more feeble as he weakened. Smoke knew the war

chief wasn't faking. Black Drum couldn't breathe, and consciousness was slipping away from him.

After several more moments, the renegade's muscles went
limp. His arms and legs fell and didn't move again. Smoke
didn't ease up on the pressure, not one single ounce. He kept
it up, holding on for all the innocent people this madman and
his followers had slaughtered. He felt it when Black Drum's
chest stopped rising and falling, but still he didn't let go. Not
until several minutes had passed and he was absolutely certain
that the war chief was dead.

With a shudder, Smoke released the rawhide sling and
shoved the limp corpse off of him. He rolled away from it and
had started to climb wearily to his feet when a familiar voice
cried, "Smoke!"

He looked up, and his heart leaped as high as Pikes Peak
when he saw Sally running toward him. A few seconds earlier,
he would have said he was completely played out after everything that had happened today. But a sudden burst of energy
fueled by the sight of his wife revitalized him, and he hurried
forward to meet her.

She rushed into his arms and he clasped her tightly to him,
heedless of the dirt and sweat that covered him. Sally buried
her face against his bare shoulder, and he filled his nostrils
with the sweet scent of her hair.

After a moment that probably lasted just a few seconds but
seemed both shorter and longer to Smoke, Sally stepped back,
looked him up and down, and exclaimed, "Smoke! You're
bleeding!"

He nodded toward the shallow cut on his forearm and the
even shallower cut on his side. "You mean these? These are
just scratches. Nothing to worry about."

"You're sure?"

"Positive. Now that I can see you're all right, I'm as fine as
can be."

She leaned slightly to the side to look past him and said, "Is that . . . ? Is he . . . ?"

"It's Black Drum, all right," Smoke told her. "And he's dead." He lifted his head and listened. No more shots rang out over Big Rock. Instead, an almost eerie silence had descended over the settlement. "I reckon it's all over now, at last."

She hugged him again and sighed. "It was so awful," she said in a quiet voice. "All the shooting and killing . . . but the worst part about it was wondering if you were all right."

He put his hand under her chin and lifted her head so he could grin at her.

"I was feeling the exact same way about you," he told her. He remembered his friends, then, and grew solemn as he asked, "What about Monte and Louis? Were either of them hurt?"

"They both got nicked by bullets. It was almost impossible not to, with so much lead flying around. But neither of them are hurt badly, at all."

"How'd you manage to avoid all those bullets?"

"Well . . ." She returned his grin and indicated a couple of torn places on the sleeves of her dress, one on each arm. "I almost didn't."

Seeing how close she had come to being wounded—or worse—made a chill go through him, but he told himself not to think about it. They were together again, they were all right, and the danger was finished . . .

"Mrs. Jensen, step away from your husband!"

The sharp, strident voice filled the alley and made Sally gasp. She turned to look, and Smoke gazed over her shoulder at the man who had given the order.

Colonel Lamar Talbot strode toward them with four of the so-called troopers at his back. There was nothing phony about the rifles the men pointed at Smoke, though.

"Colonel, what are you doing?" Sally demanded.

"Move aside," Talbot said again, instead of answering her question. He aimed the gun in his hand at Smoke. "I won't tell you again."

In a flat, hard voice, Smoke said, "You'd better think twice about what you're doing, Colonel."

"I don't have to think twice, Jensen," snapped Talbot. "I know exactly what I'm doing. I'm placing you under arrest for the murder of Captain Adam Skinner."

Chapter 29

Sally was unable to find her voice for a moment following that startling pronouncement. Then she cried, "That's insane!"

Talbot ignored her outburst and said, "Truly, Mrs. Jensen, this is your last warning."

Sally had turned to face Talbot. Smoke put his hands on her shoulders and gently but firmly moved her aside, out of the line of fire.

"Stay there," he told her. "There's no telling what these varmints might do."

"But Smoke—"

He stepped past her and said to Talbot, "I agree with my wife, Colonel. Claiming that I murdered Skinner is plumb loco."

"I witnessed it with my own eyes," Talbot insisted. "Captain Skinner was attacking the renegades in a valiant charge, and you coldly and deliberately shot him off his horse, killing him."

"He was shooting at *me*. I reckon I've had enough people try to ventilate me that I know when I'm the target."

Talbot's lips curled in a sneer. "Yes, I'm aware that you have quite a reputation as a gunman and an outlaw. But that doesn't change the facts of the matter. Big Rock is under martial law, so you'll have a military trial, presided over by me."

"So you'll be judge, jury, *and* star witness? Or the *only* witness?"

Talbot shook his head and said, "A number of troops saw you murder Captain Skinner, and I'm sure all of them will be happy to testify to that fact. Your trial will be legal and aboveboard, Jensen . . . and so will your execution." He smiled. "A firing squad would be most appropriate, I think."

"You'll never get away with this," Smoke said. "And since when was martial law declared?"

"During the battle with the renegades, of course. I've sent men to inform Sheriff Carson that he no longer has any authority in the town, and to spread the word to the other citizens, as well, that I'm now in charge."

Smoke saw what was going on. Now that the threat from the renegades was over, Talbot was moving quickly to strengthen his grip on the settlement. In the aftermath of battle, with the townspeople still in a state of shock, Big Rock would be ripe for looting.

Talbot probably still had enough men to get away with it, too. A couple of dozen ruthless killers were enough to tree a town the size of Big Rock. Some of the male citizens had clashed with Indians and outlaws before, but the only truly seasoned fighting men were Smoke, Monte, and Louis.

And Pearlie, Smoke suddenly recalled. He hadn't seen Pearlie or the other hands from the Sugarloaf with Skinner's forces when they came thundering in. Maybe the man he had told to fetch them hadn't done so.

If Pearlie was on the loose, there was still a chance of turning the tables on Talbot, although Smoke couldn't try that at the moment. Not with Sally and the rest of the townspeople potentially in the line of fire.

As much as it galled him, he had to play along with Talbot's madness . . . for now.

"All right, Colonel," he said. "I surrender."

"Smoke, no!" gasped Sally.

He turned to her and rested his hands on her shoulders. Holding his head so that Talbot and the troopers couldn't see his left eye, he let that lid droop in a meaningful wink. Although Sally's horrified expression didn't alter, he saw understanding flicker in her eyes.

"It'll be all right, honey," he told her. "I have to cooperate with the colonel. I'm sure all this misunderstanding will get hashed out before much longer."

"Very soon, indeed," Talbot put in. "I see no reason why your trial can't be held as soon as order is fully restored in the town. As early as this evening, perhaps. In the meantime . . ." He turned to the troopers. "Lacking a proper military stockade, take Mr. Jensen to the local jail and see that he's locked up. And while you're at it, lock up Sheriff Carson, too, so that he can't attempt to interfere with us."

"You figure you've got Big Rock in the palm of your hand, don't you?" said Smoke.

Talbot smiled. "Not just the palm. I've closed that hand into a fist. An iron fist that will never let go."

The next couple of hours, as the afternoon waned, were extremely frustrating to Smoke. With at least four rifles covering him at all times, Talbot's men had marched him to the sheriff's office and jail, then prodded him into one of the cells.

Smoke had been locked up before, but he hadn't liked it then and he didn't cotton to it now. The clang of the cell door closing was almost like a knife in his guts.

A short time later, more troopers brought in Monte Carson. Monte was groggy, with a swollen lump on his head. Somebody had walloped him, probably with a rifle butt. He had a soldier on each side of him, holding him up. They half shoved, half dragged him into the cell block and pitched him in one of the cells. He rolled across the floor and came to a stop near the bunk.

"Put up a fight when you came for him, didn't he?" Smoke drawled. "I'm not surprised."

"Nor was I," Louis Longmont said as he entered the cell block, too, with three troopers around him. One had a pistol pressed against the back of Louis's head. "I tried to persuade these gentlemen that it would be unwise to take the sheriff and myself into custody, but they weren't inclined to listen."

Louis's handsome face was bruised and scratched from the struggle. When Smoke saw the shape his two friends were in, he felt bad because he hadn't put up a fight. He hadn't wanted bullets to start flying in that alley while Sally was there.

The troopers put Louis in another cell, leaving only one empty. But as long as Pearlie stayed out of that last cell, they still had a chance, Smoke told himself.

When the troopers were gone, Smoke went to the door of his cell and grasped the iron bars as he looked across at Louis.

"How's the town?" he asked. "Did that fire spread very much?"

Louis shook his head. "One building was heavily damaged but not completely lost. As soon as the fighting was over, everyone rushed to form a bucket brigade and contain the flames." The gambler's mouth twisted wryly. "All the towns-people rushed to fight the fire, I should have said. Colonel Talbot had other uses for his men."

"Seizing power," Smoke said.

"Exactly. He moved quickly to arrest you, and then, before Monte and I heard about what was happening, they came for us. It appears that he considers the three of us to be the only real threats to his continued reign in Big Rock."

"How many men does he have?"

"Counting the ones who returned to town with Captain

Skinner and the men from the camp who scattered at the first attack but then regrouped later . . . approximately thirty-five."

"Thirty-five men," Smoke mused. "That's not much of an army."

"It is when you've gotten the drop on the citizens and managed to disarm most of them," said Louis. "Oh, by sheer force of numbers, there are enough people in town to overcome Talbot and his men, of course. But doing so might mean that quite a few of them would die . . . and no one is in a hurry to be first in line."

Smoke shook his head. "Can't blame them overmuch for that, I reckon. They came to Big Rock to settle down and lead peaceful, productive lives, not to fight outlaws."

"Sometimes one has to be done before the other is possible," Louis pointed out. "This has all the makings of one of those occasions."

The two men fell silent for a few minutes, then Smoke said, "You know that I didn't actually murder Skinner, don't you?"

"Of course. I saw what happened. It was the other way around. Skinner was trying to kill you. What you did was purely self-defense."

Smoke smiled. "I reckon I can count on you to testify to that at my trial?"

A contemptuous snort came from Louis. "Trial!" he repeated. "It'll be no trial, but rather a farce of justice instead. Talbot will pretend to hear testimony from his hand-picked witnesses, and then . . ."

"Yeah," drawled Smoke, "he's already decided on having a firing squad."

"Why is he going to so much trouble for even a pretense of legality?"

"You mean instead of just shooting me himself?" Smoke shook his head. "I don't know for sure, but I think it has something to do with him being loco. He's not right in the head,

Louis. If you're around him for very long, you can see that in his eyes, especially now that he thinks he's got all the power."

"Someone like that is more monster than man," muttered Louis.

Smoke couldn't argue with that sentiment.

Monte Carson regained his senses a few minutes later, grabbed hold of the bunk in his cell to help pull himself into a sitting position, and let out a groan. He started to shake his head, then stopped the motion abruptly and winced.

"Got a headache?" Smoke asked. Monte was in the other cell on the same side of the aisle where he was locked up.

"Feels like a herd of buffalo stampeding through there," Monte replied through clenched teeth. "I don't want to open my mouth too much for fear the whole top of my head'll fly off."

"We don't want that. Just sit there for a minute and let it settle down."

"I'm locked up in one of my own cells, aren't I?"

"I'm afraid so," Smoke confirmed.

Monte muttered curses under his breath for several moments, then hauled himself onto the bunk and sat there with his head in his hands. Smoke and Louis waited patiently, knowing what was coming.

After a while, Monte lifted his head, and now anger and determination gleamed in his eyes.

"Well, boys," he said, "what are we gonna do about this?"

"Did either of you see Pearlie this afternoon?" asked Smoke.

"I didn't," Louis replied.

"Neither did I," said Monte. "Was he supposed to be in town?"

"When one of those troopers brought word that Black Drum was attacking the town, I told him to have Skinner swing by my ranch on his way and bring my hands with him," Smoke explained. "He didn't do it. Maybe he was already thinking about taking advantage of the opportunity to gun me and didn't want Pearlie and the boys at his back when he did it."

"If Pearlie finds out what's going on, he won't stand by and do nothing," Monte said. "I've known that old boy for too long. He'll be spoiling for a fight."

"And I've got a hunch that Bob, Max, and Jed will ride— and fight—for the brand, too," Smoke said.

"That's only four men," Louis pointed out. "They'd be badly outnumbered, Smoke. Almost four to one."

"Yeah, but sometimes all it takes to start a fire is a spark to set it off."

"The townspeople," Monte said. "That's what you're talking about."

Smoke nodded. "But before that can happen, somebody will have to get word to Pearlie."

"You think anybody in town can do that?"

"I can think of somebody who's probably had the same idea and is going to try," Smoke said.

Sally hadn't seen Smoke since Talbot and the four soldiers hustled him away from her. She had started to follow, but Talbot swung around and blocked her path.

"Please, Mrs. Jensen, either return to the hotel or, if you'd prefer, help with tending to the wounded," he said. "There's no need for you to accompany your husband. You'll see him again soon enough."

She would have argued, but Smoke, who had paused with the troopers around him, looked back over his shoulder and said, "The colonel's right about one thing, Sally. There are probably a lot of folks in town who could use your help right now."

She let out a frustrated sigh and said, "I suppose you're right."

She stood there while the little group left the alley and turned toward the jail.

Since then, she had indeed stayed busy helping people. A makeshift hospital was set up in the recently constructed school. There were too many wounded for Dr. Colton Spaulding, Big Rock's only physician, to deal with all of them by himself. He concentrated on the more seriously injured while Sally and some of the ladies from town served as volunteer nurses, cleaning wounds and bandaging the ones that didn't require stitches, as well as providing words of comfort and reassurance. Big Rock had suffered a lot today, but the town was resilient, as had been proven already in its short existence, and it would recover from this attack.

But there were things it might *not* recover from, thought Sally as she tried to keep her mind off what had happened to Smoke. The idea that Colonel Talbot was going to hold a military trial and charge him with murder was insane. She had to do something . . .

That growing resolve became even stronger when one of the wounded men said to her, "Did you hear what happened to Sheriff Carson, Mrs. Jensen?"

Sally stopped wrapping a strip of clean cloth around the man's wounded arm and felt a stab of fear. "No," she said. "What happened?"

"That colonel fella had him arrested and hauled off to his own jail. Louis Longmont, too. They put up a scrap, o' course, and the sheriff got clouted pretty good with a rifle by one of those fellas. I hope he's all right."

Sally did, too. She understood instantly why Talbot had moved quickly against Monte and Louis. They were Smoke's staunchest allies in Big Rock. If anybody was going to try to help him escape from that ludicrous murder charge, it was them. But they couldn't do anything if they were locked up, too. There was even a good chance that Talbot would come up with some excuse to have them executed, as well.

Sally finished what she was doing, then went over to Dr.

Spaulding. The young, bespectacled physician had just stepped back from a table on which a man lay. His shirt was heavily bloodstained. Spaulding reached out and closed the man's open, staring, but sightless eyes, then arched his back to stretch stiff muscles and sighed wearily.

"Oh, hello, Mrs. Jensen," he said, noticing Sally. "We just lost another one, I'm afraid. The man was wounded too badly for me to save him."

"I'm sure you did your best, Doctor," Sally told him. "And you haven't lost many patients."

"This is the third," he said bleakly. "And I'm told that at least a dozen townspeople were killed in the fighting. This is a terrible blow for Big Rock." Echoing Sally's thoughts from a few moments earlier, he went on, "We'll recover, I suppose, but still, this is a sad day for our community."

"It is," she agreed, then changed the subject by asking, "Have you seen Pearlie Fontaine?"

"The foreman from your ranch?" Spaulding frowned. "No, I don't believe I have. Was he in town today? Do you have reason to think he may have been wounded?"

"No, in fact, I think it's more likely that he's still out at the Sugarloaf, along with the rest of the hands. I need to find them, Doctor, and bring all of them back here if I can."

Spaulding nodded and said, "Because of what Colonel Talbot's in the process of doing, I take it."

"He's already done it," Sally said. "He and his men have taken over the town."

"I heard rumors, but I've been so busy . . . You know, I think there's something not quite on the up-and-up about those soldiers."

Sally could have said quite a bit in response to that comment, but instead she just nodded and told him, "I have to go, Doctor."

"By all means. You've already been a tremendous help. I mean . . . just look at your hands."

Sally looked. They were stained with blood, and the sleeves of her dress were red almost to the elbows. Under other circumstances, she might have been horrified by the sight, but right now, there just wasn't time to be as shaken emotionally as she might be later.

"Good luck," she said.

"And good luck to you, Mrs. Jensen, whatever it is you're doing."

Sally turned and left the school hurriedly. She headed down Center Street toward the livery stable. She knew that Mr. Patterson, the man who owned it, wouldn't mind if she borrowed a horse and a saddle . . . although she could ride bareback if she needed to.

The only thing that was really important now was for her to get to the Sugarloaf so she could tell Pearlie and the other men what was happening in town. She wasn't sure what they could do to help, but she knew they were the best hope right now for foiling Colonel Lamar Talbot's deadly schemes.

She averted her eyes from the sight of the dead renegades still sprawled in the street. The bodies of the citizens who had been killed had been carried to the undertaking parlor already. That man would be very busy over the next few days, and so would the gravediggers.

No one stopped her as she hurried along the street. She reached the livery and saw that the doors were open. Stepping inside, she called, "Mr. Patterson? It's Sally Jensen. I need a horse."

There was no response. She hoped Patterson hadn't been injured, or worse, during the battle. But chances were, he was just off somewhere else in town, trying to help people. She walked along the wide center aisle, checking the horses in the stalls on both sides, searching for one that looked like a good saddle mount.

She had just decided on a chestnut mare when a hand fell roughly on her shoulder and a harsh voice rasped, "Hold it, lady. What the hell do you think you're doing?"

Chapter 30

Sally turned her head. One of the troopers stood just behind her. The hard planes of the man's face were beard-stubbled. She had seen enough hard cases to recognize the breed. She knew this man wasn't a real soldier. He was an outlaw, just like the rest of the First Colorado Rifles.

"I thought I would go home, now that the threat from Black Drum is over," she said, trying to make her voice sound casual.

The man shook his head. "Forget it, lady. Nobody goes in or out of town. Colonel's orders."

"But I really need to check on things at the ranch—"

The trooper leered at her. "You're Jensen's wife, ain't you? The cap'n had a real yen for you. I think maybe the colonel does, too. And I can sure understand why."

He moved his hand from her shoulder down to her upper arm, squeezing gently now.

Sally jerked away. Coldly, she said, "Keep your hands off me."

His face hardened. "Gonna be stuck-up, are you?" He grabbed both of her arms and jerked her toward him. "Maybe we'll find a nice pile of hay in one of these stalls. What the colonel don't know won't hurt—"

Sally lifted her knee into his groin as hard as she could.

That took him by surprise. He gasped in pain and bent forward as he let go of her arms to clutch at the injured area. Sally twisted away and darted behind him. She rammed her shoulder against him from behind and knocked him facedown on the floor.

A pitchfork leaned against the gate of a nearby stall. Sally snatched it up and brought it down on the back of the trooper's left thigh, putting all of her weight and strength behind the blow. The outer tines missed his leg, but the middle one went right through the flesh, pinning the leg to the ground.

The trooper screamed.

Sally knew that outcry would get the attention of anybody who heard it. She ran to the chestnut's stall, grabbed the harness that was hanging on the gate, and opened the gate just enough to slide through. She slipped the harness over the horse's head. The animal was a little skittish, but Sally was good at handling horses and calmed her down quickly. She climbed onto the gate and swung from there to the chestnut's back, pulling up her dress so she could ride astride. Then she kicked the gate wide open and charged out past the wounded trooper, who was still writhing on the ground and yelling as he tried to yank the pitchfork tine out of his leg.

The chestnut was already moving at a gallop as Sally burst out of the stable. She hauled on the reins, turning the horse to the west. From the corner of her eye, she saw several troopers running toward the stable, drawn by their comrade's screams and shouts. One of them yelled for Sally to stop. She ignored that and leaned forward, just in case the men started shooting.

They did. She heard the guns booming behind her. But the chestnut, running smoothly now, never broke stride as Sally raced along the street, legs bared, hair flying out behind her. A crazy thought crossed her mind.

If she'd been blond, she would have looked like one of the Valkyries, riding down from Valhalla to gather the souls of the warriors slain honorably in battle.

Instead, she was riding to save the life of *her* warrior . . . Smoke Jensen.

The light in the cell block was faded, telling Smoke the afternoon was about over and evening was coming on, when Colonel Talbot came into the jail, followed by six of the troopers.

"All right, Jensen, we're ready to begin your trial," Talbot announced.

"You mean that farce you're going to put on," Smoke countered.

Talbot glared at him. "It will be a proper military trial."

"Doesn't the military usually hold a tribunal?" Smoke asked. "Where are the other two judges?"

"Since I am the only officer present in this command, I will preside over the proceedings," Talbot said stiffly.

Smoke shook his head disdainfully. "None of this is legal, and you know it . . . *Colonel*."

The emphasis he put on the rank made it clear he considered that as fake as everything else Talbot was doing.

Talbot's face flushed. He nodded to the men with him. Two of them positioned themselves in front of the doors leading into Monte and Louis's cells and aimed their rifles at the prisoners.

"If you resist, those men will shoot your friends," Talbot told Smoke. "And these other men will shoot you. You're heading for a firing squad anyway, so if you insist on hurrying matters along . . ."

"See?" Smoke said. "You admit the verdict's already predetermined, and yet you insist this is a real trial you're putting on."

"Never mind that." Talbot rattled a key on the door's lock. "Just come along and don't give us any trouble."

Monte said, "Jump the son of a buck and make him eat his own saber, Smoke. Don't mind about us."

Louis added dryly, "Normally I'd tell Monte not to volunteer me to be sacrificed, but in this case, he's correct. Don't cooperate with these scoundrels, Smoke."

"Sorry, boys," Smoke told them with a shake of his head. "I reckon I'll take my chances."

Talbot smirked. "That's a wise decision, Jensen. There's no reason these two have to die. They'll learn who holds the power here."

Smoke didn't believe that for a second, but he didn't say anything as he left the cell when Talbot swung the barred door open. The troopers fell in around him and escorted him out.

Talbot strutted along behind as the soldiers marched Smoke along the street. They were headed toward Longmont's, Smoke noted, prompting him to ask, "Are you going to have this so-called trial in a saloon, Colonel?"

"That's right. It seems appropriate since you and Longmont are friends. Also, it's large enough to accommodate such a proceeding. I considered the school, but it's being used as a hospital."

Something about the way Talbot fell silent prompted Smoke to glance back at him. The colonel was scowling.

"Your wife assisted Dr. Spaulding there for a while, as you suggested," Talbot went on. "But then she got it in her head to flee, although I'm not sure what good she thinks it will do. I gave my men strict orders that no one was to leave town—"

"Is Sally all right?" Smoke interrupted. Even with all the rifles covering him, if anything had happened to his wife, he was going for Talbot's throat . . .

"She appeared to be fine when she galloped out of town after attacking one of my men and injuring him rather severely," Talbot snapped. "That's the report I got."

The tension inside Smoke eased slightly. If Sally had gotten away from Big Rock, she would be headed for the Sugar-loaf to fetch help. More than likely, Talbot had figured that out, too, and that was why he was in a hurry to get the trial over with and put Smoke up in front of a firing squad.

Once again, Smoke was a little thankful that Talbot was loco, otherwise the colonel might have given up on the idea of holding a joke of a trial and just have Smoke killed out of hand. This way, there was still a chance of turning things around.

As they walked along the street, Smoke noticed quite a few townspeople gathered on the boardwalks, watching anxiously. Each little group had a trooper standing nearby with his rifle ready in his hands. An air of tense expectation gripped the settlement. Talbot had people cowed at the moment, but they might not stay that way.

They reached the saloon and went inside. All the tables had been shoved to one side, clearing a large area in front of the bar. Louis's private table, with its polished hardwood sheen, had been carried forward and placed so it commanded that open area. Talbot went to the chair behind the table and sat down. Smoke's guards stood him up in front of the table and then backed off a little but continued covering him with their rifles.

Several of Big Rock's leading citizens, including Don Baker from the mercantile, Haywood Arden, the editor and publisher of the *Big Rock Bulletin*, and Norman "Hog-jaw" Lambert, owner of Lambert's Café, were lined up along the side wall. Talbot nodded to them and said, "You gentlemen have been brought here to serve as observers, so you can see for yourself, on behalf of the other citizens, that this proceeding is being conducted in a fair and impartial manner." He didn't wait for them to acknowledge that ludicrous statement. Instead he clasped his hands together on the table in front of him and went on, "This trial will now begin. Kirby Jensen, you are charged with the murder of Captain Adam Skinner. How do you plead?"

Smoke was a little surprised that Talbot had gone to the trouble of finding out his real name. When a man was crazy, there was no telling what he might do or where his obsessions would lead him.

"Not guilty," declared Smoke. "I shot Skinner, but only because he was trying to shoot me. I killed him in self-defense."

"This is not your time to testify," Talbot said. "The first witness will be Sergeant Gerald Rafferty."

The sergeant smirked at Smoke as he stepped forward. Smoke wouldn't get a fair shake from Rafferty, and he knew it.

"Sergeant Rafferty," Talbot began, "please tell the court how you saw the accused, Kirby Jensen, murder Captain Adam Skinner in cold blood . . ."

Pearlie glanced over his shoulder as he, Bob Dutton, Max Collier, and Jed Hightower galloped toward Big Rock. The sun had dipped below the mountains, and shadows were falling swiftly over the landscape. According to Sally, Talbot had said that Smoke's trial could be this evening. Pearlie could only pray that they would reach the settlement in time to prevent his best friend and employer from being stood up in front of a firing squad.

Not that Smoke would ever let things get that far, thought Pearlie. If Smoke knew he didn't have any way out and was doomed to die, he would go down fighting, one way or another. And he'd probably take a good number of those phony soldiers with him . . .

Pearlie wasn't going to let himself think like that. With a little shake of his head, he cleared his brain of such dire possibilities. He and the boys with him would be badly outnumbered, but he planned to make the odds a little better by hitting the jail first and freeing Monte Carson and Louis Longmont. With those two hombres on their side, he figured that he and the other Sugarloaf hands would be almost a match for that bunch of owlhoots pretending to be soldiers.

He was distracted enough by everything going through his head that he didn't see the mounted, blue-clad figures charging out of the trees on both sides of the trail until it was too late and he and his companions were surrounded, forced to rein in sharply and bring their mounts to a halt because of the rifles leveled at them.

The parade of liars continued until Talbot had heard half a dozen troopers testify that Captain Skinner had been firing at the renegades as he led the charge, until Smoke cruelly and treacherously blasted him out of the saddle.

While that was going on, Smoke glanced at the assembled citizens. He could tell from their expressions that they didn't believe a word of what they were hearing. But outnumbered and outgunned as they were, they couldn't do anything about it without risking their lives.

He didn't expect them to do that for him . . . but they might have to take action for themselves, if they didn't want Talbot and his gang to steal everything they had.

Finally, Talbot said, "Very well, I've heard enough. I'm ready to render a verdict—"

"Don't I get a chance to speak up for myself?" Smoke broke in.

Talbot let out a bark of laughter. "What are you going to say? Are you going to repeat that ridiculous claim of self-defense, a claim that's been obliterated by the testimony of half a dozen good men and true? If such is the case, I see no need to waste the time listening." He rose to his feet. "Kirby Jensen, I find you guilty of murder and sentence you to death, sentence to be carried out immediately by firing squad. Men, take him out and—"

"Just a moment, please!"

The unfamiliar voice came sharply from the saloon's entrance. Smoke looked around to see a blue-uniformed figure stride into the room. The newcomer was fairly young, medium-sized, and wore spectacles. He had a determined, intelligent look on his face.

"Who the devil are you?" demanded Talbot.

"Lieutenant Samuel Brant."

Talbot drew in a breath and glared. "You should address a superior officer as 'sir,' Lieutenant. A salute would be proper, too."

Brant's chin jutted defiantly. "Certainly, I would salute a superior officer and address him as 'sir,' *if* I were to be in the presence of one. However, at the moment, the only person I see is an outlaw and an imposter."

"How dare you? How did you get in here?" Talbot raised his voice. "Guards!"

Brant shook his head slowly. Smoke had a feeling the young lieutenant wanted to smile, but he kept the solemn expression on his face.

"If you're calling your men, you're wasting your time. Except for the ones in this room, they've been taken into custody by *my* men . . . actual members of the United States Army. You're now my prisoner as well, *Colonel*."

Scorn dripped from the rank as Brant spoke it.

Wide-eyed and pale, Talbot stood there, staring at the lieutenant. He began to tremble a little, as if something inside him, at his very core, shook with rage.

Smoke said to Brant, "So the First Colorado Rifles aren't an actual army unit?"

"They're a self-styled militia, vigilantes, I suppose you could say, at best. At worst, a gang of outlaws recruited by that man to satisfy his campaign of vengeance against the Indians . . . as well as looting all the honest people they encounter."

"Lies!" cried Talbot. "All lies! Our mission is to battle the savages—"

Brant clasped his hands together behind his back and said, "I've conducted an investigation of your activities. You and your men have attacked several peaceful bands of Indians after claiming they were responsible for various atrocities. You whip up sentiment against them, convince settlers to pay you to protect them, and then slaughter innocent men, women, and children."

"That's not true! Black Drum was a killer—"

Brant interrupted again, saying, "Yes, he was. For once, you went after an actual threat to the frontier and, from what I understand, wiped out his war party. That may be taken into account at your trial, but it doesn't excuse your past crimes."

Smoke said, "I reckon even a fella who's loco can do some good every once in a while, by accident if nothing else."

Talbot looked around wildly. He slammed a fist down on the desk and yelled, "You're the ones who are insane, all of you! You don't appreciate what I've done to save you from those savages!"

"You may have saved some people, I'll grant you that," said the lieutenant. "But you couldn't save your own family back in Texas, could you, Talbot?"

"Kill him!" screeched Talbot as he clawed at the holstered revolver on his hip. "Kill that liar! As for you, Jensen—"

Smoke leaped forward. Guns fired behind him. He didn't feel the shock of any bullets as he cleared the table and smashed into Talbot. Both of them went down, upsetting the chair that had been behind the table and rolling against the bar as they struggled. Talbot had cleared leather, and he tried to shove the gun against Smoke. Smoke grabbed Talbot's wrist and forced it up. The gun blasted, its deafening report smashing against Smoke's ears like giant fists. Sparks from the muzzle flash stung Smoke's cheeks.

Talbot went limp. Smoke shoved himself up on his left hand and looked down at the false colonel. The bullet had caught Talbot under the chin, bored up through his diseased brain, and exploded out the top of his head before hitting the front of the bar, which was now splattered with blood.

Smoke heaved himself to his feet and looked around. The other guns had fallen silent. A haze of powder smoke hung in the room. Talbot's troopers were down, except for a couple who had thrown away their rifles and stood with their hands in the air. Pearlie, Bob Dutton, Max Collier, and Jed Hightower stood just inside the saloon's entrance, bristling with guns as they covered the remaining soldiers.

Sally pushed past them and ran toward Smoke, calling out his name.

With a grin, Pearlie said, "I told her to stay behind at the Sugarloaf, Smoke, but I reckon you know how far I got with that. After we ran into Lieutenant Brant and his boys, she caught up with us."

Smoke took Sally into his arms and held her closely against him, for the second time today relishing her nearness and her strength after the tumult of battle.

This is what he fought for, heedless of the odds against him, he thought.

And he always would.

Chapter 31

"So it was what happened to Colonel Talbot down in Texas, when he was a boy, that made him turn out the way he was?" asked Smoke.

"Please don't refer to him by that rank, Mr. Jensen," Brant replied. "He was never a member of the army." The lieutenant shrugged. "Even though it's difficult to say what makes *anyone* turn out the way they do, I believe that tragedy down on the Brazos had a very large influence on Talbot's . . . obsession . . . with killing Indians."

They were sitting in the lobby of the Dunn Hotel. Sally was beside Smoke on a sofa, and Pearlie sat nearby, straddling a ladderback chair he had turned around. Monte Carson and Louis Longmont were there, too.

"His entire family was wiped out, you said?" Sally asked.

Brant nodded. "That's right. The Comanches raided the family homestead, twenty-five years ago. I found newspaper accounts of the atrocity. His parents were killed at their cabin, but Talbot's two younger sisters escaped through a tunnel but were captured as they tried to flee. You can, ah, only imagine their fate . . ."

"What about Talbot?" Smoke asked. "How did he survive?"

"He never really said. But given the hatred he felt toward

Indians . . . *all* Indians . . . I suspect he hid somehow from the Comanches. He may have known that his sisters were captured but didn't do anything to help them." Brant shrugged. "From his reaction when I implied as much, I believe something like that must have happened. The guilt he felt drove him mad."

"Well, it's over now," Monte said. "He won't be killing any more innocent people or victimizing the folks he pretended to be helping."

"And yet he *did* help," mused Smoke. "The Bagbys might have been wiped out if not for Talbot's men, and the same is true for Sally and the crew at the Sugarloaf."

Sally said, "I don't like being in debt to such a man, but what Smoke says is true. Black Drum might have succeeded in burning down the town, too. We actually owe something to Colonel Talbot."

"I reckon he's at peace now," said Smoke. "That's all the settling up we can do."

Solemn silence hung over the room for a moment before Pearlie broke it by saying, "There's a lot of fixin' up to take care of here in town, and some buryin's to get behind us, but once that's done, I figure Big Rock ought to look ahead again instead of thinkin' about everything that's happened."

Sally smiled and said, "That's a good idea, Pearlie. What did you have in mind?"

"Well, I was cogitatin' on that . . . and I thought maybe we could have a big ol' party. A reg'lar celebration of the fact that the town survived and bigger and better things are ahead. There'd be a bunch of food, and maybe a dance . . . We could even get some folks to make speeches. Like you, Smoke, since Big Rock never would've got started in the first place without you and might not have survived without all you did to get rid of those renegades *and* that bunch of owlhoots."

"Me?" Smoke said, his eyes widening. "Give a speech?"

Sally laughed and said, "I think it's a grand idea."

"I think I'd rather take on a war party again!" he declared. "Besides, it seems to me like that would just be asking for more trouble."

Sally wrapped both arms around his left arm and rested her head on his shoulder. She said, "Somehow, Smoke, I have a feeling that trouble will make a habit of cropping up wherever you happen to be!"